Life in

Chapel Springs

by Ane Mulligan

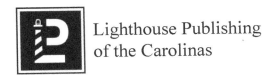
Lighthouse Publishing
of the Carolinas

LIFE IN CHAPEL SPRINGS BY ANE MULLIGAN
Published by Lighthouse Publishing of the Carolinas
2333 Barton Oaks Dr., Raleigh, NC, 27614

ISBN: 978-1-946016-13-3
Copyright © 2017 by Ane Mulligan
Cover design by Elaina Lee
Cover artwork by Terence Mulligan
Interior design by Karthick Srinivasan

Available in print from your local bookstore, online, or from the publisher at:
lpcbooks.com

For more information on this book and the author, visit: anemulligan.com

Brought to you by the creative team at Lighthouse Publishing of the Carolinas: Eddie Jones, Denise Loock, Susan Price, Brian Cross, Shonda Savage, and Christy Distler.

Library of Congress Cataloging-in-Publication Data
Mulligan, Ane
Life in Chapel Springs / Ane Mulligan 1st ed.

Printed in the United States of America

Praise for *Life in Chapel Springs:*

Looking for a down-home feel-good story with lots of laughs, romance, and a bit of intrigue on the side? You'll find it right here in the latest adventure in the Chapel Springs series. I dare you not to fall in love all over again with the characters. I couldn't help myself. Don't miss *Life in Chapel Springs!*

~ **Michelle Griep**
Author of *The Captive Heart, Brentwood's Ward,*
and the Once upon a Dickens Christmas series

Small-town story with a big heart. In *Life in Chapel Springs,* Ane Mulligan once again brings together her loveable cast of characters in a story that will bring tears and chuckles until the last page. Whether you are new to charming Chapel Springs or a long-time friend of the series, you'll be swept into Claire and Patsy's world as they deal with the little and big issues of life, doling out faith, fun, and compassion one donut at a time. Wonderful storytelling!

~ **Elizabeth Musser**
Author of *The Long Highway Home*

Ane Mulligan delivers yet again with the latest release in her Chapel Springs series! *Life in Chapel Springs* is Mulligan's best book yet, with engaging characters and a captivating storyline that make this book a joy to read.

~ **Elizabeth Ludwig**
Author of *A Tempting Taste of Mystery*

Life in Chapel Springs offers a little bit of everything—families, friendships, and homespun Southern humor, laced with a touch of mystery. You'll be charmed by the endearing residents of this warm and welcoming community, so much so that you may never want to leave!

~ **Myra Johnson**
Award-winning author of *When the Clouds Roll By*
and *Castles in the Clouds*

Interwoven lives enmeshed in intrigue, mystery, heartaches, and witticisms—that's what I always count on with Ane Mulligan's books. Ane is a master storyteller, and I guarantee you will love this one.

~ **Anne Baxter Campbell**
Best-selling author of One Step Closer fiction

What people are saying about the Chapel Springs series:

Chapel Springs: where anything can happen, and usually does. Claire and her best friend Patsy are as loveable as ever; even with all the new problems they face, they keep their sense of humor. The storyline is believable, and readers will identify with issues that are mentioned in the book. Mulligan writes with humor and wit. This book does not disappoint.

~ *Romantic Times*, 4-Stars

Pour yourself a tall glass of sweet tea and head out onto the porch with this richly woven tale of life in a small but suddenly booming Southern town. Mulligan's characters are warm and engaging, not to mention delightfully human, as they struggle to navigate problems both big and small, proving in the end that nothing is impossible when we hold tight to faith and keep our hearts open.

~ **Barbara Davis**
Author of *Summer at Hideaway Key*

With her trademark wit and Southern charm, Ane Mulligan takes us on another trip to the idyllic town of Chapel Springs, spinning an endearing tale of how far we'll go for those we love and the ones we hope will love us in return.

~ **Jennifer Allee**
Carol Award finalist and best-selling author

A touching story involving real women who face crisis, love, doubt, and desperation with love and humor. Together, they survive when courage calls.

~ **DiAnn Mills**
Christy Award winner and author of *Firewall*

Ane Mulligan ... succeeds in creating a town full of quirky characters, each endearing in their own way, who discover—sooner or later—what their hearts and their town really need.

~ **Cynthia Ruchti**
Award-winning author of *All My Belongings*

Buckle up for another bumpy and funny ride with the ladies of Chapel Springs. Characters are funny, caring and just want to do the right thing for the community, with unexpected and humorous results. Mulligan has written a wonderful contemporary novel that tickles the funny bone.

~ *Romantic Times* **4-Stars**

Readers who enjoy a good novel that will stir emotions and bring some heartfelt love and laughter into their lives—I highly recommend reading the Chapel Springs series by Ane Mulligan. Readers will fall in love with Chapel Springs and will want to travel there as a tourist.

~ **An Amazon reader**

Ane Mulligan paints delightfully imaginative word pictures and makes you wish you could take Claire and Patsy out to lunch. I nearly fell off the sofa laughing at Claire's antics. Hopefully redemptive without sappiness.

~ **An Amazon reader**

This is a wonderful story of love, forgiveness, patience, and understanding. I highly recommend this book and series to anyone who loves to laugh, cry, and enjoy a great story.

~ **An Amazon reader**

"Friends are the chocolate chips and the nuts in the cookie of life."

- Claire Bennett

Dedication

Greg, life is better for having you in it.
You turned my life and your dad's upside down and inside out.
You've found the path God has for you and I couldn't be prouder.
I love you.

Acknowledgements

Thank you to the gracious Dr. Kun Z. Kim and his office manager, Esther Meyer, who gave up paid office time to answer all my questions regarding blunt trauma and facial reconstruction. I've taken liberties for the pacing of this book. Any discrepancies from the actual healing time are mine alone.

Other medical professionals who gave of their time to me include former Atlanta paramedic, Daniel Francis. Dan, you've let me pick your brain for several books, and I appreciate you so much. You're my "other" son. I love you. To Dr. David Engstrom, PhD, thank you for helping me understand the mental process many people experience after life-changing surgery.

My local Gwinnett County Station 26 in Sugar Hill welcomed me, not realizing I would badger one of their paramedics with questions. Ryan Young helped me tremendously on procedure. I might have brought in the Air Force to act as a life flight. So thanks, Ryan, for saving me heaps of embarrassment. Any medical gaffes are mine.

Two dear friends, Fred St. Laurent, director and stage designer extraordinaire (among other things) and Karl Wagner, former set designer for the New York Metropolitan Opera, answered all my questions about theater terminology I'd forgotten. I'm blaming it on new technology in theater since I first learned it. Hey, that's as good a reason as any. Right, Phred? And it was Karl who verified Lacey's injuries were indeed possible. He fractured his cheekbone when a five-pound roll of gaffer's tape fell from a ladder and hit him in the face.

There would have been some real problems in my descriptions if not for B. Kent Snyder II, project architect with Precision Planning Inc. Your patient answers and the drawings you let me look at added authenticity to this book. Any mistakes are mine.

I have the best critique partners ever: Michelle Griep, Elizabeth Ludwig, and Patty Smith Hall, better known to me as "Genghis Griep" and "Ludwig von Frankenpen" and "Hall of the Baskervilles." You push me beyond my comfort zone. Thanks for always being there and for pulling me back from the edge. My phenomenal beta readers, Ginger Aster, Beth Willis, Gayle Mundy, and Donna Mynatt: You caught the mistakes our weary eyes miss. How you do it, I don't know, but all y'all are great!

To the team at LPC, you're the greatest. Susan Price and Denise Loock, I'm blessed to have you as my editors. You prodded, suggested, and stretched me to reach for "better." Chapel Springs is a better place because of you. Eddie Jones, my old friend, thank you for taking a chance on me. I love being an LPC author. I bless the day I met you at the BRMCWC … way back in the Stone Age.

To my family, what can I say? You encourage me and continue to provide ideas that find their way into my stories. I love you!

Most of all, thank You to the Lover of my soul for the stories You whisper to my heart and the passion given in grace.

"I have loved you, so I continue to show you my constant love."
Jeremiah 31:3

Chapter 1

The morning fog was as thick as the pea soup Great-aunt Lola used to make. Claire hated that soup then, and she didn't much like this fog now. A tourist could get lost and walk right into the lake on a day like this. She swished her hand back and forth in an impotent attempt to dispel it. Good thing Chapel Springs was small, and she knew its topography like she knew her own face. Visibility was down to five feet, if that. In the distance, the foghorn on Henderson's Island blew a warning.

Why couldn't this morning be like yesterday? The sun had peeked over the horizon and risen a quarter of its girth by the time she'd reached the boardwalk. Its golden rays had danced on the waters of Chapel Lake, sparkling like the sequins on a wedding dress.

Mist-laden air filled Claire's lungs as she made her way down the boardwalk. Why the dark mood? She should be happy. The next wedding would be for her twins, Megan and Melissa. They'd dreamed since childhood of a double wedding, and God had kept their dream safe. She glanced up toward the fickle sun, or where it would be if she could see it. The weather and the town had better be perfect for their nuptials, only three and a half months away. Not much time left.

Despite the fog, the bells above the door at Dee's 'n' Doughs jingled a cheery welcome. Her BFF Patsy waved from their favorite table by the window. Since Chapel Springs had become *the* vacation spot in the Southeast, they seldom sat at that table. Instead, they were relegated to one in a back corner of the bakery.

Claire returned her wave and went to the counter to select her breakfast. A mocha sounded good and ... she let her gaze move from left to right over Dee's concoctions. Raspberry Danish, cheese Danish, apple fritters, and oh, the pear tart Patsy loved. She moved past the pear and over the bagels. Her eyes and her appetite stopped on the bear claws. Bagel versus bear claw. Almond paste inside Dee's flaky pastry topped with a light glaze of icing versus blueberry bagel. No contest.

She grinned at Trisha Halloran behind the counter. "I'll take the smallest one you have. I can't afford to gain any weight between now and the wedding."

"I shrank all the calories just for you." With a pair of tongs, Trisha picked up the bear claw and positioned it on a plate. "Here you go."

Claire thanked her, poured her coffee, and joined Patsy. She hung her turkey tote on the back of a chair and slid into place. Designer Chartreaux Katz had licensed the designs of Claire's whimsy vases to make as totes, and the gobbler that beaned Avery Chandler, the art critic and now her agent, had become legendary. Avery even carried one. Claire loved the totes and certainly didn't mind the extra money she made off them.

Settling into her chair, she turned to Patsy. "I have something for you. My daughter-in-law sent it."

Patsy set her coffee cup down. "Which one? You do have two, you know."

"Sandi, of course. Costy doesn't have babies yet."

"Well, what is it?"

Making Pat-a-cake wait another moment, Claire took a bite of the pastry, then wiped her hands on a napkin. She reached into her tote and pulled out a stiff envelope, handing it to Patsy. "Copies of their family portrait session. The twins cooperated and the photos are adorable. We want you to choose one and paint it."

Patsy's eyes lit up. She pulled the photos from the envelope, alternately oohing and aahing. Charlie, Sandi, and their twins, now eleven months old, were dressed alike in white oxford shirts and jeans.

Patsy finally slipped them back into the envelope. "Where did Sandi find those shirts for Micah and Michaela?"

"She ordered them online. Aren't they darling?"

"The first grandbabies." Patsy frowned. "How'd we get old enough for that?"

"Count, girlfriend. We're fast approaching forty-nine." Claire wrinkled her nose.

"Oh, hush. I'd convinced myself I'm still thirty-nine."

Claire snorted and pulled off another piece of pastry. "I have a theory about that." She popped the tidbit into her mouth and savored it. Delicious. "We hit our stride as individuals somewhere between thirty-five and thirty-nine. It tends to stick." She followed the bear claw with a sip of mocha.

"Hmm, interesting theory, O Wise One." Patsy placed the envelope beside her on the table. "I think I know which pose I'll use for the portrait, but I'll study them again in the studio."

"Which one?"

"Nope. I'll make that a surprise for all of you." Patsy grinned.

"Did I tell you Micah has nicknamed his sister?"

Patsy blinked and tilted her head. "How did he do that? He's only babbling."

Claire laughed. "Prepare to be impressed. Little Micah babbled, then clearly as anything said 'Aela' and reached for his sister. Sandi and Charlie have started calling her Aela now."

The bells jingle-jangled, and the pastor's wife, JoAnn, came through the door, followed by Ellie, their town librarian. Before the door fully shut, Carin and Lacey entered. It pleased Claire the two had struck up a friendship. Both being writers, they reminded her of herself and Patsy, although theirs was a new friendship. Hers and Patsy's went all the way back to early childhood. She glanced at her Pat-a-cake. Claire couldn't imagine doing life without her best friend.

As their friends joined them, she passed the photos around the table, asking each to chime in on their favorite pose. Naturally, they all had a different opinion.

Kelly Appling breezed in the door, a stream of fog clinging to her heels. One of the most beautiful women Claire knew, Kelly's milk-chocolate complexion was flawless. She could have been a model, instead of owning a gift shop and heading up the community theater. After getting a to-go cup of coffee, she stopped by their table.

"Are y'all coming Thursday night for auditions?"

No *way* would Claire go onstage. "I'm only coming to paint flats." She took a long sip of her coffee, giving Kelly the evil eye.

A wicked gleam entered hers. "But Claire, sugar, Lacey wrote a part that has your name all over it."

"Why? You've already put enough comedy in this play."

Kelly laughed. "I'm teasing you, although I still think you should take a role sometime. You'd be good, Claire."

The woman was a good director, but she sure overestimated Claire's talent as an actor. "Thanks but no thanks. I'll stay backstage. Hey, where are we supposed to do all this? You aren't going to Pineridge, are you?"

"No." Kelly looked pleased with herself.

"Well? Where are we going then?"

"The theater."

But the— "The renovations are—"

"In the lobby. The engineer looked over the stage and everything is good. It passed. There're some small structural things to fix, but they're doing that during the day. They finished the wiring yesterday. So we're okay to be there at night."

"That's great. Then we can build the flats and paint." Claire made a note to tell Joel what they were doing tonight.

"Seth'll be there too," JoAnn said. "My husband has decided to try out. He thinks it would be good for people to see their pastor supporting it."

Claire gaped at her. "Really? Our pastor in a play?"

"Why not?" Carin asked. "Is there a reason he shouldn't?"

JoAnn shook her head. "Of course not. Lacey's mysteries are good family entertainment."

Still, it would seem strange to see the pastor as someone else.

JoAnn rose, and as she and Kelly left, Patsy nudged Claire. "I thought you said you'd try out if I would."

"Yeah, well, that was in a weak moment. Besides, you're not trying out. And I've asked Mel to help us paint." She turned to their petite librarian, who was fostering their employee. "Ellie, you don't mind if she helps, do you?"

"Not at all. She has a special heart for the old place."

They all laughed, and Ellie leaned forward in her chair. Being as petite as she was, her shoulders touched the table. "Guess who has already passed her GED?"

"Mel? Really? Wow. Barely educated and brilliant." Claire breathed on her fingernails and rubbed them against her shirt, grinning at her friends. "I knew it. So now what?"

Ellie sat back and folded her hands in her lap, clearly pleased with Mel's development. "I'm enrolling her in the summer semester at Pineridge Community College. I've also"—she looked around the room and lowered her voice—"hired a detective to find her daddy. I want to adopt her, and I'll need his release."

Adopt her? That was great but what if— "Her daddy may want to keep her if he finds out how smart she is. And from what she's told Joel and me about him, he's a scoundrel who'd use her intelligence to commit crimes."

"I'd already thought about that, Claire. That's why I'd like to do this quickly."

Patsy dunked a piece of Claire's bear claw in her coffee. "He hasn't found out about her being gainfully employed by us yet. You're probably okay."

"I'm not leaving anything to chance." Ellie wrinkled her nose. "I'll find him and somehow convince him to let me adopt her."

"When's the tattoo removal?" Claire had been glad when Mel told her she wanted to have the tattoo removed from her face and neck. It was pretty dark, and she didn't mean the color.

"Her first appointment is Friday." Ellie's forehead pinched. "I hear it takes several treatments. I hope the results are what she wants. That tattoo isn't that old."

"Does that make a difference?"

Ellie nodded. "It can."

Always the author, Carin pulled out a little notebook and jotted down something.

Claire had never seen her without it. "The funny thing is, I don't notice it anymore. What? Close your mouth, Patsy, before you catch a fly."

Coffee shot out Ellie's nose. She wiped it, alternately coughing and laughing. "I don't notice it anymore either, Claire."

"I do. I don't judge her, but I can't help it if I notice it. Uh, Ellie?" Patsy tapped her finger against her jaw, and Ellie wiped off the drop of coffee. "Got it."

"We all know you love her." Claire patted her BFF's hand. "I guess it is more noticeable since all the rest of her Gothness has been put away."

"Lacey, since the remodeling is only in the lobby area, will the grand reopening be soon?" Carin asked.

Lacey lowered her eyes. "The designs are ready but haven't been approved yet."

Her voice was so soft, Claire could hardly hear her. "How long will that take?"

Lacey raised her gaze to Claire's, then quickly dropped it again. "A couple weeks."

Claire lifted an eyebrow in question at Carin. Hadn't their friendship helped Lacey with her shyness? Was she the only one who saw the need of Lacey learning some—

"Lacey, we need to give you lessons in being assertive." A foot connected with her ankle. "Ow." Claire glared at Patsy. Maybe she was right, though. Poor Lacey looked so horrified, Claire was ready to kick herself. Still— "Then what about Toastmasters? Oh, don't look so frightened. When we start producing more of your plays, the media will want interviews. It would help you overcome your shyness."

Ellie nodded and pumped more coffee into her cup from the thermal pot on the table. "I have some information about the chapter in Pineridge, if you're interested."

Lacey shook her head in fast tight shakes. "No. Thank you. I need to go to work." She pushed her chair back so fast it nearly fell over. She hurried to the door and disappeared into the fog.

Chapter 2

Hidden in the fog outside the bakery, Lacey took slow, shallow breaths to avoid fainting. Her friends only wanted to help, but they didn't understand her fear. Or the cause. She wasn't about to enlighten them either. Her sister didn't even know. Lydia had bailed by then, leaving her alone on the farm with their cuckoo mother and the deaf aunt and uncle. The tram rumbled to a stop, thankfully interrupting any more memories.

She clutched the handrail and stepped up into the rear of the tram. Bud Pugh was driving today. He was normally at the parking lot guard shack.

"Hey, Mr. Bud." The other driver must be sick.

"That you, Miss Lacey? I cain't see through this dadgum fog."

The sweet old gentleman knew her voice. Gripping each seat back, she moved to the front and sat behind him. He was one of her favorite people in Chapel Springs. "It's the worst I've ever seen."

"Worthy of that Guinness book, I reckon. A body could become lost in this. Now, where you headed to, missy? Work or the theater?"

"Work, please."

"All aboard!" He twisted his thumb in his ear, adjusting his hearing aid. Then the motor rumbled to life and the tram moved on.

In the few minutes it took to pick up two more passengers before they reached her stop, her heartbeat slowed to where her head no longer felt like fizzy water.

"Thanks for the ride, Mr. Bud."

"You're welcome, missy. You save me and the missus tickets to your next play, you hear?"

"I surely will." Lacey descended the two steps and walked to the bank's front door, which was already unlocked. Her brother-in-law beat her into work half the time. Her low heels echoed in the cavernous lobby as she made her way to the loan department. Graham's door was open and she waved as she passed.

He looked up. "Morning, Lacey. Will you bring me the completed file on the Vaughn loan, please?"

"Sure." It had taken time, but Lacey accepted Graham as Lydia's husband now, and as a boss. He was a good man, and her sister deserved a happy marriage like she and Jake had. As long as he didn't try to move Lydia away. She did not want to lose her sister again.

In her office, she pulled the file for Nancy Vaughn, who owned the town's boutique, and walked it back to Graham's office. "Here it is." She sat opposite his desk. "She has more than enough equity and collateral. She's owned the building and the boutique for fifteen years. She's never missed a payment."

Graham looked up from the paperwork. "Not even when times were lean here?"

Lacey shook her head.

"Didn't she purchase a house on"—he paused, shuffling the papers—"Pine Drive, next to Charlie Bennett. Will that affect the loan?"

"No. She put a hefty down payment on the cottage. The mortgage payment is very affordable for her, and the business loan isn't a jumbo one."

"All right. You said the loan committee recommends approval?"
She nodded.

"And you recommend her?"

Her brother-in-law earned points there. He alone asked her opinion. She nodded. "She's an excellent risk."

He pushed the papers back to her. "Approved. You want to let her know?"

"I will, but I think she'd be pleased to hear it from you." She pushed the loan application back to him and stood. "Anything else you need right now?"

"No, thanks, Lacey. I appreciate all your hard work on this. I'll be sure to let the president know."

Like he'd pay attention. She doubted the president even knew who she was. She closed his door behind her. The irony was lost on her brother-in-law. For the past eight years, all she'd wanted was for her work to be noticed so she'd be promoted. It never happened. No one ever asked her a question during loan committee meetings, even though it was her work, her diligent research, that culled the bad risks from the good. Only Graham noticed her. He didn't really count, though. As her brother-in-law, he had to notice her.

Back in her office, Lacey pulled out the stack of loan applications. Three were for new homes. That would make a total of fourteen new homes being built on the outskirts of Chapel Springs. Only two of those were full-time residents: a retiree and a young widow named Haleigh Evans. She quickly processed the retiree's paperwork but dawdled on the widow's. Claire was playing matchmaker with the widow and her brother-in-law. Was Dr. Vince interested?

Romance played well as a red herring in a murder mystery. It threw the audience off. If a young—no, a middle-aged widow moved to a small village. Stuck to herself. What background would work best? She'd need to work. Or maybe not. Why did she choose a small town? What if shortly after she moved in, the local—who?—disappears?

Lacey turned on her computer and typed a quick page of notes. She had the beginning of a new murder mystery for the Lakeside Players. After saving the file, she closed it and emailed it to her personal address. That poor widow had no idea what she sparked. Hopefully, none of her imaginings would come true for the woman, especially the part about the dead body.

The ten-minute reminder for loan committee sounded on her cell phone. What would happen if she simply set her pile of work on the table and didn't stay? Surely someone would notice, wouldn't they? She was tempted to try it. In the conference room, Lacey placed her pile of loan applications on the table, then slipped into her seat.

The loan officer, Mr. Cleaver, picked the first application from the top of the stack. After he glanced at it, he frowned. "Are we sure this is a good risk?"

"Yes, they have a high credit rat—"

"I found everything to be in order. I think it should be approved." Mark Nicholson, the V.P. from Atlanta, talked right over her.

Mr. Cleaver nodded and handed the application folder to his secretary, Wendy, who stamped it approved. He picked up another folder. The application was from a land speculator. Lacey had done extensive research on this application. She had a feeling he was overextending his resources. Turned out she was right.

"Why isn't this one worthy of approval?"

"The group is spreading their money too thin," Lacey said.

"Does anyone know? Nicholson? Have you looked into this group?" He didn't even hear her. Lacey raised her hand.

"I don't know a lot about them." Ollie Katz reached out his hand. "Give me the app. I'll research them."

What did they need her for? Last month, when she'd had a question about a loan recommended by the bank president, no one acknowledged her raised hand then either. They talked over and around her but never *to* her. They wouldn't miss her if she went to the restroom.

Lacey rose and left the room. When she returned to the meeting, at the end of the table where they stacked the approved loans, sat her applications. Each was stamped approved. She picked up the pile and left. The conversation never stopped and no one looked at her. If the mirror in the ladies room hadn't revealed the zit on her chin, she could have easily believed she truly was invisible.

What would happen if she didn't come in one morning? Other than Graham, no one would notice. She could quit. She and Jake didn't need the money. But what would she do to occupy her time?

Write. That's what she could do. But first, she'd wait and see what that agent thought. Maybe she wasn't good enough.

Chapter 3

Claire pushed open the gallery door with her shoulder and backed her way inside. In her hands, she bore a tray with lunch prepared by her sweet hubby. As she passed through the showroom to the workroom, she called to Nicole, her apprentice and Patsy's daughter-in-law, "Come and get it! And bring Mel and 'Lissa too." The aroma of homemade tamales, fajitas, rice, and beans had her drooling on the short walk from home.

The girls wasted no time following her, and Patsy had already set plates on the work island. Joel didn't often have time to fix a big midday meal, but with Wes taking over more of the work at the marina, her hubby had time on his hands. The muscles between her brows pulled slightly. After the fun of feeding them wore off, would he begin to feel unneeded? Redundant? How many hours could he fish in one day? In a week?

"Wow, these smell good." Mel helped herself. "I miss this. Miss Ellie's a good cook, but nothing like Mr. Joel. He should open a restaurant." She perched on a stool and took a bite of tamale, moaning her pleasure. "It's a wonder Melissa and Megan don't weigh a ton, growing up with this."

"Daddy doesn't always cook things that are fattening, thank goodness." 'Lissa's hand hovered over the tamales. "Maybe one, though. I—" She grinned and her eyebrows danced. "I've found my wedding dress and don't want to gain an ounce."

A plate wobbled in Claire's hand. "You found it? Where? When? What does it look like?"

Patsy echoed Claire's words one beat behind her, "… like?"

After Patsy pushed a stack of canvases aside, they sat at the island and ate, while 'Lissa described her dress. "It's what I've always dreamed of. It's strapless but has a lace bolero that wraps my shoulders in front and goes up my neck a bit in the back. The skirt has a soft drape from one side and a small splattering of beads." She stopped, wiped her hands, and pulled a folded magazine photo from her pocket. She unfolded her dream and handed it to Claire.

Claire's hands shook as she looked at the dress. Her baby girls were getting married. The picture blurred.

"Momma! Don't cry on it."

She took the napkin offered and dabbed her eyes. "I suddenly could see you in it, all grown up, and starting a new life as a wife." She wanted to grab time and squeeze more out of it. "It's so elegant. I almost pity poor Sean when he sees you in it. He'll be undone." *Oh!* "And your poor daddy. Oh, my."

'Lissa reached over and squeezed Claire's hand. "I feel like I'm in a dream or a fairy tale." The photo was passed around.

Claire's eyes weren't the only ones misty. Patsy's were too. "I can't believe you finally found it. It's only been three months of constant searching."

"Actually, Aunt Patsy, I've been looking for it since I was sixteen. Megan isn't quite as picky, but every other one had something wrong with it."

Claire wagged a finger at Patsy. "I seem to remember a certain somebody found her dress within two weeks after Nathan proposed."

Patsy's giggle took Claire back in time. "Do you remember the first double date we went on?" Best friends since kindergarten, when Claire's parents moved to Chapel Springs, their friendship carried her through acne, the loss of her mother when she was six and her twin sister to cancer when they were fifteen. They'd been through boyfriends, marriage, and— "Do you remember the night Charlie was born?"

"How could I forget?" Claire laughed. "The ballgame was on TV, and Joel had no idea I was about to give birth on our couch." They reminisced and laughed through each birth. Now nearly all their babies were married. She blinked. "Where are the girls?"

"They rolled their eyes and went back to work about the time we started having babies."

Claire studied the list of inventory she still needed to make. "Have you looked over the tour Avery has planned? It starts two days after the twins' wedding." Who would have thought art critic Avery Chandler would become their agent? The first time he entered The Painted Loon, he ended up beaned by a turkey vase. She had thought their careers were over, but wonder of wonders, he gave them rave reviews. Last year he opened a new gallery and wanted to represent them. Finally, they were off the weekend art shows and into some top-notch galleries, all thanks to him. And her turkey vase.

With her right bum cheek still on the stool where she sat, Patsy stretched her left leg over to the wheeled stool by Claire, hooking it with her foot. She pulled it close and retrieved her copy of the list. "I think it looks great, but are you sure you want to tour with our art this time?"

"Honestly, I don't know. Part of me does and the other part doesn't." Claire gave a wry laugh. "How's that for decisive?"

"Okay, let's talk about the part that doesn't want to go. Why not?"

"We'd have to dress up. People want to see you looking artistic, and I have no idea what that looks like." Ticking the reasons off on her fingers, she grimaced. "I feel like a hunk of meat hanging in the butcher's shop with people staring at me. And I never believe the fawners."

"Claire Bennett, you sound like me!"

"I know. Ironic, isn't it?" She picked up the remaining dishes and put them on the tray. "The half that wants to go says, 'Fiddlededee on them all.' Let's have fun. Do you think Nathan will go?"

Patsy nodded. "What about Joel?"

"If you look at each gallery, there is a lake or ocean within thirty minutes. Avery arranged fishing for the fellas. He's one smart cookie."

"And he said we only had to be at the gala collectors' preview. We could use it as a vacation. A paid one, at that."

"Paid if we sell anything."

"What has you in such a pessimistic mood?"

Claire sighed. "I don't know. Hormones, maybe? I've had a few hot flashes at night lately, and it makes me feel old."

Patsy patted Claire's shoulder. "Poor thing. It could be stress."

"I suppose. I'll call Avery and tell him we'll go. And to book the fishing boats for the boys."

"I'm heading over to Dee's 'n' Doughs. Kelly's called a meeting because the plans for the theater are ready," Claire called to Patsy. "Want to come?"

"Can't right now. I need to finish this," Patsy said.

Mel perked at the word *theater*. "May I come?"

"Sure. That okay with you, Patsy? Do you need Mel for anything?"

"Nope. Nicole will be here shortly. Go ahead."

Claire smiled at her protégé. "Come on, then. Are you as excited to see them as I am?"

Mel's hair swayed with her nod, having grown out from its chopped Goth cut to shoulder length. She let it fall over her face on one side, hiding the tattoo that started beneath her ear and ran down her neck. That was about all that was left of the girl Claire had met in jail. Except for the line of mismatched earrings that ran up both ears. Those sort of defined her quirky personality. Claire tossed her arm around Mel's shoulders, and they walked to the bakery.

Kelly and Lacey were already seated. Lester Gordon, who designed the sets for the Lakeside Players, followed Claire and Mel in. Only Nancy Vaughn, the stage manager, and Mayor Felix Riley were missing. In Felix's case, that was normal. He was never where they could find him when they needed him.

Claire dropped her tote on the floor and sat down. Kelly held a long rolled-up set of papers. "Are those the designs?"

"Yes, but I'm waiting for Nancy. She should— Oh, here she is." Nancy jogged past the window to the door. As soon as she was settled at the table, Dee brought a pitcher of sweet iced tea and glasses, then stood behind Claire to watch the plans unfold.

Kelly unrolled the design. "I'm thrilled with the plans. They took into consideration the historical significance of the building and still gave us all the things we need."

Claire leaned over the paper—it wasn't blue. "Where are the blueprints?" Her eyes swept across the large drawing. "Aren't they supposed to be blue?" Was she the only one who couldn't read these? Where were the bathrooms? And what about the shower they asked for? Kelly had said they needed two. "What happened to—"

"They aren't blue anymore, and everything we need is here. There are small symbols for the bathrooms and showers. The mayor and the town council already approved the budget. I guess the council will vote tomorrow night." Kelly rolled up the plans. "What I want to see are the set designs. Does anyone have them?"

"I brought along my drawing," Lester said. He set a sketchpad on the table. "I'll redo it to scale after you approve the overall design."

Mel leaned in to see, then glanced at Claire. "What's that?" She pointed to one section of the drawing.

Claire shrugged. It looked like an Etch A Sketch to her. "I only hammer the nails and throw on paint. Lester?"

"It's the box set."

Mel frowned. "I thought a box set's a collection of CDs."

"It's called that because it boxes in the set or the stage." Lester licked his lips. "It creates the illusion of a fourth wall the audience is privileged to see through."

"What's this?" Mel pointed to another section of the drawing.

What was her interest in Lester's sketch?

"That denotes a door in the back of the stage. In this play, it goes into a hallway."

Mel glanced at Lester skeptically. "Have you built a set like this before?"

"Well, no, this is the first time we've done a box set."

"I wondered, 'cause I don't think it'll work."

Lester drew back as if he'd been slapped. "What? What do you know about designing a set?"

"What do you mean, Mel?" Kelly asked.

"If there's a break in those things—the door—then the supports won't hold this stable. They aren't long enough."

Ooh, Mel was stepping on toes here. "What makes you say that?" Claire peered at the drawing.

"Look at the angle of those … What did you call them?"

"Flats." Lester's answer was flatter than flat.

"Yeah, flats. The way they're connected, well, if you use a real door, there's not nearly enough support to hold that box set steady. It'll wave and wobble. Could fall over."

Kelly's mouth gaped open. At least Claire wasn't the only one. "Mel, how do you know that?"

She shrugged. "I see things like that. I can tell what angles work and don't."

An uneducated—or barely educated—child prodigy? "Do you see stuff like this all the time?"

"I don't know. I never stopped to think about it." She gave Lester a half smile. "I didn't mean to be disrespectful, Mr. Gordon."

Lester blinked, then squinted at his drawing. "Huh, you know, I think you might be right, kid. I know this was a preliminary sketch, but …" He erased one area, redrew the angles, and roughly sketched in some lines. "What do you think?"

Mel scrutinized his changes and grinned. "Yeah, that'll work."

Lester pushed the drawing to Kelly. "A workable set, now." He winked at Mel.

Kelly, still looking like she was a step behind—exactly how Claire felt—looked at the sketchpad. "Will this one set work for the whole play?"

"According to what Lacey showed me in the script, yes. Everything takes place here, with some of the actors going into that hallway or out the door on this side." He pointed to the left side of the drawing.

"Great. Thanks, Lester. Let me do another read-through and detail the script. I'll do it this afternoon and make my notes. I'll see everyone at auditions."

Back in The Painted Loon, Claire called Ellie and relayed what had happened. "You wouldn't have believed it, Ellie. Mel pointed out the problem to Lester, and he agreed with her." That alone was monumental. "I think she might be one of those child geniuses or something."

"Do you remember that day Sean took Mel to lunch? She told me they talked about engineering and geology the whole time."

And all Claire wanted to do was show Sean how Mel was too young for him. Although it didn't matter. The minute he saw 'Lissa, he was a goner. "We ought to have her tested or something. Put her on the right track in college. If she's as bright as I think she is, they might let her start session B."

"What's that?"

"Pineridge Community divides the sessions into two parts. I don't understand why, but they have some students start the A session and others the B. Classes start in two weeks."

"I'll check with the guidance counselor right away. Thanks, Claire. I think our girl is pretty special. And to think you met her in jail."

Ellie's chuckling echoed even after she clicked off. Except for Mel, Claire would like to forget that night. Well, and Hazel—Motorcycle Mama. She'd become a good customer. And Costy, her sweet daughter-in-law. "Okay, Lord. I get it. I get it. All things work together—"

"What are you mumbling about?" Patsy handed her a magazine and two bills.

"I was grumbling to God about our night in jail, but as usual, He reminded me that it all worked out to my good."

Her BFF's smile warmed Claire's heart. How did anyone do life without a best friend? She and Patsy had weathered many storms together. Pat-a-cake kept her secrets and supported her better than an 18 Hour Bra.

Chapter 4

Boone Clarke, newly reelected Council Chairman, banged his gavel with the enthusiasm of a cymbalist. Claire winced. Really? Did the man have to be such a showoff? The community room was filled to capacity. Felix apparently got out the word about having a surprise announcement, because Jacqueline Ford from WPV-TV was here, sporting a microphone and a new hairdo. Claire would have to catch her afterward and tell her how becoming it was.

She glanced over the printed agenda while Ellie read the minutes. It looked like the lease with Happy for the parking lot was up for renewal. She hadn't heard anything from Joel about Happy wanting more money. He loved this town and wouldn't take advantage.

"All in favor signify by raising your hand."

Claire lifted hers and wiggled her fingers. She'd read the minutes and knew Ellie had recorded everything. Never had their librarian missed so much as a jot or a tittle.

"Any old business to discuss?"

Doc waved his hand without lifting his elbow off the table. "It's time to renew the lease with Happy for the parking lot. I spoke with him, and he's fine leaving the price where it is." Felix stopped playing with the rock he held and nodded. "He told me the same, and I'm good with that. How about y'all?" He flipped the rock from hand to hand. What new annoying habit was this?

Nancy Vaughn made the motion on the lease, Claire seconded it, and it passed unanimously. After they dispensed with the old business, Boone called for new. Felix asked for the floor.

"I need the council's advice on something I found on my property.

When the feds finally cleared the marijuana my brother planted on my land, they turned the soil and sprayed. Nothing will grow there for years." He set his stone in the middle of the table. "But they also turned up a lot of quartz."

Boone, who hadn't grown up in these mountains, picked up the rock. "What's the big deal with quartz?" He turned it around in his hand, then stopped. "Is this gold?"

Felix shrugged one shoulder. "Probably. Those of us who grew up here are used to finding bits of gold in the streams. There were some large mines here at one time."

Doc nodded. "Sure were, and even a mint was built in Dahlonega in 1837."

"Why didn't I know about that?" Boone asked.

Claire nudged Nancy Vaughn. "Do you think he's seeing a story for *The Weekly Voice*?"

Nancy shushed her but smiled.

Tom Fowler pulled his unlit pipe out of his mouth. He'd quit smoking but never lost the habit of having that thing clenched between his teeth. "The first gold was found in 1828 and started a rush."

"Well, I've seen too many people become excited about finding gold only to have it turn out to be a small vein worth less than the cost of extracting it. Prospecting is risky business." Felix scowled at Tom. "I'm more interested in the quartz. Stone countertops are all the craze, and I heard the quartz ones are antimicrobial, or some such thing. I'm looking into it."

Boone's brow wrinkled. "So what does that have to do with the council?"

Yeah, that's what Claire wanted to know. She reached for the rock in the middle of the table. Felix's hand beat hers to it, and he slipped it in his pocket.

"If I decide to actually do it, I'd need a permit to quarry the quartz. I'm still looking into what problems it could potentially cause for the town." He looked straight at Claire. "I know some of y'all question my decisions, but I love this town. It's my home, and I won't cause her any harm."

She was right. Felix was growing softer in his old age. Claire bit back a smile. "I know you and I butt heads a lot, but I have never questioned your love for Chapel Springs, Felix. That's saved your bacon a number of times."

He snorted. "I'd like to have Sean look into what is involved. Can I simply dig it up? What do I need to do? Or what steps do I need to take?"

Tom raised his hand. "I move we let Sean look into this for Felix since it would potentially have an effect on the town."

"I second it," Claire said. She only hoped it wouldn't interfere with the wedding plans since Sean was 'Lissa's fiancé.

Boone raised his gavel. "Any more discussion? All right, then all in favor raise your hand."

All hands rose.

"Opposed?"

Why did he do that? No one was left to oppose it. Silly rules. She gathered her things as soon as Doc moved for the meeting to end, then rose and made her way toward Jacqueline.

"I love your new haircut."

The reporter's hand brushed a strand of hair off her forehead. "Thanks." She turned as Felix walked by. "Mayor, may I have a word with you?"

Felix sighed but stopped.

"Why are you not interested in the gold?"

"Like I said, these mountains are littered with gold, but you rarely find enough to make a living, given the cost of mining. If—and that's a big 'if'—someone were to find a large vein and set up a major mining operation, costing thousands of dollars, they might make some money. But probably not as much as the rig cost." He winked at Claire.

She winked back. She knew what he was telegraphing. That would never happen in Chapel Springs. No matter how much gold there was. Life as it was in their little village was worth more than a pot of gold.

"Now, if y'all will excuse me, I've got a date." He nodded and lumbered toward the door.

Jacqueline scribbled a couple of notes, then said good night and left.

Claire eyed her retreating back. Now, why would she be so interested?

Claire flipped on the stage lights while the director and stage manager headed to the audience seating. She crossed the stage, and in her echoing footsteps, voices from past productions marched around her in a ghostly procession. A line from *Auntie Mame*, a soliloquy from Shakespeare, a song from *Guys and Dolls*. Claire turned to Lacey.

"Can you hea—"

Holy moly. Lacey had quit staring at the floor. Like a starving banquet guest, she took in her surroundings with wide-eyed anticipation. At least, until Kelly called her name. Then Lacey's eyes went to her toes, and she moved off the stage and down the aisle. No question about it, though, the theater was in the girl's blood.

After setting a handful of brushes and Lester's sketches on a crate in the wings, Claire strode to center stage, shaded her eyes against the spotlights, and searched for Kelly. There she was in the third row, flipping through what Claire guessed to be audition forms. "What do you want us to do tonight?"

Kelly looked up from the pages and peered over her glasses. "Since the set design is approved, y'all can go ahead and start painting. Just try to do it quietly, please."

The new side stage door opened and a small crowd entered, led by Ellie Grant. Even though Kelly knew everyone's acting abilities, she always held auditions—her way of being fair. Besides, sometimes a person from Scarlet's Ferry or a summer resident tried out.

Claire had been in a play once in high school. She grimaced at the memory. That was when she learned she was a better painter than actor. Waving at her friends gathered around Kelly, Claire headed backstage, twitching her nose against the smell of greasepaint and sawdust. Though the theater had been boarded up for years, the aroma clung to the old place, seeping from pores in the wood and wafting from the curtains.

Claire grinned, remembering how she and Patsy had played backstage while Great-aunt Lola rehearsed whatever play they were producing. Actors didn't have microphones back then. They projected their lines to the back row, using vocal technique and strong diaphragms. When she closed her eyes, Claire could almost hear them. If the theater was truly haunted, it was by memories of the past.

Raucous laughter rang out. Time to end her walk down memory lane and go to work. Joel and Nathan had spent several hours over the weekend with Lester, building new flats with lumber donated by The Tool Box. Claire stepped back as Joel and Lester placed them in order against the back wall.

Now, all she and Patsy needed to do was sketch out Lester's design and paint it. Claire picked up her pencil. "Thanks. Where're Patsy and Nathan?"

"Getting the paint out of the truck."

Claire checked the drawings against the line of flats. "Honey, the one that has the door in it needs to move two places to the left. Can you do that, please?" She pointed to where she wanted it, then squatted to set the drawings on the floor.

"Sure, but I may have to stop after a few minutes." Joel moved the set piece.

Claire turned her head to peer over her shoulder. "Why?" Was Joel blushing? She stood. "What's going on?" He wouldn't look her in the eye but pushed his foot against the crate where her brush bucket sat, moving it an inch closer. "Joel?"

"I'mtryingoutforapart."

She couldn't make out his mumbled reply. "You're what?"

"I'm trying out for a part."

He definitely blushed. This was exciting. Her Joel, an actor. How about that? She gave him a hug. "I think you'll do great." She hoped he won the role he wanted, whichever one—"What part are you reading for?"

"Kelly asked me to read for the fisherman. He's the one who finds the body. I guess she's typecasting." He chuckled and smoothed out the canvas he'd wrinkled. Then he lifted his head, his eyes meeting hers. "You really think I could do it?"

Claire put her arms around his neck and gave him a peck. "I think you'll be terrific." She gave him a second little kiss. "I haven't a doubt in the world."

Nathan and Patsy arrived, and Joel moved away to help his buddy. Was that a little swagger in his walk? It did Claire's heart good to see her sweet hubby step out of his comfort zone. This was going to be a fun play.

"Hey, Clairey-girl. I'm ready to paint." Patsy set down two buckets and four brushes.

"Are those the special fire-resistant paints?"

"They are. We don't want another episode with disappearing scenery, do we?"

Claire snorted a laugh. "At least that one wasn't my fault. I wasn't even there that night."

"Quiet, everyone!" Kelly's voice hushed them. "Auditions are starting."

Chapter 5

The man with ferret eyes rounded the last curve and arrived in Chapel Springs. That's all there was to it? He pulled over and stopped by a boat launch. This had to be the tiniest hamlet he'd ever seen. One street faced the lake and one t-boned off that. No big box stores. No supermarket. Nothing but water and trees and a few Podunk shops. He grinned. The Happy Hooker … he'd have to see what that was all about. He moved on and came up to a guard arm blocking the road. They had to guard the town? From what? He snorted and rolled up to the guard shack. An old man stepped out and approached his window, which he rolled down.

"Mornin'. Ain't seen you before. Renter?"

Nosy too. "Yes, my good man. I'm renting one of …" He pulled a paper from his shirt pocket and unfolded it. "Ah, here it is. Glen Tabor's cottages." He offered the old man a one-hundred-watt smile. "I'm in the raccoon cottage." *Appropriate too.*

"How long?"

None of your business. "I've got some business in town. Might be a couple of weeks. I'm not sure. I may stay to fish some."

"Cheapest is the monthly parking. Then you'll receive a free tram pass."

Restricted driving? That fit well into his plans. He gave the hillbilly an enthusiastic nod. "Sounds good to me. I like to save a dollar as much as the next guy."

The old dude pointed to a parking lot he'd not seen. "Leave your car there, and the tram will be here in"—he looked at his watch—"four minutes." He slapped a permit on the windshield.

"Thanks. See you around."

He pulled into the parking slot, grabbed his suitcase, and hustled to the tram stop. Interesting way to get around the town—it seemed small enough to walk everywhere you wanted to go. During the tram ride, he'd scope out the lay of the land. If the information provided to him was accurate, the goods were easy pickings. He'd start tonight. After dark.

Lacey settled next to Kelly and opened the notebook on her lap. As she glanced over the audition sheets, she inhaled deeply. Even out in the audience, Lacey could smell the heady aroma of theatrical production and a slight tinge of dust burning from the spotlights. The theater had something magical about it. This was her real life. She wasn't sure why or how, but when she was in the theater, she felt fully alive. Different. Unafraid. No time to pursue the thought, though. Kelly called for quiet. Auditions were starting.

Lacey glanced over the audition list. She'd been delighted when Kelly asked her for input in the casting selection. She wasn't sure about Ellie for the lead part of Alexa, but she was open to it and anxious to hear the librarian read. Flipping through the audition sheets everyone had filled out last week, Lacey searched for another person reading for the lead and finally found two more. She should have taken the time to put these in order.

Laying the applications side by side, she glanced up. "Is anyone else, besides Ellie and these other two, reading for Alexa?"

Kelly rifled through her audition forms. "That's it. I don't know the woman from Pineridge. Do you?"

Lacey shook her head.

A loud crash boomed from behind the backdrop. "Quiet on the set!" Kelly's shout made Lacey jump more than the crash did. "Anybody hurt?"

"Everyone's fine," Patsy replied. "Claire fell over a pile of lumber."

"Is she okay?"

"I'm okay. Bruised but okay."

Claire's disgusted admission made Lacey chuckle. Never in her life had she met such a klutz. With Claire for a friend, they had to keep a mop handy and, sometimes, a doctor. Even so, Lacey couldn't ask for a more lovable, loyal chum.

Kelly stood and faced those seated in the audience who were auditioning. "We'll begin with the lead character of Alexa." She glanced at her list. Lacey smiled. Kelly had that list memorized too. "Brenda Jerald, let's have you read first."

The new woman took the stage and read—rather nervously and without inflection, in Lacey's opinion. Not a speck of Alexa in her. The other person trying out was Esther Tully, who'd agreed to read only after much coercion. And Eileen Carlson. She said she'd read for the sidekick. She was the casting director for Lakeside Players. This was the first time Eileen had ever tried out for a part, as far as Lacey knew. She chewed on that thought for a moment. This would be interesting.

Ellie and Eileen took the stage. Though diminutive, Ellie commanded attention simply by her presence. Lacey couldn't take her eyes off the tiny, quiet librarian. How could she seem so large onstage? The moment she opened her mouth and read the first line, Ellie became Alexa. Lacey didn't need to hear any more. Strange, how the outside package hid what was inside the woman.

Eileen read her first line and the magic happened—the chemistry between two actors that lit up the set. Eileen had flair and Ellie played off it. Lacey's characters came alive onstage. Was this thrill of creation what women felt when they had a baby? Lacey marked Eileen's audition form with an asterisk for Alexa's sidekick. She set Ellie's audition sheet to one side, also marked with an asterisk at the top. Eileen joined Lacey and Kelly in the first row. Lacey handed her the forms from those who had already auditioned. When Eileen saw the one with her name and "sidekick" penciled on it in Lacey's handwriting, she quirked her mouth and one eyebrow.

The next character was the fisherman. Claire's husband, Joel, stepped out from the wings. He'd never been to a play before, to Lacey's knowledge. But when he read, he took ownership of the dialogue. Amazing. He was one of those people who had an untapped natural talent. His inflection was perfect. She'd have to remember that for future scripts. After Joel came the church pastor. Goodness, she was learning things about her friends tonight.

"What about me?" An Amazon strode onto the stage. While physically intriguing, her demeanor wasn't at all what Lacey imagined for the sidekick. No humor was apparent in her. The character of Bonnie needed to be a … well, a character. Quirky and wacky, yet the straight man—okay, woman—to Alexa's comedic lines. Like Eileen.

Lacey glanced at Kelly, who struck through the woman's name on the form. Eileen frowned at them.

"You're up now." Kelly looked down at the sheet. "Helen ... Hayes?" She raised her head to stare at the woman again.

She drew her shoulders back, making her appear even taller. "Yes, great-grandniece of the First Lady of the American Theater. I inherited her talent, as you'll see."

Lacey raised her eyebrows at Kelly. Was this woman for real? Helen Hayes was tiny and a sweet soul.

"Okaay. Uh, well, Helen, begin on page fourteen. Ellie, read with her, please."

Helen moved upstage from Ellie/Alexa, struck a commanding pose, and looked down her nose. "You didn't search his pockets, did you?"

No, no, no. Derision wasn't right. Helen had the wrong idea. Lacey wrinkled her nose at Kelly, who crossed her eyes.

"Helen, excuse me," Kelly said. "Let's start over. The character of Bonnie is Alexa's staunchest supporter."

"I don't see her that way." Helen planted her fists on her hips. "I see her as wanting to take Alexa's place."

The author in Lacey bristled. Helen wanted to upstage Ellie, pure and simple. She sure didn't have her ancestor's stage etiquette.

Kelly shook her head. "No, that's not the way she's written."

"She should be. It would add more conflict between them."

"That's not the story here, Helen. Please read it again without the attitude. And never upstage any actor in my theater."

The woman took two steps downstage and stared out at Kelly. "I don't think so. You obviously don't appreciate a *professional* opinion." She tossed the script down and stalked off.

Ellie turned and watched the retreating Amazon. She flinched when the backstage door slammed. "My, my, my. If that was a *professional* opinion, I'm six-foot-three." It took a moment for the laughter to quiet.

"Okay, let's get back to business. I believe we have our parts, right? Lacey? Eileen?"

Lacey nodded at Kelly. Together, Eileen and Ellie were spellbinding.

The only thing better would be if she, Lacey, could become Alexa, or at least like her—afraid of nothing. But how does one cast off their fears? Or being shy, for that matter? Every time Lacey tried, her heart raced, her tongue stuck to the back of her teeth, and her brain refused to compute.

Joel took Claire's hand and turned her toward the back of the theater. "We'll go the back way through Springs Park."

What did he want to talk about? Going this way took longer, which meant he didn't want to return home too fast. She walked in silence. He'd say it when he was ready.

"Do you think I made a fool of myself tonight?"

That didn't take long. She stopped, stepped in front of him, and took his face in her hands. "Oh, Joel. I was so proud of you. You're perfect for the part. If you were nervous, no one could tell. I thin—"

"Shh." Joel pointed over her shoulder. "Don't say anything but look across the park. There's a small light, like a flashlight, bobbing around near Felix's property."

Claire turned and squinted. "You're right. What do you suppose Felix is doing?"

"Felix isn't doing anything. He's walking Eileen home."

He was? "Then who do you think it is? And what is he doing?"

Joel scratched his head. "I don't know. I want to move a little closer to see." He pointed in the direction of home. "You go on. I don't want you here if there's any trouble."

That made her heart pound. She grabbed his sleeve. "I'm not leaving you. We'll go together, or I'll holler right here and now."

Joel sucked in his lower lip. "Claire, I—"

She crossed her arms and planted her feet.

He blew out his breath. "Okay, but stay behind me and be quiet."

She nodded and followed him. He took a path through an area wet from the rain. They'd be muddy when they arrived home, but they didn't make a sound as they crept through the forest.

Joel stopped and she almost ran into him. He put a finger to his lips and pointed with his other hand. A man was digging a hole. Why in the name of Van Gogh was he doing that? She looked at Joel wide-eyed. He turned her around and they headed home. Claire wanted to hurry so she could find out what Joel thought. Finally, they entered their back yard.

She stopped. She couldn't go another step without an answer. "Honey, who do you think that was? And what was he doing?"

Her hubby shook his head. "I don't know for sure. Something about him seems familiar, but I can't put my finger on it. I'm going to call Felix and Sheriff Jim Bob." He pulled off his shoes at the back door, leaving them in the wooden box he'd made for the kids' shoes. They hadn't used it in a long time. She slid hers off and set them beside his. She'd clean them in the morning.

When she came into the kitchen, Joel was talking on his phone. "No, we didn't get that close. But he was definitely on your land and he was digging ... uh-huh. Yeah, I called Jim Bob too ... all right. I'll meet you there." He tapped his phone, hanging up. "I'm meeting Jim Bob and Felix. You stay here."

As much as she wanted to, she didn't argue. He'd tell her when he came home, and the sheriff would be with him, so he'd be safe. Besides, it was probably some drifter ... but why would he be digging in Felix's backyard? *Gold.* That had to be it. Whoever it was, he must have been at the last town council meeting.

She closed her eyes and tried to picture everyone who'd been there. That hole digger had to be a renter. Most of the gold had been mined in the late 1800s. A person could dig for a month and not find a thing except blisters.

Twenty minutes later, Joel called her from Felix's house. "Whoever it was ran off as we came into the house. We searched but didn't find anyone. What he was doing, we aren't sure. He left a large hole in Felix's back forty."

"Gold. That's what he was looking for. I'll bet he was at the council meeting."

"Hmm. I'll tell Jim Bob, and we'll try to come up with who it could be. I'll be home in a bit."

Claire called Patsy and told her what they'd seen. "Be on the lookout in your yard at night. I have a feeling as much as everyone said they don't care, gold fever is hitting Chapel Springs."

Chapter 6

L acey closed her book and laid it on the sofa beside her. She couldn't concentrate after experiencing the joy of seeing the right people play her characters. If only she could be as open and free as Alexa or Bonnie. Whenever she tried, her heart pounded until she thought she'd faint.

Except for Jake. She pulled up her legs and hugged her knees. Talking to Jake never made her anxious or fearful. He'd proved his love for her long before she agreed to marry him. He could have had any girl he wanted. His good looks had women flirting with him all the time. They still did. But he loved her. She didn't understand it, but he saw something in her that nobody else did. And he never flirted back with women. She was one lucky girl.

Headlights shone through the window and bathed the living room in light. Her real-life hero pulled into the driveway. Lacey went to meet him at the door.

"Hey, sweet stuff." Jake kissed her and lingered, his fingers playing with her hair. He never hurried his hugs or kisses. After a moment, keeping his arm around her, he led her into the living room. "How did the auditions go?"

She took the mail from him. "Great. You'll never guess who's playing Alexa." He knew her characters as well as she did by the time she finished writing the scripts.

Jake scrunched up his eyes and his mouth. After a moment, he opened his eyes wide. "You?"

Lacey laughed. "Right. No, Ellie Grant."

"You're kidding."

"Nope. She's wonderful, Jake. She *is* Alexa."

"But she's so tiny. I always pictured Alexa as tall and commanding."

"Me too, but when she started to read, she became Alexa."

He emptied his pockets of his keys and change, dropping them into an abalone shell on the sofa table. "Then who's playing her sidekick, Bonnie?"

"Eileen Carlson. Together onstage, they have the magic. I've only seen it happen a couple of times, but when it does, it creates such magnetism, the audience is beguiled."

Jake flopped onto the couch. "But it takes a powerful script for them to read, babe. And this one is. I think it's your best."

He thought anything she did was the best. For Chapel Springs, she wasn't bad. Still, a sliver of excitement shimmied up her spine and sparked a dream. An unrealistic one, but a dream nonetheless. She tucked it away to ponder later.

Dark smudges accentuated hollows beneath Jake's eyes. She reached out to lay her hand against his cheek. "Can I get you anything? You look tired."

He patted the seat next to him. "I don't need anything but you."

When he didn't head straight for the shower, it meant he'd faced problems at one of the restaurants and wanted to talk. She snuggled in next to him. "What happened?"

"What didn't? Trey Appling and Billy Eisler got into a shouting match. Something about the football team. Billy threatened to quit." He put his arm around her and pulled her closer. "But when I'm with you, it all goes away." He closed his eyes and took a deep breath, blowing it out slowly.

She didn't try to fill the comfortable silence. Their living room, decorated in monochromatic tones, encouraged relaxation. Jake dozed off most nights; however, it wasn't a good place to work. Normally, her laptop sat in the sunny kitchen. There, her creativity pulsed.

"Sometimes," Jake mumbled, "I think it would be cool to have a restaurant somewhere like New York, where the waiters are professionals and not high school kids."

"I thought you'd gone to sleep. You realize those waiters would be starving actors, who would quit at the first casting call." She breathed in his scent and sat up. His regular citrusy cologne was overpowered by hickory and applewood. "You smoked meat tonight."

He laughed and stood. "Yeah. I'll go shower." He headed to their bedroom. "Hey, Lacey?" He stopped in the doorway. "You ever think about having one of your plays performed on Broadway?"

Leaving the question hanging midair, he walked down the hall.

The dream spark. Somehow, he'd picked up on it. How did he do it? Lacey walked to the window and looked out over Warm Springs Park. The lights on the gazebo twinkled between the trees. Everyone in Chapel Springs and Pineridge liked her plays, but she was a local writer. People always liked a local writer. That didn't mean her scripts were good enough for Broadway, though. Sure, it was the goal of every playwright, but …

Besides, would she even want to leave Chapel Springs? She wasn't raised here like her friends, but the town had welcomed her and made her feel safe. In New York, she'd feel lost. She wouldn't know anyone but Jake.

The whir of the shower stopped. Lacey left the window and went into the bedroom. She'd sort through it later. After all, it was only a dream, and a baby one at that.

The morning dawned bright and sunny, a nice change from the fog they'd had lately. On her way into the bank, Lacey passed Bud Pugh on the boardwalk. She raised her hand in greeting.

"Morning, Mr. Bud. How's your daughter getting along?"

"Fine as frog's hair, missy. She's all done with the chemo treatments and gaining her strength back. Thanks to you, she has a right pretty wig to wear."

Since her hair was thick and grew fast, every couple of years she cut it and donated it for wigs for women like Bud's daughter. She pulled up her collar around her neck and smiled to herself.

"It's my pleasure. I'm glad to hear she's doing so well."

The tram soon left and she walked on to the bank. A few moments later, she was settled at her desk and organizing the day's work. In front of her sat a stack of applications to present to the loan committee this week. The sun topped the trees, and a shaft of light illuminated the pile before her. She picked up the first one. This mound of loan apps represented hope for so many people. Hope for a new business or expansion of an existing one. To Lacey, they were neighbors, town merchants, and friends. She knew who was a good risk and who wasn't.

The first one was from Gloria Jenkins, who wanted to put another wing on her B&B. An addition made sense, considering the influx of tourists. They'd been booked solid for over a year now. The Eisler's Inn had been renovated last year. They'd added several guest rooms and a larger dining room. Gloria waited, though. Said she wanted to be sure the tourists continued to come. They did. Lacey set hers in the approval pile and continued to work her way through the stack.

When the clock chimed ten, she stretched a kink out of her back and hurried across the lobby to unlock the front door for the day's first customer. With a grateful smile, Mrs. Chester's eyes disappeared into her wrinkles, making her look like a sweet grandma elf. Her smile was infectious.

Lacey returned it with one of her own. "How's your arthritis today, Mrs. Chester?"

Taking her elbow, Lacey helped her cross the slick marble floor to one of the desks set aside for their senior depositors.

"Arthur is loud and sassy this morning." She gingerly lowered herself into the upholstered chair. "I have to expect that at my age." She tapped her cane against the floor. "Tell me how that handsome husband of yours is treating you. Thinking of leaving him yet?"

Lacey laughed and took the seat beside her. "Not even."

Mrs. Chester asked her that every time she came into the bank. To be fair, she asked every woman over the age of thirty. She had a single great-nephew, whom she was determined to see wed. Lacey let her chat for a moment.

"Are you making a deposit or withdrawal today?" She slid the two pads toward her.

"Deposit." Her gnarled hand covered Lacey's. "And I wanted to thank you for bringing me such a delicious supper Thursday evening. When I'm done here, I'll be on my way to Lunn's to pick up a soup bone." She handed Lacey her deposit. "I'll be at the opening night of your play. Are rehearsals going well? I hear it's your best script ever."

"Rehearsals are going very well, thank you."

"Good. Chester's bringing me. Break a leg." With a wink and her elf-smile, Mrs. Chester put her deposit receipt in her purse and toddled out.

That great-nephew of hers, Chester Nelson, was one of the business loans Lacey had fought hard for. She'd learned from comments over the years that Chester was conscientious and a good businessman. And he made a mean hamburger. At first, the committee had balked—said

Chapel Springs had enough restaurants, but Lacey knew competition was good for business. The more eateries they had, the more people they'd draw. If one place were too busy, they'd have another to go to. The suits finally saw the light, but only after she asked Chester to cater lunch during a loan committee meeting. The Burger Gourmet had become a reality four years ago.

Lacey loved helping people achieve their dreams. But what about hers? The bank no longer played a part in her aspirations. Her job was merely a means to an end—but what end? To write plays full time? She could. After all, she and Jake didn't really need her salary. Their retirement was secure. They had invested her earnings from the day they married. So why did she keep working here?

Still, what would she do without a full-time job? She couldn't write plays all day. After all, the Lakeside Players couldn't produce more than five a year. Who would want what she wrote? But if she didn't write, what would occupy her time? She and Jake didn't have children. He said they didn't need to know whose fault it was. They were okay with that. Besides, what did she know about being a mother?

Back in her office, Lacey answered emails from customers checking on the progress of their loans. She clicked Send on the third email. A fourth came in, but it was spam—an advertisement about publishing, which brought her thoughts automatically back to her scripts. Were they good enough to publish? According to the local theater reviewers, they were. Maybe she should check into some of those plays. She could buy one of the scripts from the publisher. Read it. Just to see. At lunch, she pulled up the Internet, went to a script publisher's site and bought a script of a play that had been on Broadway to use as a comparison. As soon as she printed her receipt, her heart began to pound.

Chapter 7

Claire sat at the banquette in her kitchen with Megan and Melissa flanking her. Dozens of photos lay in messy stacks all over the old table. Cakes, invitations, flowers, bridesmaids' gift ideas, catering flyers, bubbles, birdseed, or rose petals—the decisions were enough to boggle the mind.

Claire touched the border of one of the photos. "When your daddy and I married, we reserved the gazebo in Springs Park, and Patsy helped me make finger sandwiches. You sure y'all don't want to elope?"

The girls giggled, knowing she was kidding. And she was—sort of. Joel worried about the cost. She'd tried to reassure him last night. After all, the weddings and the reception were a two-for-one affair, so they ducked a double hit. He pointed out her flawed math.

"Momma, we need you to cast the deciding vote. Both of us like this invitation." Megan pointed to an off-white, lacy-looking cutout. "But we like this one too." She held up one with clean lines and block print.

Neither looked like her girls. She sorted through the pile until she found the one she'd brought home last week. "What about this one? Did you even look at it?"

'Lissa picked it up, and her eyes opened wider. "Meg, it's perfect. Did you see this before?"

Megan peered around Claire, reaching out her hand. "Uh-uh." When 'Lissa gave it to her, she huddled over the invitation created from puzzle pieces. "Did you show this to us, Momma, or just slip it in the pile?"

Claire shrugged. They wouldn't have even considered it if she'd handed it to them.

'Lissa ran a knuckle beneath her eyes. "I love how it says we found our missing piece because that's what happened with both of us, huh, Meg?"

Megan tucked her bottom lip between her teeth and grinned. "I love it. That's the one. We can put all the pieces in one envelope, and our guests can put them together to see who's marrying who."

"Can we have them cut so only the right groom goes with the right bride?" 'Lissa dropped the invitation back on the table, then slid her fingertips over it.

"You can. My friend Unity Jones makes them, along with all her other artistic labors. She's a woman of many talents."

"Not to mention electroplating illegal leaves." The twins giggled.

Claire groaned "Please. I had no idea those leaves were marijuana."

"Aw, Momma. We love our necklaces."

"Thank you, Megan, but the resulting night in jail I prefer to forget. Well, except for meeting Mel." The jury was still out on Hazel— Motorcycle Mama. She'd become a good customer, but— "Anyway, Unity said after they're printed, she does the cutting. Each will have its own pattern and size, so the pieces can't be placed in the wrong puzzle."

Megan swept the rest of the invitation samples into a wastebasket sitting beside the table. "Done. Next, the cake." She pulled out photos of Dee's creations. Since they knew what Dee's concoctions tasted like, an hour later, they'd settled on the style, flavor, and filling.

Claire put a check next to "cake" on the list. "What about the groom's cake?"

"Dane and Sean already chose one together. Chocolate, obviously." 'Lissa stretched. "I'm going cross-eyed. We made two major decisions tonight. Can we save the rest for tomorrow after church?"

Claire put her hands on the table and pushed herself up. "Sounds good to me. I have a couple of errands to run, anyway. See you at supper."

'Lissa shook her head. "Not me. I'm babysitting Micah and Aela. Charlie and Sandi have a date night."

Claire paused as she reached for her tote. "What about your supper?"

"I'll make a sandwich at their house."

The gallery's front-door bell jingled and the handle rattled. The clock showed seven thirty-four. Who could be here at this late hour? Patsy had gone home, but Claire was working to finish another whimsy urn for the art tour. She grabbed a rag to wipe her hands on her way to the door. Felix. She flipped the deadbolt and let him in.

His shirt was disheveled, and one tail hung outside his pants. Their mayor might be a large man, but he was always meticulous in his dress, shirttail tucked in and suspenders straight. She grabbed his arm and pulled him inside.

"Felix, what's wrong? Come on in the back where we can talk."

"I've been over at the county seat researching the title on my land."

Claire stopped. "What did you find out?"

"That I own the land but not the mineral rights."

"What?" Claire gestured to her desk chair. "Sit. I'll bring some water." She removed two bottles from the fridge and gave one to Felix. While he opened his water and took a long swig, she pulled Patsy's stool over near him and sat.

"So tell me how can you own the land and not the mineral rights?"

"Gotta go back four generations. When my great-great-granddaddy homesteaded this land, it was 1873. The mint in Dahlonega had closed at the onset of the late unpleasantness in 1861."

"I know that, Felix. What does that have—"

He held up his hand. "Just wait. After the War of Northern Aggression, gold was getting harder to find. The miners had left long before that, headin' to the gold rush out West. The point is, people knew there was still plenty of gold left in the mountains. But it wasn't as easy to mine, so old Frank McIlrath, who my great-great-granddaddy bought the land from, kept the mineral rights. He was one smart hillbilly."

Claire fingered the gold loop in her ear. Made of Dahlonega gold, they had belonged to Great-aunt Lola. "Where does that leave you? Can you find the descendants and buy the rights?" And what would he do with them if he had them? He probably couldn't find enough gold on his land to buy a vacation in Myrtle Beach.

"I'm researching that now. After the end of the war, McIlrath moved his family to Kentucky. Makin' things harder is the last son in the family died in the flu epidemic in 1918. A daughter survived, though, so I'm starting by looking at the marriage records there."

She might regret this, but her nemesis wasn't quite as irascible as he used to be. She kind of liked him, not that she'd tell him that. "How can I help you, Felix?"

He finished off the water, crushed the bottle, and screwed the cap back on. "I don't rightly know, Claire. Without those mineral rights, I can't do anything. But if I can find the daughter's married name and the descendants, maybe I can buy them. The rights, I mean. I don't plan on mining for gold. I might set up a small panning outfit for the tourists, though. Like the one in Dahlonega. They might like that."

Not a bad idea. "What about the quartz? Didn't you want it?"

"Changed my mind. I looked into it, and quarrying the rock would destroy Chapel Springs. I couldn't do that. Not for any amount of money."

Claire's heart melted. "Felix, that's where you and I will always be of one accord. We may disagree on a lot of things, but I've always known your heart for this town."

He leaned back like she might try to hug him. "Well, don't you tell folks that. They'll think I've gone soft."

"Never. Now, if we're going to find the daughter, I'd suggest—rats, I'm not sure what to suggest. It's not going to be easy."

"Don't I know it? He pushed his ball cap back on his head and scratched his ear. "I might take a trip to Frankfort and see what I can find."

"Why don't you call first? You might find a sympathetic clerk, especially if she knows you're the mayor here."

Felix stared at her like she was brilliant. "Who would I call, though?"

"Vital records. Start there."

"If I don't get those mineral rights back, I can't do anything. Not to mention the state could buy them and then force me to sell to them."

"What are you talking about?"

"If the state decides there is more than quartz there, like gas or oil, they can claim that eminent domain thing and force me off my land."

Claire's heart skipped a beat, then accelerated. "Felix, could this happen to everyone?"

"There's that potential. If someone puts his hands on enough mineral rights, even if he doesn't find gold, he could bring the state in, show them there's gas or oil there, and they could claim all of Chapel Springs."

Claire dipped her fingers in the bucket beside her, bringing up a slight amount of water to wet the clay. Her potter's wheel spun at the same speed as her thoughts. Felix had told her Deputy Farley was on his way home last night and fell into a large hole left in the forest. A hole nearly as deep as a grave but round. Whoever dug it didn't bother to fill it in. Farley could have broken his neck instead of his arm.

Who was digging up Chapel Springs? And why? She hadn't shared her thoughts about the cause being gold, but gold fever affected some people in strange ways.

"Pat-a-cake, remember when we were little and one of the summer people found a small nugget of gold in one of the lake's feeder streams?"

Patsy's head popped out from behind her easel. Her grin revealed a smear of vermillion paint on her front tooth. How she always seemed to get it on her teeth was a wonder. "I remember that. That nugget turned all the summer people and a lot of us kids into gold miners. I still have the pan Daddy bought for me."

Claire shook her head. "Collectively, what did we manage to net? About twenty dollars' worth?"

"About that, but to a couple of six-year-olds, that was a fortune."

"And we gave it up as soon as your daddy paid us the twenty. But do you remember that one couple?" She lifted her arm to scratch her temple. Oops, she was covered in clay. She tapped her foot instead. "Oh, what was their name? Something to do with ducks."

"You mean Quackenbush?"

"That's it. How'd you come up with it?"

Patsy waved her paintbrush in a circle. "Easy. Ducks quack."

"Good one. Well, Mr. Quackenbush was panning every day for a month. When it was time to go home, he told his wife to go without him. He was staying on his 'claim.'" Claire chuckled. "My daddy said he'd caught gold fever."

"What happened?"

"You don't remember? His wife had their grown son come for him. All the rooms and cottages were rented. Mr. Quackenbush pitched a tent beside the north fork of Benson Creek."

"I didn't think that was allowed." Patsy dipped her brush in a pot of odorless turpentine, then wiped it.

"We didn't have a sheriff back then, so he got away with it until his son came and threatened to have him committed to a home for the delusional."

"What made you think about that?"

Claire rested her hands on her clay-covered overalls. "Felix and his quartz. There are more holes being found too. I think the word is out that there's gold in Chapel Springs."

Patsy laughed until she hiccupped. "A person can't find enough gold to buy the Goldmine burger at The Burger Gourmet. Why, Bud Pugh has more gold in his teeth than can be panned anymore."

Claire shivered. "Unless someone builds a serious mining operation." One that could reach gold deep inside the earth. "Whatever happened to that huge vein of quartz containing gold that was so big, they didn't measure it in inches but in feet?"

Chapter 8

Claire left the girls gathering up their samples after yet another session of selections. This one was for the table décor for the reception. They decided to keep it simple since it was to be outdoors. No table coverings to blow away. They chose two-inch metal pots planted with geraniums as a table favor. Then people could have a permanent memory of the weddings.

Claire closed the front door behind her. As she walked toward the pharmacy, she rubbed the back of her neck. An octopus of a headache had its tentacles wrapped around the base of her skull and was squeezing. This morning, she checked the calendar and her fears were confirmed. Her period was five weeks late. The only times she was ever late she'd been pregnant.

The implications were earth shattering. Her personal forty-eight-year-old earth, anyway. What would she do? What *could* she do?

Lean on Me when you're not strong.

"I try to, but this? Oh, Lord, what am I going to do?"

I'll be your friend. I'll help you carry on.

"This isn't funny." Although, if she looked at it from God's perspective, maybe it was—to Him. She bit back a grin. *As if.*

Wishing she were invisible, Claire crept into the drugstore. Tom waved at her from behind the pharmacy window. Terrific. Now he knew she was here. How was she going to manage to buy a pregnancy test without him wondering or even asking whom it was for? What if he thought it was for one of the twins? And he would. He sure wouldn't think it was for her. She gulped. Gossip would fly all over town, and the twins would be mortified.

She turned toward the hair color aisle. If she picked up a box of color, she could hide the test beneath it. Then, if she waited until a long line was at the register, in the rush to hurry everyone through, she could check out without anyone noticing her purchase.

How long could she dawdle without drawing attention? She picked up the first box and turned it over, pretending to read the instructions. Holding on to that first box, she picked up another color, then a third and a fourth. This should do it. Balancing them in her arms, she glanced to her left and then her right. Nobody was in the aisle. Good.

Juggling the four hair color boxes, she found the pregnancy tests after going up and down several aisles. There were so many brands. She moved the boxes to her left arm, rearranging one to keep from dropping it, then picked up the first test and turned it over to read.

She had to do what? Oh dear. Were they all like that? She picked up another and read the back. Same instructions. What a revolting' devel—

"Well, hello." Voices in the next aisle sent her heart into hyperdrive and boxes popping out of her grip. After rousting them back into submission, she tiptoed closer to the voices.

"How are you, Vince?"

Claire froze. What was her brother-in-law doing here? She scurried to the incontinence end of the aisle. Wait, no, not there either. Why had she thought this was a good idea? How could she make a clean getaway? She still held all the boxes of hair color and was in the wrong aisle to put them back. Well, tough luck. It would give Ralene something to do later. Shoving all but one back onto a shelf in the middle of the Depends, she turned and headed to the checkout with a single box of dye.

"Claire! Hey! Over here."

Rats. And caught like one too. She turned with what she prayed resembled a non-guilty smile on her face. "I thought I heard a familiar voice."

Vince put his arm around her. The woman he'd been talking to raised one eyebrow. Good, she was interested in Vince.

"Haleigh, this is my sister-in-law, Claire." The eyebrow resumed its natural place. "Claire, this is Haleigh Evans. She recently moved to Chapel Springs."

Claire reached out her hand and gave a genuine smile. She wanted Vince to meet someone, and she'd already heard about Haleigh. A military widow.

Claire clasped her hand. "I'm very pleased to meet you. Thank you for your late husband's and your service to us all. Why did you choose Chapel Springs?"

Haleigh's open smile revealed a tiny space between her front teeth and her right eyetooth. It made her grin endearing. "Thank you, Claire. Vince has told me a lot about you and your husband. I'm delighted to meet you. I'm teaching at the community college in Pineridge."

Vince eyed her hands. "Thinking of becoming a redhead, Claire?"

"What?" She looked down at the box she held. "Oh. Uh, no. I guess I grabbed the wrong color." She crossed her eyes, making Vince laugh and giving her an excuse to go. "I'd better find the right one. Nice to meet you, Haleigh. Come join me and my friends some morning at Dee's 'n' Doughs."

Claire hurriedly set the box of red dye back on the shelf and left empty-handed. Maybe Monday morning—no, that wouldn't work either. Ralene worked the register then, and Tom's wife was almost as big a gossip as Faye Eisler. Didn't matter if what she saw was true or not, she'd create a story around it, telling everyone within a hundred miles.

Should she adopt Patsy's way of facing problems? Pretend it didn't exist and maybe it would go away? Until she started to show. Then what?

The bells at the bakery clattered as Claire opened the door. A yawn stretched her lips. She'd managed to fall asleep last night, but a little after midnight a jumble of horrible images woke her. They'd started in a dimly lit doctor's office off some back alley. She'd run out, screaming. Then the dream changed. An old decrepit Claire in a wheelchair pushing a stroller occupied by another set of twins. All night long, her stomach had rolled and bounced like the Harlem Globetrotters on exhibition.

"Morning, Claire. What's your choice today?"

"Tea, please. Herbal."

Dee froze, her hand poised over the coffee pots. "I think my hearing's gone. I thought you said herbal tea."

"I did. I think I ate something that didn't agree with me." *Please believe me.*

Dee tsked sympathetically. "You poor thing. I have the perfect tea. It's mint with some other soothing herbs. I'll bring it over to you."

"Thanks, Dee." Claire took two deep breaths, attempting to settle her stomach on the way to the table. Haleigh was sitting next to Patsy. Claire finagled a smile. "I'm glad to see you made it."

Ellie's head bobbed up and down. "Claire, you aren't going to believe this. I managed to register Mel in the B Session at the college like you suggested. And guess what? Haleigh is teaching two of her classes." Ellie turned to Haleigh. "What were they, again?"

"Introduction to Engineering and Problem Solving and Introduction to Computing Environments. From what Ellie tells me of Mel, I'm anxious to meet her. She sounds a lot like me when I was young." Haleigh blushed a deep red.

Claire was a sap for blushers. It usually meant the person didn't carry an overly high opinion of herself. "You were a child engineering prodigy? How did that affect you?"

"The social part was a bear. I was so much younger than everyone else. I was fifteen. Mel, at least, is almost seventeen."

"I'm so glad none of us knew how brilliant she was until now. Her father—" Ellie clamped her lips together and shook her head.

Claire patted Ellie's hand. "She'll do fine. She's very street-wise." Her gaze returned to Haleigh. "So, tell me why you chose Chapel Springs over Pineridge or Scarlet's Ferry?"

The blush crept up Haleigh's neck again. Claire hoped it meant Vince was the reason. "I'd visited here before and met a few people." She blinked and looked at her cup.

Time to let her off the hook. "Well, I'm tickled you did. Not only for Mel's sake." Claire winked at her. "Ellie, what does Mel need for school? Patsy and I want to help."

Ellie nodded. "I appreciate it, Claire. I'm putting all the money the state gives me into an account for her tuition. I want to talk to your Wesley about investing some of that money for her. So, if you really want to help, I'll accept it."

"Wes invested some of the money my dad left me," Carin said. "It's done very well. Enough so that I don't need to substitute teach."

Claire frowned. "I thought you were still doing that."

"I am but not as often. They only call me if they can't find anyone else."

Patsy pushed her chair back and angled it toward Carin. "How's JJ getting along in school?"

"Fantastic. He loves it here, and he and Mikey have a new friend too. They both have fallen in love with Haleigh's little girl, Belle."

A little girl for Vince to spoil? It couldn't be more perfect. A kick to her ankle pulled her from her thoughts. Ouch. Claire leaned toward

Patsy. "What did you do that for?" she whispered.

"You're matchmaking again."

"Did I say a word?"

Patsy laughed. "You didn't have to. Come on, we need to go to work." She picked up her cup and napkin.

"What's the hurry?" Carin asked.

"We're going on a national tour right after our kids' wedding, remember? We have a lot to do."

The tour. She'd forgotten. Her stomach flopped over again. What if she started to show? God wouldn't. He couldn't. Well, He could, but would He? *Please, no.* Oh, how could her own body betray her like this? She had to get over to the drug store in Pineridge. People didn't know her there, and if she were seen buying a pregnancy test, no one would think anything of it—except that she was too old for it. Could a person die of mortification?

From what the redneck said, renters here got involved in village life, and that's what he would do. That way, if anyone saw him, they'd think he was a local too. He wasn't positive about that, but then he wasn't a redneck and had no way of plumbing their minds. He hoped what's-his-face did. He slipped on the plaid shorts, a shirt, and the fisherman's sandals he bought at the boat launch. That had been an eye-opener. No wonder the redneck said these people were ripe for them. That hayseed kid could have sold them for twice what he did and gotten away with it since there wasn't anywhere else to buy them.

The street was fairly busy, although that depended on what you called busy. Sure wasn't like New York. A couple hundred people would overwhelm this backwater town. He was on a mission to gather information, so he followed the mini-crowd to a bakery. While he waited his turn, he kept his eyes and ears open. The residents were pretty easy to separate from the non-residents. The renters, as the guard called them, dressed like he did. Denim seemed to be the choice of the hillbillies, although some dressed a little better in khakis. He started to snicker, then pulled it back.

His turn came up at the counter. The food looked pretty good for a backwoods bakery. "Do you make everything here or ship it in?"

The round-faced woman behind the counter smiled pleasantly but bit off her words. "Here, of course. Nothing is shipped in except the flour and sugar."

"No offense meant, ma'am." It wouldn't do to insult the natives. "It all looks delicious. What do you recommend?"

She held the tongs like a weapon. "Depends on what your tastes are."

She was no pushover. "You select for me."

Using her weapon, she selected a hunk of pastry and set it on a plate. "Enjoy. That's four-fifty, includes a beverage. Coffee is over on the coffee bar." She slid a cup toward him.

He found a table as close to the middle of the place as he could. Did she own this bakery or rent it? It would suit his purposes if she rented. A group of women sat with their heads together at a table near the window. He leaned back to enjoy his breakfast and listen.

Chapter 9

Claire used her wrist to push her readers into their proper place on her nose. For the intricate detail work necessary to make the animals come to life, she needed to see. A supply of toothpicks lay beside her, and she picked one up, using it to make tiny grooves in the clay. Those quickly became the otter's fur. She smiled at the playful turn of its head. He'd make a wonderful large whimsy pot. She rotated her neck to work out the kinks. Tomorrow, she'd blend his body into a clay pond she'd prepared for him. Wouldn't it be wonderful if she could scratch out her problem as easily as she scratched fur onto this otter?

Patsy was hard at work on a new painting, but Claire had done enough. "You almost finished for the day?"

"Not anywhere near. I've got a vision, but I'm struggling to put it onto canvas."

"That's not like you, Pat-a-cake. Is something wrong?" Here she'd been so focused on her own mess she'd missed Patsy's.

"Claire?"

Patsy's voice was barely audible. Claire had to strain to hear her. The hairs on the back of her neck stood at attention. "What's wrong?"

"I'm scared. This tour is turning me into a quivering ostrich, ready to stick my head in the sand."

Had Patsy lost her marbles? "That's the nuttiest thing I've ever heard come out of your mouth, girl. You're talented, even more so than your mother. Why are you so scared?"

"You said why—Mama. Her artwork is world renowned. She's in the collections of some of the world's major collectors. Who am I? Just a small-town artist."

That painted mad all over Claire. She threw down her apron. "Patsy Louise Kowalski! I'm insulted." She glared at her friend. "Where do you come off calling me and my business partner the equivalent of a couple of backwoods hick artists? We've received great reviews. Even Avery Chandler became an agent so he could rep *us*. And we're in the collections of some well-known collectors." Claire turned her back and crossed her arms. She had to help Patsy snuff this creativity-killer fear—and fast.

Patsy's stool scraped the floor, and a moment later, her hand rested on Claire's shoulder. "Claire?"

Good. Her outburst worked. She turned, a half smile tugging at one corner of her mouth. She pursed her lips to stop it. "What?"

"Thanks. I hadn't thought it through. You're right. I only hope I can live up to my mama's reputation."

Claire waved that away. "Your mama has a completely different style. You've never been compared to her." She let the smile come. "Even Avery didn't do that, and he fawns over your mother's work."

Patsy squared her shoulders. She grabbed a rag, dipped it in odorless turpentine, and wiped her brush. "You're right. I'm being silly. What time is it?"

Claire slid her phone from her back pocket and checked. "It's four thirty. Let's go catch the boys' baseball game. We can start fresh in the morning."

They let Nicole know they were leaving and went out the back door, crossed the street, and strolled into Springs Park. Last year, the men in town had cleared enough trees from the back corner of the park to add a baseball diamond. Then they formed a team and joined a Southeast men's league. Dee's Dough Boys, sponsored by the bakery, hoped to win the pennant this year. Vince had joined the team. He and Joel both had excelled in baseball in high school and Vince in college. And having a doc on the team eased Claire's mind.

The game was in the bottom half of the second inning when they arrived. They settled onto the bleachers by JJ and Carin Jardine and in front of Tillie Payne, JoAnn Hanson, and the team's sponsor, Dee Lindstrom.

"It's about time y'all got here," Dee said, keeping her eyes on the game. "Hey, batter, batter, swing!" A cheer went up from the home bleachers as the batter struck out.

Claire squinted at left field. "Is that Ryan Graves out there?"

"Yep," Tillie said. "He does better with one arm than most do with two. Just watch."

Patsy waved to Nathan, who was the first baseman. Joel played shortstop. The next batter knocked a fly into left field. Ryan ran beneath it and caught it on a dead run. Then, while sprinting toward third, he tossed the ball in the air a couple of feet, dropped his mitt, re-caught the ball, and fired it to third base for the out. A double play. Carin and JJ jumped up, screaming.

JJ tugged on Claire's sleeve. "He's great, isn't he, Miss Claire?"

"He sure is." She had heard on the NASCAR circuit gossip that Carin's ex hooked himself to a new bride. She was glad JJ had a father image in Ryan since his own daddy didn't have time for him.

"And you should see him at bat. Nothing stops Ryan." JJ wiggled in between her and Patsy. "Mama said you were going on a tour." He frowned. "Is your tour in Afghan'stan like Ryan's was?"

She smiled and chucked him under the chin. "No, sugar. This isn't a military tour."

"I thought Mama was wrong."

"Well, she wasn't wrong. I am going on tour, but this is an art tour."

JJ nodded. "Yeah, I thought you were too old for a military tour."

"JJ!" Carin rolled her eyes. "You don't say that to a lady."

"Oops. I'm sorry, Miss Claire. You aren't really old. Not like Miss Tillie. She's so old, she farts dust."

Carin screeched and hid her face. Claire cracked up, and everyone within hearing distance laughed—Tillie the loudest. She tapped Carin on the shoulder. "Don't y'all be mad, now. It's me who should apologize. I told him that."

Carin shook her finger at Tillie, but she was laughing so hard, she couldn't say anything. JJ reveled in the attention.

The other side retired, and it was the Dough Boys' turn at bat. Joel hit a single and Nathan walked. Farley Taylor struck out. Then Vince hit a homer, and the score was three to one. This was going to be an exciting game. Mikey Akins called to JJ from beneath the bleachers. After asking his mama, he slid through the opening and dropped down to play with his best buddy.

Tillie dug in her pocket, pulled out some money, and held it between the bleachers. Her hand came up empty. Claire chuckled. "You're going to spoil those boys."

"Those two are far from spoiled, and they're my best readers. They come to my store to read the old children's books."

"You don't mind that they don't buy?"

"Nope. Instill reading when they're young, and they'll buy when they're grown."

Tillie hadn't lived in Chapel Springs but two years, yet she was already investing in the children. Funny how Esther Tully had despised Tillie when she'd first opened her store. Now—

She turned in her seat to face Tillie. "You and Esther have become good friends, haven't you?"

Tillie chuckled a moment. "It took a bit of time. She was sure I was trying to put her out of business."

"How'd you convince her you weren't?"

"Started buying books from her."

"You're kidding, right?"

"Nope. Esther needs her store for her livelihood. Mine's for my sanity." She took her eyes off the field and glanced at Claire. "And I needed friends. Someone to talk books with. Carin gave me the idea."

Carin turned. "I didn't do it, but if I was supposed to, it's done."

Tillie waved her silliness away. "You told me Esther's past, so instead of being put out, I understood her. A little love—well, a lot of love and persistence won her over. Now she, Ellie, and I meet for dinner once a week to talk books."

The loud crack of a bat connecting with a baseball propelled them to their feet. Joel had hit a homer. "Run, baby, run!" Claire screamed. The bleachers bounced with foot stomping—and it was for *her* hubby.

After they resumed their seats, Patsy's knee bumped hers. "Thanks for the attitude adjustment today."

"Anytime. You do the same for me. In fact, I could name several times."

"I think between the weddings and the tour, I'm stressed."

Claire glanced at her. "I don't know why. So far, everything's going fine. Neither of us has to worry about the in-laws."

"Thank the good Lord for that. Did you ever think we'd see our families unite like this?"

"I'd always hoped, but the last two kids I'd have put money on were your Dane and our Megan." Claire shaded her eyes and scanned the bleachers. "Speaking of the kids, have you heard where they want the reception?"

Patsy looked at her, eyes narrowed. "Where?"

Claire dropped her hand to her lap to look at her. "Sandy Shores Drive. Apparently, the girls asked Felix, and in a moment of weakness, he said yes. They told him streets are already closed to most traffic, so stopping the rest during that time shouldn't be a big thing. Felix started to protest, then Meg kissed his cheek and pleaded with him, said that Chapel Springs is the prettiest town in the South. And that everyone in town was invited. They laid it on thick."

"And he said okay? That's amazing."

Felix was definitely getting soft, not that she'd ever say that to him. That would be the quickest way to make him change his mind.

"It's really a great idea. Tables along the beach side, the street open for dancing."

Patsy waved at Hazel and Oscar Jones, climbing up the bleachers. "What about tourists?"

Claire leaned close. "From what I hear from Faye and Gloria, nobody has any available rentals for that weekend—at least not until Sunday night."

The crowd cheered, and they both looked up to see why. Earl Appling scored.

"That's awfully nice of them. It's a financial loss."

"I know. Sweet Lydia started it. Faye Eisler wouldn't be left out to be labeled a curmudgeon. Warren grumbled, but Gloria seems to have grown a backbone and said if Felix was letting them use Sandy Shores, and the other B&Bs were closing, there was no way she would open. If he wanted to do all the work, then he could do it alone."

Patsy laughed. "He hates hard work. I'm so touched by this. I had no idea."

"That's because you're the mother of the groom not the bride. Those boys don't worry about details."

"Wow, that means we have a lot to do in the next few weeks—besides make art. What about Sean's parents? Where will they stay?"

"At his cottage."

"Hey, girls." Patsy's dad climbed onto the bleachers and sat next to them.

Patsy craned her neck looking behind him. "Where's Mom?"

"Working on a new painting."

"Is she sleeping better? I know the meds she was taking gave her insomnia."

"We're both sleeping better." Doc grinned, then jumped up. "He's out!" The umpire turned and pointed at Doc until he sat down. "Stan needs glasses."

Funny how at first Doc ignored the signs of Alzheimer's in Patsy's mom, and now he was researching new medicines. Claire leaned forward to talk across Patsy. "How'd you do that, Doc? Find the new meds, I mean."

"Even old doctors can use the computer, Clairey-girl. There's a lot out there in the way of information."

Maybe she could find some information on pregnancy at her age. "Where would someone look if they were interested in … say a diagnosis for—" *Think!* "For acid reflux?"

"You having trouble?"

"No, merely curious. You know me."

Doc's eyes drilled into her. "Yes, I do. And if you have a problem, come in and see me or Vince. Stay off WebMed. That will confuse you."

WebMed. *She scores.* Claire logged it in her mind. When she went home, she'd take a look. Then she'd know. She hoped.

Joel strolled to the plate. He tapped his bat and looked over at her, winking. He looked almost like he did back in high school. Ten pounds heavier and a little gray at the temples, but he still made her heart flutter. What would he say when he learned she was pregnant? At their age. Claire closed her eyes, then opened them quickly. She didn't want to miss it if Joel hit another homer.

Chapter 10

Lacey stayed her hand, mid-knock. Through the glass in the front door, two women lounged on the sofa. Carin had company. Lacey whirled and started back down the steps. Just as her foot hit the last one, the door opened.

"Lacey? Hey, it's good to see you. Come on in."

Lacey shook her head. "No, no. You've got company."

Carin slipped out the door and caught her arm. "They're not company. They're customers—authors, staying here on a writing retreat. I've turned my house into a moneymaker, so come on in. They're about to go out, anyway." Carin had hold of Lacey's arm, so she didn't have much choice. She followed her inside, where the two women eyed her curiously.

"LuAnn, Celeste, meet Lacey. She's a playwright."

The heat started in her neck and swept upward into her cheeks. Why did Carin tell them that?

The redhead—LuAnn or Celeste?—looked Lacey over from her dishwater-no-color hair, past her too-big nose, to her non-brand loafers. "What plays have you published?"

Carin lifted her chin. "She hasn't submitted them to anyone yet, Celeste, but they've been produced here and in other community theaters. They're excellent."

The other one, LuAnn, rose. "Speaking of shows, let's get this one on the road. I'm hungry. Nice to meet you, Stacy."

"It's Lacey," Carin said and handed LuAnn a key. "In case you stay out late. You can leave it on the kitchen island when you come in."

After they left, Lacey relaxed. "Friends of yours?"

Carin laughed. "Not likely. Most of the writers I claim as friends are nice. But I'll take their money." She rubbed her hands together, grinning. "They arrived about an hour ago and have been trying to impress me since they walked in. Celeste asked me straight out for a referral to my agent."

"You signed with a new agent? When?" That was good news. Lacey dropped onto the sofa.

Carin beamed. "I did. I've known her for years. She called me as soon as she heard I'd been cut loose. Blythe has been a long-time encourager for me." She leaned against the island separating the great room from the kitchen. "So, what's up with you?"

Lacey pulled at a loose thread on her T-shirt's hem.

"Come on, Lacey. Tell me." Carin joined her on the couch, sitting beside her.

Lacey picked up a throw pillow and hugged it to her galloping heart. "Jake said to ask you how to go about getting some of my plays published."

"He's right. They're really good. You have a gift for dialogue."

She did? A gift? Carin could be saying that to be nice, though. Lacey glanced sidelong at her friend.

Carin shifted on the couch so she faced her. "I mean it, Lacey. Your wit makes the dialogue snappy. That's money in a stage play."

Her toes hung over the edge of a rocky precipice. She took a deep breath. "What would I have to do?"

"To publish? I don't know a lot about plays, but I'll call Blythe." Carin picked up her cell phone from the coffee table and tapped it a couple of times.

Her friend didn't waste any time. A butterfly danced to "Great Balls of Fire" in her gut.

"I'll help you write a query letter and a synopsis—Hello, Blythe? It's Carin. Good, thanks. You? … Great. Hey, what do you know about stage scripts?" Carin's eyes widened and she grinned at Lacey, nodding her head. "Really? Yes, I do. I have a friend who's a good playwright. I'm pretty sure she's *very* good. Would you ask him if he'd look at one of her scripts? Uh-huh. Sure. Like a novel query? Oh, all right. I can do that. Thank you." Carin swiped her finger across the phone. "There's an agent at her agency who represents playwrights."

Breathe. Lacey tugged at her collar. "So what do I do now?"

Carin flopped her head against the back of the sofa. "We'll get your query and synopsis ready to send in the next couple of days."

"How can I ever repay you?"

Carin laughed. "You can't. You're my friend, Lacey. Friends don't need to repay."

"But you said you don't refer people to your agent, but you referred me."

"Because I already know you're good. And I didn't refer you to Blythe. I asked if she knew anything about stage plays."

"Well, it never would have happened without you making that call. At least I can treat you to a great dinner. You and JJ." She scanned the hallway and stairs. "Where is he?"

"Hiding out back with Edgar."

That made Lacey laugh and settled the butterflies. "Tell me about the writers' retreat. Doesn't having people here interfere with your writing?"

Carin rose. "Come on up and see."

Lacey followed her up the stairs.

"This is where I write."

The office was in the attic, but it sure didn't look like any attic she'd ever seen. Painted in a soft gray with white crown molding, the room had a long dormer, maybe ten feet in length. Overlooking the lake, it let in a lot of natural light. Flanked by white bookcases, a built-in desk ran the length of the dormer. On the other side of the room sat an overstuffed chair and ottoman, covered in a soft blue, tan, and gray pattern, like abstract flowers. Here and there were pops of red and yellow accents.

"That's my reading nook. Those low bookcases by the chair contain my reference books."

"What a wonderful place to write. And your guests don't try to come up here?"

"I keep it locked when I have paying guests. But let me show you what I've done downstairs. You can't see it from the front, but with the money I received from my dad, I decided to add a wing with three large guest bedrooms."

Back on the first floor, Lacey saw that each guest room had a desk and overstuffed chair. One room overlooked mountains, one had a view of the lake, and the third had a corner window with glimpses of both.

She let out a soft sigh. "They're beautiful." And inviting.

"Thanks."

"Why would writers need to come on a retreat?" Lacey never had any trouble writing. She could write anywhere. Anytime. Of course, that didn't mean she was a good writer, only that she was prolific. Jake said it was because she talked so rarely, she saved up all her words.

Carin leaned on the doorjamb of the last bedroom, her hands in her pockets. "Usually, they have a deadline and need to get away from all the normal distractions at home. But sometimes writer's block can be the culprit. With these two, Celeste and LuAnn, I'm not sure."

"Maybe they like the idea of being a writer more than writing."

"Good point. You may be right. LuAnn said she has four different novels in the works but hasn't finished any of them."

JJ's head poked through the open back door. "Mama?"

"Come on in, doodle bug. They've gone out to dinner."

"You sure? I heard you talking to someone."

"And I was. Come see who." Carin grinned at Lacey and put her index finger to her lips.

JJ skidded around the corner. His eyes lit up when he saw her. "Ms. Lacey!"

He threw his arms around her waist. That kid sure wasn't lacking for love. Carin gave him enough for three parents, and it overflowed onto others who needed it. Usually, Lacey was fine with her childless status. She and Jake had come to a point of acceptance. But when JJ gave her one of his hugs, and she inhaled his little-boy scent—then she wished.

"Where's Mr. Jake?" JJ looked around.

"He's at work, and I'm fixing to take you and your mama out to dinner. What's your pleasure? Ribs or fish?"

JJ giggled. "What about ribs of fish?"

"How about chicken lips?" Their standard joke always made JJ laugh and tell her chickens didn't have lips. They settled on ribs.

Over dinner, Carin showed Lacey the structure for a query letter and a synopsis.

She frowned at one of the pages. "What if I broke the synopsis into the three acts?"

"No, Blythe said less is more with a play synopsis. Brevity is the byword. So opposite of a novel synopsis." Carin pulled out her phone. "She said she'd email a sample—ah, here it is." She tapped the screen a couple of times. "There. I sent it to you. Look it over tonight."

He put in the number of the rental agency he'd found the cottage through. "Xander Barlow here. I need to rent this cottage through the summer. Yes. I find I like the fishing, and I heard there's a tournament coming." Heartburn crawled up from his gut as he listened. "What do you mean it's rented? Well, move them. I'll make it worth your while." That would do for enough of a reason. If it kept going like it had been, he'd need it through July at least. He tossed a couple of antacids into his mouth and crunched. These rednecks moved slow. "Thank you, my good man. I'm putting a check in the mail for the entire amount plus extra for your help." He ended the call.

Next, he called Newlander and told him about the timetable change.

"Do you think it will take that long?"

Did this yahoo think he was an idiot? "The people here are not fast to trust strangers, and from what I overheard, they don't take well to *you*. You should have told me about that, Newlander." He pulled out a chair and sat at the cottage's kitchen table.

"Uh … they're … uh …"

"Don't bother with excuses. I need to gain their trust. I have a job for you. Find out what properties are for sale closest to the mayor's."

"Why?"

This particular redneck would try his own mother's patience. He drummed his fingers on the table. "Because I'm going to buy it and move in."

"Why do you need to do that?"

"Newlander, do you purposely act stupid or are you really that dumb?"

"I don't see why you have to move in."

"Once more. The people here are slow to trust outsiders. They tolerate the renters because they spend their money here."

"Actually, they're pretty welcoming to renters and tourists."

"Welcoming, maybe. Trusting? Get real." The man was making him rethink this partnership. Maybe he'd send Newlander to Alaska to have him learn about gold mining. Once he found a cabin or house for Xander to buy. "Get busy finding me a house. Let me do the thinking."

He slipped his phone into his pocket and left the cottage by the back door, which faced the lake. That put him right at the beginning of the boardwalk. It held appeal for the tourists, so he'd play tourist for a while. See what he could learn.

The first shop was called Front Row Seat. He wouldn't mind a movie. They rolled the sidewalks up at dusk here. He stepped inside.

What the—? Most of the inventory was videos not DVDs. The cottages were equipped with DVD players. A young woman approached him.

"By your expression, I'm guessing you're looking for the DVDs?"

"What's the deal?"

"I can't get my granddad out of the twentieth century. I have stocked one section with DVDs, though. Come on back here." She led him to a single display of maybe a hundred DVDs.

As he pulled a few out to check the titles, he kept one eye on the girl. She'd already outed her old man. Maybe she'd dish up some more info. "Why do you think your grandfather is against progress?"

She gave him a frank appraisal. "He and the mayor are stuck in the sixties and seventies. Granddad still uses his video player. Thinks everyone does."

Phrasing his next question could be critical. "Is everyone in Chapel Springs like them, stuck in an earlier decade?"

She laughed. "Not at all. Most are quite progressive. The mayor eventually catches up, and Granddad follows whatever Mayor Riley does."

Okay, that was good information. "So you like the town?"

She lifted one shoulder, then dropped it. Her wide mouth quirked. "It's home. What's not to like?"

Another customer entered the store, so Xander chose two DVD movies he hadn't seen. After paying for the two-night rental, he left. The next shop was Happy's Hobby. Really? The owner was named Happy, or was that a play on words? This town was beyond quirky. Still, he might learn something.

When he entered, a tall older man with silver hair and an open face approached him. He thrust out his hand to Xander.

"Welcome to Happy's Hobby. I'm Happy Drayton. What can I find for you?"

Xander didn't have to conjure up a fake smile. This old dude made him grin. "How'd you get the name Happy?" What struck him as strange was he really wanted to know.

Drayton shook his head. "Totally by clerical error. When my great-great-grandfather emigrated from Lebanon, the folks on Ellis Island misspelled Habib, and he became Happy. I was named for him."

He didn't look Lebanese. "Uh, Drayton's English, isn't it?"

"Indeed it is. My ancestor married an Italian." He raised one hand and ticked off on his fingers. "His daughter, my great-grandmother, married an Irishman, and my grandma married an Englishman. And so on. I'm quite the Heinz-57-variety American."

Quite the tale, if it was true. Xander peered around him. What could possibly interest him in here?

"Are you looking for something specific?"

"Uh, no. I'm really getting a feel for the town. I'm considering purchasing a cabin. I … like to fish." Happy had better not ask him any questions about that, or he was in trouble.

The man lit up. "Well, your timing is perfect. Our next tournament is coming up in a few days. It's pretty open. Bluegill, crappie, perch, pike, walleye."

Xander sighed. "Now you've caught me. I should have said *want* to fish. I'm … trying to learn to relax. Doctor's orders." That sounded reasonable.

Drayton nodded. "Chapel Lake is one of the best places to learn. The lake is full of lots of varieties." He eyed Xander. "You aren't going for trophy mounting, are you? We don't cotton to that. Around here, we either eat our catch or release 'em."

"I'm not into having a fish stuffed, if that's what you mean." Man, this dude was passionate about their lake's fish.

"Glad to hear it." Drayton actually thumbed his suspenders. "We've seen a lot of yahoos come to catch trophy fish. A plumb waste, if you ask me. Which you didn't."

Xander almost squirmed under Drayton's stare. He thrust out his hand. "It's been good to meet you, Happy. I hope we become friends. According to my realtor, the town is small enough that most people are neighbors."

The grin returned. Interesting. *Neighbor* seemed to be the byword. He needed to get a feel for the people and gain their trust. "Maybe I could get you to give me some pointers on how to fish?"

"Delighted to, but the best one in town is my fishing buddy, Joel Bennett, or his son Wes. They own the boat launch."

Ah, yes. He'd seen that on his way into town, across from where he had to leave his car. He thanked Happy and took his leave. Next door to the hobby shop was the bakery, where he'd gleaned some information the other day. The coffee and food were good. Maybe another visit was in order. These yahoos would be easier to fleece if he fully understood them.

Chapter 11

Claire glanced out of the corner of her eye at the young man chopping vegetables beside her. Sean O'Keefe had become family already, even though the wedding was still a little over three months away. She was so glad Melissa waited to find the man God had prepared for her. He was already deeply embedded in Chapel Springs. Her BFF's son Dane and Megan were perfect for one another too. They'd grown up together and would soon unite the two families forever. As a momma, Claire couldn't have been happier.

Sean paused in his chopping. "Will you come with me tomorrow to look at a house?" he whispered.

She took a quick peek at 'Lissa who was stirring a pot and laughing with her daddy. "I can. What time? And is it a secret?"

Sean grinned. "I've found a house I want to surprise Melissa with, but I want to make sure it's right by having you and Megan look at it."

"That could be dicey, choosing a house she hasn't seen."

Sean picked up his knife and made fast work of the zucchini, rendering it into bite-sized pieces for the salad. "I know, but we've talked about houses, and I happen to know she loves it."

"She does?" Claire scooped her chopped celery into the salad bowl. "I thought she hadn't seen it."

"It's the old Belford farmhouse, out on Church Street, beyond Happy Drayton's. She said it's always reminded her of this house." He gestured with his knife to the kitchen. "But a bit smaller. I figure we could add onto it in a few years."

Sean turned red, but Claire liked the sound of that. No one could have too many grandbabies. And he was right about the old Belford house.

"She does love it. She used to visit Ed and Leola when she was little. They adored her and she loved their stories. Plus Leola was an artist of sorts. She painted in the primitive style and encouraged 'Lissa to paint the way she wanted. But …" Claire leaned back to look around Sean to make sure 'Lissa wasn't listening. "If you know she loves it, why do you need me to look at it?"

He exchanged his knife for the grater and attacked a carrot. "It's in pretty bad shape. I want to buy it now. The bank only wants back taxes, so it's dirt-cheap. I've already qualified for a loan to renovate it, but I need you to tell me if it's too far gone."

"Tell you what, I'll bring Mel along. You know she's our engineering prodigy."

"That would be great." He grabbed a head of lettuce and tore it like she'd shown him.

"Did Felix talk to you about his quartz find?"

"He did. He's going to have to research the mineral rights."

"He already has and he doesn't own them. Now, he has to try to locate the descendants of the original owner." Claire wiped her hands on a towel and folded it on the counter.

Sean rinsed the grater and picked up the towel, wiping his hands. "There are a lot of ifs. Even *if* he finds who holds the mineral rights, *if* that person bought the rights from the state of Georgia, the state may have withheld the rights for oil and gas." He looked down at Claire. "Those withheld rights may or may not include the quartz."

Leaning against the counter, Claire crossed her arms. "Well, that sure puts spit in the pudding."

Sean snorted. "Indeed. It'll take some real sleuthing and a whole lot of legwork."

Claire rolled over to Shiloh's cold nose against hers. The mastiff stood beside the bed, his chin resting on the mattress. As soon as she opened her eyes, he licked her nose.

"Go away, boy. I need more sleep."

Nightmares kept her awake most of the night. First, she was pregnant with quintuplets, and her giant belly kept her from reaching her pottery wheel. Then she was emaciated with cancer, a walking skeleton.

Claire rolled over. Joel lay there, staring at her. He smiled and pulled her close. "What has you so agitated, babe? You had the covers twisted in a knot."

"I'm sorry. Bad dream." She couldn't worry him until she knew whether her lot was the grim reaper or a fast creeper.

"Oh, is that all?"

Claire sat up. "Yeah. I'm worried about the tour." That sounded reasonable. "What if it's a flop?"

Joel pushed himself up against the headboard and put his arm around her. "Clairey-girl, you of all people know what God can do. Look at me. Give Him a chance."

"But you don't know what I went through before you became a believer." She regretted her words the minute her blasted tongue spit them out. The sorrow on Joel's face broke her heart.

"Was it that bad?"

She laid her head against his chest. "No, not always. But there were times when I wanted so badly to tell you something God had shown me. Something that meant so much to me, and I couldn't share it with you."

A sigh rumbled from his chest. "I guess I can understand that now. I wish I could go back and change the past, but I can't. All I can do is try to make your future happy." He squeezed her.

"I know. And I don't regret our past, Joel. It's been good. You've been the best husband for me. Funny, for a while, I thought you weren't the one God meant me to have. But I've come to realize He had you handpicked for me from the beginning."

"I'm kinda glad. You make life fun, babe."

"Thanks, I think."

Joel sat up and stretched. The way her mouth tasted, she was glad when he kissed the tip of her nose instead of her lips. "Why don't you go back to sleep?"

"I can't now. I think I'll go to the gallery."

The sun wouldn't break the horizon for another hour, and in the dark, Claire made her way to the gallery. Joel went fishing. Her tossing and turning had kept them both awake. Against advice, she'd gone to an online medical site, trying to diagnose herself. It didn't give her peace of mind. It only added to her worry.

In the gallery's workroom, she threw on her apron and pulled clay from the barrel. She needed to think and did it best at her potter's wheel. As she punched and kneaded a fresh lump of clay, images from her search paraded through her mind like cartoon boxes of popcorn and Cokes at the movies. One, in particular, blared its trumpet solo. Change-of-life pregnancy. That "P" word again. Then the dreaded "C" word waved its baton. Her stomach churned and roiled. She was caught in the middle of an alphabet war.

She had grandbabies she wanted to see grown. The twins' wedding. Adrianna hinted an engagement might be announced soon. As tears filled her eyes, she let the wheel slow to a stop. *Lord, what's happening to me?*

Fear not. Trust in me.

Claire sat for a moment, letting the Lord's words flow over her. She'd trusted Him with Costy, and it had turned out wonderful. She'd trusted Him with 'Lissa's broken heart and choosing the right boy/man for a husband. God had even helped with Chapel Springs and neutralized Howie Newlander's bid for mayor.

I trust You, Lord. The fear part she didn't have a handle on yet.

She started the wheel turning again, wet her fingers in the water bucket at her feet, and leaned into her work, smoothing the clay upward. If it was perimenopause, she had no worries. Some frustration, yes, but nothing to worry about. If it was cancer—her stomach turned on its own—she could get through it. Most cancer was curable nowadays.

Unless it—no. She would trust. The clay reached the height she wanted. She stopped the wheel and, using piano wire, released the bowl from the wheel.

But what would she do if she were pregnant? *Oh, Lord.* To have grandbabies older than her last-born? And what would Joel think? Ha! He'd probably swagger and think he was the king of virility. She groaned. But what would her kids think? She set the bowl on the drying rack.

What if the baby had Down syndrome? A lot of change-of-life babies did. She flopped into her chair at her desk. She was forty-eight. Who would take care of him when she couldn't? Was it fair to subject her children to this? Oh, sure, the children she knew with Down's were sweet blessings, but they still needed lifelong care. How could she do that? *Lord, what am I going to do?*

Claire dropped her head into her hands and wept.

The bells jingled on the gallery's front door. Claire sat up with a start. Oh! She must have dozed off because her right arm was a dead weight from her head resting on it. She rubbed her cheek where her watch had left an indentation. Before Patsy or 'Lissa saw her, she dove into the bathroom and splashed water on her red face. She could explain her puffy face, but red eyes from crying, not so much. Thank goodness she'd left some eye drops in here.

"Claire?"

"In the bathroom, Pat-a-cake."

"Why are you here so early?"

"Couldn't sleep." Claire opened the bathroom door. "I had an idea for some bowls and decided to get a head start on the tour inventory." Not really a lie, a mere exaggeration.

Patsy looked around, then back at Claire with a piercing gaze. "You didn't get much done."

"No." She closed the bathroom door and went to the clay barrel. "I discovered I wasn't as awake as I thought I was." Patsy always knew when something was wrong, but for the first time in her life, Claire didn't want to tell her anything. Not yet. Not until she knew for sure, and they could form the right action plan, and not waste time on conjecture. She motioned toward the door. "Want to go to Dee's? I need caffeine."

Thankfully, Patsy let it drop. Wow, maybe hanging around the theater had rubbed off. Whatever the cause, Claire was thankful. She and Patsy linked arms and headed to the bakery. During lunch, she'd go to Pineridge and buy a pregnancy test.

After a good natter with their friends and two large cups of Dee's high-test java, Claire felt awake enough to go to Pineridge. Praying as she drove helped relax her tightened nerves. She turned right into the strip mall that housed Hill's Pills.

In the parking lot, Claire glanced over her shoulder as she locked her SUV. Not a single car she recognized … unless that blue Sonata belonged to MaryLou Peterson. Last time Claire had seen her, she'd said her husband bought her a new Hyundai. Claire made her way into the pharmacy, keeping an eye out for her.

Inside, she didn't see anyone she knew, but not about to take any chances, she grabbed a hand basket and started down the first aisle. After all, she could always use shampoo and conditioner. If she buried the pregnancy test beneath other items, the clerk would never notice. Too bad they didn't have one of those self-help checkout lanes.

The next aisle contained deodorants and shaving cream. She grabbed a deodorant and turned into the next row. Oh, good. Greeting cards. She'd stock up. After selecting several cards, she rounded the end of the aisle and turned up the next and almost laughed. The pregnancy test display was next to the condoms. Irony at its best. Or worst. She reached for one.

"Claire Bennett. Fancy seeing you here. It's been ages."

Ages nothing. It hadn't been long enough. The last time she'd heard that voice, she was desperate to keep the woman away from Joel and blabbing about the cooking class.

Claire turned. "Hello, Trixie." The woman took every cooking class offered at Henderson's Fresh Market. Took them and considered herself the queen.

Claire crossed her arms over her basket. "What has you in Pineridge?"

"I live here, silly." Trixie craned her neck to look past Claire at the display case, then back at her. She could feel it coming. "What are you doing buying condoms?"

She got it wrong. *Thank You, Lord.* "I'm not buying condoms. I thought they were —" *Think, Bennett. And fast.* "Individually wrapped hard candies. Joel loves butterscotch."

Trixie gaped at her. Then she giggled. "Claire, you are such a hoot. Hard candies! Ha ha." She put her hand on Claire's arm. "Sweetie, they really are condoms." She hooted again. "I can imagine that handsome hubby of yours thinking he was opening a butterscotch and—"

"Yes, I get the picture, Trixie. Thanks. I won't be buying any of these. See you."

Van Gogh's ear. Foiled again. Claire scurried to the checkout. At least the trip wasn't a total loss. She did score some good cards. But what were the odds of seeing Trixie again? At least a bazillion to one.

In the car, an idea dawned. Scarlet's Ferry was far enough around the lake that the chances of anyone she knew being there were slim. She started the car and called Patsy. "I'll be a bit late getting back. I've got one more errand."

The scenic drive to Scarlet's Ferry wound through the pines, staying in close proximity to the water, but the beauty was lost on Claire today. Her mind kept interrupting her with visions of herself in a wheelchair pushing a stroller. That and a red car was behind her that looked vaguely familiar, but with the clouds playing hide-and-seek with the sun, she couldn't see who it was.

Finally, the drugstore's sign appeared. She glanced in her rearview mirror as she braked. The same bright red sports car pulled in behind her. The driver quickly pulled the visor down, but not before Claire saw who sat behind the wheel. Trixie would never make a detective. But why had she followed her? Better question was, now what would Claire do? She didn't have time for another Trixie encounter.

Okay, so she'd try to find time to come back to Scarlet's Ferry tomorrow. No, she couldn't tomorrow. She and Joel had the grands. It could wait until Monday. Then she'd take the test and be ... she'd be what? Home free? No way. No matter how it turned out, she was in deep. If she was pregnant, what would she do? And if she wasn't, then why was her period so late? The alternative scared her more than the first option.

Chapter 12

"Claire, can you spare a minute?" Felix stood in the doorway to the workroom, his cap in one hand. Where was his usual I-got-this demeanor? Something wasn't right.

"Sure, come on in." Claire glanced over her shoulder at Patsy's easel. "Uh, Patsy's here too."

"That's good. She can help us."

Pat-a-cake appeared from behind her easel. She grabbed a rag and wiped her hands while Claire washed hers.

"Sit down, Felix. Grab that chair and pull it up to the table." Claire swept a pile of drawings aside and cleared a spot. "What's up?"

He glanced between them. "In an effort to find out who owns my mineral rights, I called every county clerk in the state. What a waste of time and money that was."

"Don't you have unlimited long distance?" Patsy asked. "I thought everyone did."

"No need. Everyone I know is here. On the off chance that Bobby is gone somewhere, our conversations aren't long. Anyway, I learned all the really old records are kept at the state level, so I drove up to Frankfort yesterday."

Claire elbowed Patsy. "Nice day for it too. I'll bet the drive was gorgeous."

Felix whapped his cap on the table. "You gonna listen or tell the story?"

"Sorry." Why didn't he get on with it, then? "Wait. Why did you have to go to Frankfort? Your land is here."

"I was hoping the McIlraths still owned the mineral rights. I wasn't sure whether they recorded the sale in the state it took place in or where the property was located. But that's not the point. What I came to tell you is the mineral rights have been bought up already."

That got Claire's attention. "What? When?"

"Two days ago."

"That's crazy. Why, after all these years, did someone buy them now?" She sat up straight. "Is this the first time they were sold?"

"It is." Felix rearranged his bulk in the chair. "Aren't you curious who bought 'em?"

"You found out?"

"Of course. It's public record."

"Where? Here or Frankfort?"

"Both. The clerk there called the county seat for me."

"That was nice. So who was it?"

Felix's mouth screwed up like he'd sucked a persimmon. "Howard B. Newlander."

Claire jumped up, knocking her chair over. "What? How did he find out?" She righted her seat. "More importantly, why is he poking around here again?"

Patsy set three water bottles on the table. "Howie always was one to exact revenge. He hasn't forgiven the town for foiling all his get-rich-quick schemes."

"Don't forget, Jacquelyn Ford did a story on it." Felix unscrewed the lid on his water. "Apparently, another network picked up the story and turned it over to an investigative reporter, who pried his nose into all the land sold without mineral rights." He guzzled and wiped his mouth.

Jacquelyn's story wasn't at fault, but it sure was a crying shame that another network picked up the story. Claire paced. Did Howie plan to mine the land? And if so, for gold or quartz? He grew up here. He knew there was gold buried deep. Unless someone opened a huge mine capable of digging two to three hundred feet down, it wouldn't be worth the effort.

"It has to be the quartz." She switched her gaze from Felix to Patsy and back. "God help us. Those operations are huge, with large earthmovers and dynamite causing all kinds of havoc. Sean showed me online what a big mining operation looks like." Her heartbeat accelerated to an alarming speed. She sat down. "It would decimate Chapel Springs."

Felix took another drink, wiped his mouth, and pocketed his

handkerchief. "My sentiments exactly. What I'd like to know is how did he get the money? He paid seventy-three thousand for my rights alone."

Now her heart stopped. "What do you mean, your rights alone?"

"He now owns the mineral rights to three properties west of Springs Park. Two of those butt up against your family's land, Patsy. I don't know how many other properties are without the mineral rights, but so far, he's spent a little over a hundred and fifty thousand."

Claire tilted her head and frowned at Felix. "Where could he have gotten that kind of money?"

Patsy's eyes snapped open wide. "You don't suppose he called Mr. Shoulders, do you?"

The investor from the wild high-rise hotel scheme Howie tried to foist on the town? They never did learn the man's real name, but he had shyster written all over him. He bilked other towns out of their money, but he met his match when he came to Chapel Springs. If Howie had him involved again—

Claire's mouth tasted like she was sucking a copper penny. "We need to call an emergency town council meeting. Tonight."

Felix rose. "And alert every resident to be there. We have to get to the absentee landlords, too—before Howie does."

The noise level in the community room at the bank would have penetrated the most expensive earplugs. Even half-deaf Bud Pugh shook his head, then stuck his thumb in his ear and turned down the volume on his hearing aid. It seemed everyone in Chapel Springs showed up. It did Claire's heart good to see the response and, judging by the tone, the outrage.

She and Patsy had called the shop owners in town. Felix had called Fay Eisler, who rousted the rest. That woman had a direct line to the best gossips in three counties. They could pass the word faster than a beaver could fell a tree. And it showed. Claire gazed out over the room. There were a lot of faces she didn't recognize. If these were some of the absentee landowners, Faye rose in Claire's esteem. Some could be summer renters, although she knew most of those.

Boone's gavel tattooed a dent in the table. Felix rose and let loose an ear-splitting whistle, settling the room. Claire cringed.

"Thanks, Mayor." Boone stood. "This meeting is called to order. Pastor Seth, open us in prayer, please."

Seth prayed for unity and tolerance. His "amen" echoed all over the room.

Boone rapped his gavel again. "Mayor Riley, will you tell the council and these good people what you've discovered?"

Felix rose and took the hand microphone from Tom Fowler. "At the last meeting, I revealed how I discovered I didn't own the mineral rights to my own land. Basically, my ancestors bought the land without the mineral rights. That detail had been lost over the years. As soon as I learned that, I set out to buy them." He walked around to the front of the table so he was closer to the audience.

"Unfortunately, I discovered the mineral rights to my land had been bought two days ago by none other than that scoundrel Howie Newlander. I skedaddled back here and went to the county seat. I also found out other mineral rights have been bought up by Newlander."

Pandemonium broke out.

"He couldn't have bought without us knowing, could he?" Warren Jenkins shouted.

"If you didn't own them, he could."

"I didn't sell mine!" Bud Pugh slapped his ball cap against his thigh.

"I warned my son about buying land without the mineral rights."

Claire didn't recognize the last voice.

Felix walked back to his chair, dropping heavily into it. Boone banged his gavel.

Tom hollered into the microphone. "Quiet! Quiet, please. The Chairman will take your questions one at a time." He took the microphone and its stand and set it in the center aisle. Immediately a line formed.

"State your name, if you're a property owner, and your question."

The first man in line appeared to be in his sixties—if Claire could judge by his gray hair, bifocals, and wrinkles. He leaned forward, tapped the mic hesitantly, and then spoke.

"Name's David Adams. My wife recently inherited her grandfather Chet Bascom's house. After the funeral, we renovated and then decided to move here. We've grown to love Chapel Springs and would hate to see the town changed. Buying up mineral rights sounds like someone plans to mine something or drill for gas or oil. Any of those would ruin this town. Do you have any idea of Mr. Newlander's plans?"

Felix rose. "Newlander read a story in the newspaper that confirmed there is quartz on my land. Where there's quartz, there's generally always gold. However, anyone who has lived here long enough knows that mining gold nowadays isn't a cheap operation, and the return is highly risky. My guess is they're after the quartz."

The next man in line was much younger. Maybe mid-forties. His suit tagged him a businessman. "Good evening. My name's Alex Nordby. I'm a property owner, but I rent it out. My property has given me a good return on my investment. But this Newlander person has offered me a tidy sum for my land. Can you give me a reason not to sell it to him?"

Claire just bet Howie offered him a bunch. A bunch of baloney. She raised her hand. Boone nodded to her.

"Mr. Nordby, I've known Howie Newlander all my life. He's a get-rich-quick schemer who has tried to scam this town in the past. His ethics aren't the highest, and anything he offers needs to be examined carefully. Very carefully. On his last scheme, he told his investors that permits would be granted without any questions asked. That's illegal as well as unethical."

Mr. Nordby nodded. "Okay. Thanks for the warning. Mayor, how much quartz do you think is there?"

Claire's spirits plunged. Probably a lot. She sent Sean a pleading gaze. He shook his head. She raised her hand again and Boone acknowledged her.

"Most of us have lived here all our lives. We love this little mountain town. And the tourists love it. Your return on investment proves that, Mr. Nordby. And there are dozens like you. Yes, there's enough quartz for a mine to make money, but it would destroy the lake and the property values for every person here."

More people stood and vowed they wouldn't sell their land no matter how much Howie offered. Doc gave an impassioned speech aimed at the environmentalists and what the mining would do to the land and the forest.

"The mining operation would have to be right behind Springs Park, because most of the forest land here is national forest. They couldn't mine there, and you can't hide a mine when it's basically in the middle of town."

By the time everyone had his or her say, it was after midnight. Then Boone called for a concerted effort to stand in solidarity against any mining. Even Mr. Nordby came around to their way of thinking, saying the long-term rental would net him more income than selling his land.

But there were several landowners who didn't live in the state. Had

Faye's troops broadcast the word to them? And if one of them sold, would others in town capitulate and sell?

The moon hid behind a thick layer of clouds. How convenient. Xander picked up the shovel and softly closed the cottage door. He crossed Cottage Row and slipped into the woods. There were three small cabins nearby. He stayed within the tree line as he approached the first target. No light shone from any of the windows. Apparently, the sidewalks were taken in at dark. No matter, it suited his purposes. He rolled up his sleeves and soon the shovel bit into the dirt. He'd dig down three feet. If he found no quartz, he'd move on to the next one.

Newlander said something about finding gold in the streams too. He'd researched that and ordered some dredging equipment. But first, if he could find gold or at least quartz, he'd have an idea of which properties to purchase. His investors' pockets were deep and they wanted gold.

Sweat poured down his brow, stinging his eyes. He should pay someone else to do this. Then again, the way these people noticed anyone new in town … no, he was better off doing it himself. Maybe his gut would shrink an inch by the time he finished. By the burn in his arms, his biceps would benefit, anyway. He bent into the work, but after another ten minutes, he stopped. He'd reached waist level and found nothing but clay. Time to move.

He drew close to the next cabin, but a dog barked and a light came on. He slunk past it and headed to the third. The blasted dog kept yapping. Lights flooded the third place. Xander stepped deeper into the woods to wait. A door opened. The yapper came outside by the sound of its bark. He made ready to flee.

"Hey, Ray, is it another bear, trying to get your trash?"

"Nope. Don't know what set off Gus, but whatever it is, it's still out there. Worthless dog won't shut up, but it won't chase whatever it is neither."

Lucky for me. And Gus did shut up. Finally.

"Aw, it's probably gone by now. Night, Mitchell."

Xander waited for the lights to go out, and then waited another five minutes before he moved away from the cabins.

Chapter 13

Lacey stole through the backstage door and took a deep breath. The aroma of greasepaint filled her nose. She flipped a switch, flooding the empty area in light. How could she smell greasepaint when none had been used here in forty years? She peered over her shoulder. Maybe a theater ghost lingered. A delicious shiver slithered up her back.

According to Claire, it couldn't be her Great-aunt Lola. If Lacey strained and stood very still, though, and closed her eyes, she heard lines echoing from ages past. It didn't matter if it was her imagination. She related to them.

The door opened behind her, and Claire backed in carrying a bucket of paint. Lacey took a quick sidestep before Claire collided with her.

"Oh! Sorry, Lacey." Joel followed her in, pushing a handcart loaded with boxes.

Lacey took a bucket of paint from Claire. "Where do you want this?"

"Anywhere for now. Happy is outside, getting another ladder. We're hanging these spotlights." She pointed to the handcart Joel set to one side.

Lacey's heart pulsed. She'd been studying lighting and how it could affect the mood, so she'd been waiting for these to arrive. She set down the paint and checked the boxes. "A Fresnel, a PAR56 can, and an ellipsoidal."

"Easy for you to say." Claire wrinkled her nose. "I know the pictures are different and they're heavy. That's the extent of my knowledge."

Lacey answered a rap on the door, and Ellie, holding part of a long ladder, preceded Happy Drayton. Joel replaced Ellie and helped Happy set it up near Lacey. An empty light truss hung above them.

She stood center stage as people swarmed around her, organizing everything. She smiled at them, but no one asked her to help or do anything. She empathized with the ghost if there really was one. Claire and Kelly were the only people who saw her—other than Jake—and even they overlooked her at times.

Nearby, Kelly turned in a circle. "Where's Rick?"

"Here I am." He leaped out from behind the curtains. "I was setting out the donuts Mom sent over."

So that was Dee's son. Lacey heard he was taking a class on theatrical lighting at college. But a student?

"Do you have the lighting design?" Kelly held out her hand.

"Yeah. My professor looked it over. He said it would work for what y'all want."

Lacey's pulse kicked in an extra beat as Rick climbed the ladder with the Fresnel. He had two grid clamps with what he called receiver arms on them. She didn't know what that meant but didn't want to ask while he was climbing that tall ladder.

Rick set the spotlight on the grid. "One of these days, y'all need to replace this old rigging system with electric winches. We could lower the lights instead of raising the installer."

Kelly wrote on her notepad. "I'll ask the council. It's a matter of safety, I would think. Maybe we'd get a lower rate on our liability insurance."

Lacey's neck developed a kink as Rick worked. He dropped a bolt, and she jumped back a step.

"Smart move. Stay there, please." He went back to his work.

Rick slid the clamp onto the metal bar but didn't tighten it yet. A chain dangled, unconnected to anything but the bar. Lacey tried to remember what it was for. Of course. The safety chain for the Fresnel spotlight.

Rick lifted the light, slipped it into the clamp, and looped the safety chain through one of the Fresnel's brackets. Holding the spot in place with one hand, he pulled his gloves from his tool belt with the other, letting one glove drop to the floor. He gripped the other in his teeth, sliding his free hand into it. That was a pretty slick move.

He leaned to tighten the clamp with his gloved hand. The ladder pitched to the left. Rick grabbed for the light bar. Lacey ran to grab the ladder. A clanking rang out above her. The safety chain danced in the air. Where was the new Fresnel? Lacey craned her neck to see, then pain exploded.

Everything went black.

Nobody moved as the spotlight fell and hit Lacey in the face, knocking her down in an explosion of blood. The moment frozen in time, Claire couldn't process what she'd witnessed. Then a scream clawed its way up her throat, and everyone yelled at once.

"Help Rick!"

"Call 9-1-1!"

Joel and Nathan rushed past Claire and righted the ladder for Rick, who dangled from the light truss twenty feet in the air, with only one foot preventing the ladder from crashing to the floor. With her heart in her throat, Claire grabbed Kelly and ran to Lacey. Blood splattered everywhere. Kelly and Tom lifted the light off.

For a moment, Claire could only stare. *Dear God.* Could she survive this? Blood stained Lacey's shirt and pooled around her head. Claire gagged but swallowed and took a deep breath. *Lord, help me!* She gently touched Lacey's neck. She had a rapid, erratic pulse.

"She's alive! Call nine-one-one!" Tears choked off Claire's breath.

"Already done," Ellie shouted.

"What about Jake?" Nathan asked.

"On his way." Patsy had turned white and looked ready to faint.

Stomach, don't betray me now. Claire sucked in a deep breath. How could Lacey breathe with all that blood? It gurgled in her throat. Her face was crushed and already swollen beyond recognition. Her eyelids bulged; the skin was blue and gray. Claire's stomach roiled, but she forced the bile down. She didn't know what to do. If she tried to staunch the blood flow, she could hurt Lacey worse. "Where are the paramedics?"

Kelly clapped her hand over her mouth and hurried away. A towel landed next to Claire, and she placed it beside Lacey to catch the blood. It was soaked within seconds.

Joel's hand squeezed her shoulder. She looked up at him. "I feel so helpless. I don't know if she can breathe, but I'm afraid to touch her."

The stage door opened with a bang. Two paramedics rushed in with bags of equipment and a gurney. Felix and Sheriff Jim Bob followed them in. The sheriff immediately moved everyone back. "Let the medics take over."

A young man—was he old enough to be a paramedic?—touched Claire's hand. "Thanks, ma'am. I'll take over. Are you her mother?"

Claire untangled her feet, grabbed Joel's hand for support, and rose clumsily. She shook her head and stepped back. A lone tear trailed down her cheek. Lydia. She turned to Joel. "Call Lydia."

Felix handed her his handkerchief. "What happened?"

"A light fell off the truss."

Felix blanched and shuddered. "Is she alive?"

"Yes, but barely as far as I can tell." Claire peeked around Felix to see what the paramedics were doing.

Rick stood behind them, sobbing. "I tried to catch it. I'm so sorry."

"It's not your fault, sugar," Ellie said, holding him.

Everyone stood in small clusters, watching the young men work on Lacey. The brown-haired EMT checked her vitals. As he called them out, the other boy relayed the information to someone—at the hospital, Claire guessed. She glanced at his name badge. Jesse Appleton.

"Patient is unconscious. She was struck in the face by a ten-pound spotlight falling from twenty-two feet."

Jesse said something to his partner—Claire didn't see his name badge—then pulled out a contraption with something that looked like a balloon. She saw the tube and had to turn away as he threaded it down Lacey's throat. They worked so fast. Jesse looped his stethoscope into his ears and listened to Lacey's lungs and then her stomach. Why was he listening to her tummy?

"Anyone her family?" Jesse asked.

"Her husband should be—"

The door flew open and Jake ran inside. He stopped dead still when he saw Lacey, the color draining from his face. Claire's heart broke as he knelt beside his wife. He reached out to her, but his hand stopped short, then came to rest on her shoulder.

"Are you her husband?"

"Yes." He swallowed. "Is she going to make it?"

"I'll do everything I can to make sure, but time is critical. Is she allergic to any medications?"

Jake shook his head. "None that I know of."

"Any medical conditions? Is she on any meds?"

"No. None, no meds."

With a sharp nod, he continued to relay her condition. "Patient is non-responsive. Left pupil is blown. Pulse is rapid and bounding."

Claire strained to understand what he said. Patsy clung to her arm. "BP is inverting. Respiration?"

"Labored and shallow. Ten per minute." The men shared a glance. Jesse nodded and—Dan. His name was Dan something. Claire couldn't begin to pronounce it. He stood to talk with Jake. Claire stepped closer.

"We're in the golden hour and time is of the essence. We need to move her now. You can ride with us."

"Golden hour?"

Dan nodded to Jake. "Yes, sir. We have about an hour to save her life. That's it."

They slid a board beneath Lacey, strapped her to it, and then lifted her onto the gurney. Jesse held a cloth-wrapped cold pack to her face. Claire thought Lacey's bleeding had slowed. Just before Jake followed them to the ambulance, he turned back to Rick.

"It's an accident, son. Don't blame yourself." Then he was gone.

Claire had known Jake all his life. She even babysat him when she was a preteen. Changed his diapers. Jake might be only five-foot-ten, but right then, he stood among giants.

It seemed like forever, but within five minutes, the paramedics had Lacey in the ambulance. Jake climbed in behind her, and the door closed. Jesse had told them they were taking Lacey to Pineridge—the closest hospital with a trauma unit. Then, they were gone.

No one moved or spoke. Only the siren pierced the still night air.

Felix, bless his heart, reached out his hands and called them together to pray for Lacey. "You heard them. She's in a bad way."

After the final amen, he turned to Claire and Kelly. "We're going to replace the light system with what Rick suggested. Y'all can rehearse with house lights, but no stage lights go on until that system is brought up to code. I'll handle it personally. What in tarnation are y'all gawkin' at, Claire?" Felix took his normal pose with his hands on his ample hips.

"I … uh …" A smile began in her heart. Felix *had* grown soft. He even forgot to blame her for the old lights. "Nothing."

Felix cleared his throat. "Chapel Springs takes care of its own. I'm going to pick up Lydia and take her to the hospital." He turned to Claire and Joel. "You two coming?"

Chapter 14

Claire picked up her phone to see if Jake had left any messages. None. They had all stayed with him until they knew Lacey had made it through surgery. Felix left shortly before they got word, called away by the sheriff. She and Joel went home when the doctor came out to speak with Jake, leaving Lydia and Graham with him. Lydia had called early this morning to say Lacey was still critical, but the doctor had given them some hope. If all went well, and they were all praying it would, she'd still have to undergo facial reconstruction. Claire shuddered. What must she look like right now? All she could see was that spotlight embedded in Lacey's face.

Claire needed to get the image out of her head, and she knew how to do it. The answer was right in front of her. She raised her iPhone and clicked the video icon. Through the viewfinder, Aela waddled toward her, grinning and vamping for the camera. Only eleven months old and already a ham. The little dickens must have inherited the drama gene from Great-aunt Lola. Micah on the other hand—Claire turned the camera toward him—was oblivious. He was too busy trying to stack blocks on Shiloh's back. The mastiff snoozed, not bothered at all by the babies.

When Aela saw the camera wasn't on her anymore, she tottered over to her brother. She patted his head and then pushed his blocks off Shiloh. Claire bit back her chuckle.

"You little scamp. It's a good thing your brother is so easygoing." Aela grinned at Claire, then lay down on top of Shiloh and popped her thumb in her mouth. Micah turned and leaned against the dog and stacked his blocks on the floor. Oh, how Claire loved these grandbabies.

But that didn't mean she wanted to have a baby herself. She had to get that pregnancy test. Joel and Sandi should be nearly finished with the lesson on sauces. Claire wandered into the kitchen, keeping one eye on the babies in the family room. Sandi stood at the sink, rinsing a pot.

"Are you two finished?"

Joel kissed Claire's cheek. "We are. What's up?"

Distraction first. She held up her phone. "See the cute video I took of the twins? Aela is so funny—such a vamp."

Sandi shook her head. "Charlie's already put a moratorium on dating ... until she's thirty."

"I think they're both about to take a nap with Shiloh." Claire grabbed a travel mug and filled it with coffee. "I've got to run an errand, then get back to the gallery." She grabbed her keys and left.

The drive to Scarlet's Ferry was uneventful, and no car followed hers for more than a short distance. Thank goodness. Now she could get this business finished. In the pharmacy, Claire walked the aisles until she found the tests displayed. There were several from which to choose. She reached for the first one.

"I declare, every time I turn around, I'm seeing you, Claire. I do think we're destined to be best friends."

Claire didn't need to turn around to know who it was. She was only surprised that neighborhood dogs weren't howling at Trixie's high-pitched voice. Claire dropped her arm. "Is this *Groundhog Day*?" That movie flashed in her mind, where the hero's day kept repeating itself.

Trixie eyed her. Her head tilted to the right, then the left. "No. That was last month. Are you all right, Claire?" Trixie took her arm and led her over to a chair by the pharmacy.

And Claire let her. She couldn't have planned it better. Trixie never noticed what she'd been standing in front of. Now, she only needed to get out of there. Fast.

"I'm fine. I ..." Brilliance struck only so often, and Claire was going to take advantage of it. "I was thinking about my next project. Groundhog whimsy vases." She stood. "You merely interrupted my musing."

"You were musing over pregnancy tests?"

Uh-oh. She *did* notice. "Uh, yes." *Think!* "They're expectant groundhogs."

Trixie bought it and started to giggle.

Thank you, Lord! Claire took advantage. "Toodle-oo."

Trixie's hand on her arm stopped her. "Claire?"

Good gravy, she couldn't get away from this woman. "Yes?"

"I heard about y'all's theater in Chapel Springs. When's your first show? I'm fixing to come try out."

"Oh, what a shame. They already cast the show." *Thank goodness.*

Trixie pouted. "Phooey. Do y'all need any understudies?"

"How many shows have you been in?"

"Well, none, but my Carson—that's my new boyfriend—he thinks I'd be great onstage."

I'll just bet he does. "The director wants people with experience. Why not try the community theater right here in Pineridge?"

Trixie's expression changed. She looked at the floor.

Claire was doomed.

"I did. They didn't want me."

She was going to regret this. "Come to rehearsal next Tuesday night. Seven o'clock. I'll see if I can get them to give you a part. Only a walk-on, though. No lines. And you'll have to help out backstage."

Trixie lit up like summer sunshine. On steroids. Claire left. Without the test she came for and her mission unaccomplished.

"That Claire. She's such a hoot. We're friends, you know."

Claire had no idea who Trixie was talking to, but she thanked her lucky stars she'd made it out of there safely. Once in the car and on her way, however, her humor fizzled. She still didn't have one of those blasted tests. She'd worry later about how to keep Trixie quiet at the next rehearsal. Claire didn't want her blabbing about being in the pharmacy in Pineridge or in Scarlet's Ferry. The last thing she needed was everyone in Chapel Springs to know her business. Even though they'd find out eventually, Claire wanted to be in control of when.

Why she had that mental lapse and told Trixie she could have a part was beyond her. She had duties like being part of the stage crew. She didn't have time to babysit Trixie. They were setting the lighting tomorrow night.

"Why did I say I'd help with the play?"

Do you really want an answer?

She didn't and drove in silence, going over her mental list of what she had to do when she got back to the gallery. On the top of that list was dusting. Oh, joy.

As soon as she stepped into The Painted Loon, she pulled out the ladder and climbed to the fourth rung. Standing on her tiptoes, she dusted the top shelf of her pottery display. She lifted a fat hedgehog vase, its spiny protrusions poking her hands. She really should make a few more of these little guys. Parents said they were the one vase their kiddos didn't try to pick up. She chuckled to herself and set "Harry" back in his place.

The front door opened. Claire turned, holding on to the edge of the shelf for balance. "Good morning."

A gentleman poked his head inside. "Are you open?"

"Yes, come in. We're open until six." With the kids all grown, neither she nor Patsy had to get home early. "Did you have something in mind or simply browsing?" He had a familiar face. Or was it his stance?

"I'm really just getting ideas." He picked up a whimsy mug and handed it to her. "I'll take one of these mugs, though. I'm staying in town for a couple of weeks and prefer my own coffee cup instead of using what's in the cottage."

Claire frowned. "Were the dishes not cleaned?" She'd have to tell Glen about that.

"Oh no, they're fine. I simply prefer my own coffee cup." He turned and crossed the gallery, stopping in front of one of Patsy's paintings.

What an oddball. While she kept an eye on him, she pulled two pieces of newsprint to wrap the mug. He didn't spend a long time at any display, but moved around the gallery, looking at everything. What bothered her about him?

"Very nice work. Yours?"

Claire handed him the wrapped mug and took his money. "Yes, and Patsy Kowalski is the brush artist. I'm Claire Bennett." She gave him his change.

"Nice to meet you. Have you lived here long?"

Now that was a question none of the tourists had ever asked her. "Nearly all my life. I was a toddler when we moved here."

"Ahh. So you like it?"

This was getting odder by the minute. "Definitely. I wouldn't have stayed if I didn't."

"No, I suppose not. Well, thank you. Good day." He pocketed his change, picked up the mug, and left.

If anyone had asked her about the past ten minutes, she'd have been hard put to explain her reaction, but that man bore watching. She wasn't sure why. She locked up the gallery and walked home. As she opened the front door, it hit her. She'd seen him before. Where, she wasn't sure, but she had definitely seen him.

Chapter 15

Claire slid the wire beneath the clay, releasing the groundhog whimsy vase from the wheel. It had turned out better than she'd hoped. Its pregnant belly stood out prominently under an apron with a toddler groundhog pulling at the strings. At least the run-in with Trixie the other day had produced some results. What if Claire looked like this groundhog in a few months?

Trixie! Claire had promised to get her a walk-on in the play. She groaned. With everything she had on her mind, that particular task had flown out.

Patsy's head lifted from the art magazine she was reading. "What's wrong?"

"I ran into Trixie the other day, and she all but begged me for a part in the Lakeside Players production. To get away from her, I said I'd try to get her a walk-on."

"Oh, Claire, you didn't." Patsy sniggered. "You are a softie."

Softie nothing. More like a calculated move to make that groupie owe her. Okay, not calculated, but definitely serendipitous. She plucked a towel from the bin and wiped her hands. "I was afraid she'd keep hounding me. I'd better call Kelly."

After explaining to Kelly, who graciously agreed to Trixie having a non-speaking walk-on, Claire went into the gallery, where Nicole was making notations on a tour inventory sheet.

"I'm going to have to work night and day to complete all I need for this tour." Claire shook her head. "Why did I think it was a good idea?"

Nicole paused, her pencil poised over the sheet. "To spread your fame across the country, of course." Her grin was devoid of sarcasm.

Claire refrained from rolling her eyes. Her apprentice's youth lent a different perspective to things. "How's your own work coming along? I haven't had any time to help you." Her own words hit her broadside and she frowned. Sure, the girl was talented and quick to learn, but even so, she needed some guidance. With mentoring, she'd be a master potter within ten years. Claire's frown deepened. It'd taken her longer than that. Absently, she pressed a hand to her tummy. In her defense, she'd had babies to deal with, though. Yikes. Babies. She had to get that test.

"It's good," Nicole said, pulling Claire from her musing. "I have an idea for a vase I want to try. The sides will fold in somewhat if I can keep them from collapsing." She bent her head back to the list she held. "You need a tall vase. The list says four feet. Why would someone want one that tall?"

Claire shrugged. "I don't know, but Avery thinks a commercial building or maybe a museum might want it. I've never done one like that, but I like the challenge."

Or she would if she wasn't preoccupied over Lacey and her own trouble. The display of coffee mugs needed some attention, and right now her creativity needed a break. She moved a raccoon mug beside a loon. That loon had been a difficult one to make, but she'd finally settled on having its neck and beak form the handle. The sleepy loon appeared to need caffeine and turned out to be a best seller. She patted its handle and moved to another shelf.

The gallery door opened and Mel stepped inside, looking adorable. Her tattoo was definitely lighter this time. It still had a ways to go before makeup would hide any residual color while her body absorbed the last vestiges of ink. She said the doctor told her it would take about eight treatments over a few months.

"Hey, girl. How's school?" Claire moved to envelop her in a hug.

"Even the first time you met me in the hoosegow, you hugged me." She laid her head on Claire's shoulder.

Putting her arm around the girl, Claire led her into the back. "So, tell me everything." She plopped into a chair next to Mel. "Are you teaching the class yet?"

Nicole brought her list into the workroom, looked at the first sheet, and typed it into the computer as Claire and Mel caught up. When the buzzer rang out front, Nicole stopped. "Maybe Mel can do this for you while y'all catch up, and I'll take care of the gallery." She wagged a finger at Mel. "Just be sure you don't start typing in some quantum physics formula."

Mel giggled. What a delightful sound. Like a normal teenager.

"Sure, I'll be glad to." She took Nicole's place at the computer.

Claire scooted her chair next to Mel's. "So, tell me about your classes and the kids you're meeting."

"Classes are great. The other students are okay. They don't bother me, but they're not real friendly."

"That's too bad. They're missing out." Claire looked at the computer screen. "Change that one"—she tapped the monitor—"to a groundhog mug."

The keys clacked as Mel made the change. "Haleigh said they might be intimidated by me."

"Why?"

Her hands hovered above the keyboard. "Because I started mid-semester and I'm not behind." She started typing.

"But you're not that much younger."

"It's not about age, I don't think." She shrugged one shoulder. "It's not a big thing. I'm not there to make friends."

"Are you happy, sugar?" That's what Claire really wanted to know.

Mel stopped typing and turned to face her. "I really am. I love learning. Until I looked at those plans for the theater, I didn't know I was interested in engineering or architecture. But I realized I've always noticed angles. I haven't decided which to focus on yet, but a lot of the same classes are needed for both. I have the next two years to make that decision."

"I hope when you aren't in school and you want a part-time job, you'll come back here."

"Thanks, Claire. I will. Can I ask you a question?"

"Sure."

Mel's brows dipped, dangling her remaining eyebrow ring next to her eye. "How come all y'all are helping pay for my education?"

Claire picked up the pages Mel had already entered in the computer, tamping them into a neat stack. "Because everyone loves you, kiddo. You're part of Chapel Springs now. You represent the best of who we are. Even Hazel sent a check."

Mel curled her lip and blushed. "It's embarrassing."

The lip thing reminded Claire of the first night she met her. A small bit of the old Mel still lingered. The part she loved. Then a crease marred Mel's brow.

"What's wrong?"

"Oh, nothing. Well, it's something, but I think Nicole could help me better than you."

"Why her?"

Mel snickered. "You're old. I mean older. Okay, it's about a guy at school. But I think Nicole is closer to my age and ..." A deeper flush crept over her cheeks. "I think my foot's stuck in my mouth."

"Ya think?"

Claire dragged her feet as she walked to the theater. The last thing she wanted to do was introduce Trixie to Kelly. She forced her chin an inch higher. "Can't be helped."

"What are you mumbling about?" Joel nudged her with his elbow.

"Remember Trixie?"

"Ha! The gossiping groupie. Who could forget her?"

Claire kicked a pebble off the sidewalk. "Yeah, well, she's being given a walk-on in the play."

Joel stopped. "What? How come?"

"Temporary insanity?"

"What happened?" He took her hand as they walked.

How could she tell him what happened without revealing her suspicions? Claire shifted her tote, containing the items she'd need tonight, to her right hand. "She kept pestering me, and I finally promised to ask Kelly. It was that or have her camping on our doorstep."

They arrived at the theater, and Joel opened the door. Inside the lobby, work was nearing completion. Wall sconces, purchased from an antiques dealer, cast a soft glow over the gilt walls. They didn't remodel as much as restore the old theater to her former splendor.

"Yoo-hoo! Over here, Claire. Hey, Joel."

Claire crossed her eyes at Joel and he chuckled. "Hang in there. I promise not to believe anything she tells me." He dropped her hand and went backstage, avoiding Trixie as she zeroed in on Claire.

Trixie threw her arms around Claire's neck, nearly knocking her over. "Thank you, thank you, thank you. I'm really excited about this. I've heard so much about Lacey's plays, I have to be in one."

Claire backed out of Trixie's hug. Heard about Lacey's plays, had she? Layers of secrecy and near-truth surrounded the woman like skin on an onion.

Trixie looked around. "Say, where is Lacey?"

Claire wasn't about to tell her that and then be forced to listen to her launch into an hour-long gossip session. "Let's find Kelly." Then she could escape to the scene shop. She had props to make tonight. Claire led Trixie to where Kelly was sitting in the front row. She introduced them and made her escape.

Crossing the stage, Claire could still see visions of Lacey being struck by the spotlight. She shivered and hurried downstairs where Felix and Joel stood over a set of plans, while Lester explained what they would build and how it fit into the set design.

For two hours, the men cut and nailed and Claire painted. Lester called a halt to everything and pulled out the Shop-Vac to clean up the sawdust. "Don't blow any of that on my paint," Claire warned. "Can't that wait until next time? Start with cleanup? That way you don't risk contaminating the scenery."

Lester scratched his ear. "Sounds reasonable to me. I can do it as well tomorrow night." He scanned the room. "We could do with one of those exhaust systems that sucks up the sawdust as you cut."

"Claire?"

For one split second, Claire contemplated hiding, but she wouldn't be able to explain crouching behind a set prop to Lester and Felix. She sighed and lifted her head. "Over here, Trixie."

"There's a gigantic blood stain on the stage up there, and it's fresh. What happened?"

Claire glanced at Joel and Felix, then back to Trixie. "An accident."

With his hands planted on his hips, Felix glared at Trixie. "They cleaned that stage floor yesterday. How do you know it's blood?"

Trixie blinked. "I, uh, I know what blood stains look like."

"Do you now?" Felix moved closer. What was he up to? "When has a pretty little thing like you seen blood stains? Even Claire didn't notice them."

Claire snapped her gaze to Felix, frowning. Of course she'd noticed them. "What's that supposed to mean?"

He lifted a hand to stop her protest. "I'd like to hear what Miss Trixie knows about this."

"I don't know anything. I noticed the stains, and people avoided that area. If you don't want to tell me, that's fine." She turned to leave.

"Hold on there, missy. Are you with the insurance company?"

Lacey's insurance company? What was Felix doing?

"I'm an old friend of Claire's."

That stretched things a bit. "Felix, I met Trixie when I took that cooking class at Henderson's."

He nodded but kept his eyes on Trixie. "I don't cotton to some outsider coming in here and causing a stink. If you're from their insurance company, fixing to deny payments for some trumped-up reason, you can haul yourself right outta here. Now."

Claire narrowed her eyes. Was this why Trixie followed her? "Trixie? Where do you work? And don't try to lie. I know you have a job. You told me you did."

Felix and Claire together were more than Trixie could handle. She folded like a bad poker hand. "Okay, yes. I work for the insurance company. But you can't blame them. A homely girl now needs"— Trixie actually made air quotes—"facial reconstruction? That caused some questions." She glared at Felix. "Well, you can't deny it sounds suspicious."

Felix snorted. "Well, you can go back and tell them quacks on your board this ain't one of those kind of deals. That girl's life is hanging by a thread right now."

"I'm sorry to hear that, but it doesn't change the fact that I have a job to do."

Trixie turned to go, but Claire grabbed her arm, stopping her. "For your information, Lacey was comfortable with her looks. Your company is way off base. As for you wanting to be in the play, it was all a front for this?"

Trixie whirled. "Well, you have to admit it was a good idea. But I can see why you wouldn't want me around anymore."

"Not so fast. Kelly gave you a part, so you can't back out now."

Felix gawked at her like she'd lost her marbles. Then, as if a light bulb had gone on, he nodded.

Keep your enemies close ... that's what Claire wanted, and right now Trixie definitely counted as an enemy.

Chapter 16

Pain surrounded her. Submerged her. Held her in its claws. Stabbed at her eyes.

"Easy, Lacey."

A hand touched her shoulder. At least that didn't hurt.

Her throat was dry. So dry, she couldn't swallow.

Ice touched her lips. She opened them and it slipped in, dissolving on her tongue. Not enough to swallow. More. Another chip followed the first. This one was bigger. Then another. So good.

"That's enough for now, dear."

But she wanted more. Something near her buzzed. Then the pain receded into blackness.

Claire stepped up onto the boardwalk and headed toward Dee's 'n' Doughs. The bright sun warmed her shoulders. Were poor Lacey's shoulders warm? Claire shook her head to rid herself of the image of Lacey lying in a pool of blood, the spotlight on top of her. A week had passed, but the image was as fresh as if it had happened yesterday.

The bells on the bakery's door jangled on Claire's frayed nerves. By the look on Dee's face, her nerves weren't the only ones affected by Lacey's accident. For a quiet, shy girl, she sure had worked her way into all their hearts.

"Morning, Claire. Coffee or tea?"

"Tea." Claire grimaced. Her stomach rebelled at coffee, much to her disgust.

Dee set a steaming mug on the counter, the teabag inside already brewing. "Have you heard an update on Lacey?"

Claire looked at the selections in Dee's display case. Nothing appealed to her this morning. "The last I heard is she turned the corner and will be okay. Now, they have to reconstruct her face." She shivered. "That always sounds so strange to me. Like she lost hers, and they're making a new one."

Dee nodded. "Well, she did in a way."

Claire picked up her mug. "I guess."

"I heard about that investigator for the insurance company. My goodness, they swooped in fast." Dee pulled out a cloth and wiped the counter. "You don't think they'll deny the claim, do you?"

"I hope not. If that Trixie tries to say anything against Lacey, I'll … I'll … see her banned from Henderson's cooking school."

"You're a good friend, Claire." Dee moved to the next in line.

The bells jangled and Claire turned. Patsy, followed by Ellie, Carin, and JoAnn. Her friends weren't chattering like normal. Claire waggled her fingers in a wave and went to secure a table. The only people who were oblivious were the tourists, yapping away as if nothing had happened.

Patsy pulled out a chair beside Claire. "I saw Lydia drive by as I came in. She's on her way to the hospital to give Jake a breather. He needs to check in on the restaurants." She emptied a sweetener packet into her coffee. "Can I borrow your stir stick? I forgot one."

Claire handed it to her. "I'd like to go over this afternoon, but I don't know if she's able to have visitors yet."

JoAnn joined them, setting her coffee and bagel down before pulling out her chair. "Talking about Lacey?"

Claire nodded. "Have you and Pastor Seth seen her yet?"

"We're going tonight. We've been to see Jake but didn't try to see her until she was awake. He called a little while ago. She's talking as well as she can through all the bandages." She paused and smiled at everyone. "She's out of danger and will be okay. There's no permanent brain damage. That's why she's rebounding so quickly."

"What if, when all this is over, she's badly scarred?" Patsy asked. "She's already so shy. What will that do to her?"

JoAnn's smile faded. "I don't know. Somehow, I don't think she has a strong faith to fall back on."

Ellie arrived at the table, arms loaded with her own breakfast and an extra pot of coffee. "Dee will be over in a minute. Were you talking about Lacey?"

"I don't think any of us has talked about anything else since last week." Claire removed the gold hoop from her left ear and pulled her lobe to relieve an itch. "She still has to go through reconstruction. Jake said the doctors would put steel or titanium plates or something inside her to hold it all together." Claire shuddered. "I try to put myself in Lacey's place. How would I feel if my face were scarred?"

"I doubt you'd become a hermit." Patsy picked up her cup with both hands, inhaling its aroma before she sipped.

Pat-a-cake was right. Claire wouldn't be that bothered. Maybe. "But Lacey might. She hates to be the center of attention. Do y'all remember when I made that frog for her? She almost didn't take it because we all made such a big deal out of it. If she knew she was the subject of this conversation right now, she'd be mortified. She'd probably hide for a month."

"What can we do to help her?" Patsy asked.

Of all Claire's friends, Patsy's heart was the most tender and put Claire to shame sometimes. "Don't stare at her, no matter how badly scarred she is. Ignore her like we've always done. Not that we ignored her on purpose. More like overlooking her." Claire groaned. "I feel so bad about all the times I've done that."

Ellie reached over and patted Claire's hand. "You aren't alone in that. She so rarely talks and moves just as quietly. No wonder we don't notice her."

"I think Claire has a good point," JoAnn said. "We'll try to act normal around her—not pay attention to her scars."

"Maybe I should talk to Graham. He knows, of course, but I'll bet he hasn't thought about the other employees' reaction to her when she gets back to work."

"I'll go with you," Patsy said. "To make sure you don't put your foot in your mouth." She winked.

"If you weren't my best friend—"

"But I am. Hey, anything on the romance front with your brother-in-law? I saw him and Haleigh having lunch yesterday."

Leave it to Patsy to change the subject. "Where?"

"On the beach. I was helping a customer. I saw them through the window."

Dee's grin looked like Tweety's when he snookered Sylvester. "Vince ordered a picnic lunch for them."

"Well, I'm glad. I hope they do fall in love. My brother-in-law needs someone." And Haleigh seemed perfect for him. Claire finished her tea and nudged Patsy. "So, are we going to talk to Graham?"

"Yes." She pushed her chair back. "Let's do it now before a lot of people are in the bank and Graham's too busy."

"See y'all later." JoAnn waved them away. "Ellie and I will decide on some flowers to take her from all of us."

That was a nice idea. "Thanks, JoAnn. See y'all tomorrow." Claire grabbed her tote and followed Patsy out the door. Once they cleared Dee's 'n' Doughs' windows, she stopped her BFF. "Okay, what's the deal? Why did you want to come with me? And don't say to keep my foot out of my mouth. I'm only going to talk to Graham. He knows all about my feet."

Patsy laughed. "You're right. There is something else." She started walking, and Claire hurried to keep up with her. "It's about Mel. I didn't want to say anything in front of Ellie, in case Mel hasn't told her. And somehow, I doubt she has."

"Is it why she wanted to talk with Nicole yesterday? The stinker told me I was too old and wouldn't tell me anything. Should I be worried?"

Patsy stopped, picked up a piece of paper on the boardwalk and tossed it into a trash can. "I'm not sure. Some boy has been following her at school. Or at least every time she goes to her locker, he's nearby. She sees him in the student union, the library. Everywhere she goes, he's there."

"He probably likes her." Claire wasn't sure how she felt about that. Mel was younger than all the other college students. She said that much herself.

"That's what Nicole said, but Mel told her he hasn't said a word to her."

Claire's stomach clenched. "Could he be a stalker?" Wait ... surely not. Mel knew how to handle herself. "What does Nicole think?"

"That it could be as innocent as a tongue-tied boy or as crazy as a stalker. She told Mel to always have someone with her."

"But Mel doesn't know many people at school. It's only been a few weeks." Claire couldn't wrap her mind around someone stalking Mel. Still, the world was full of crazies. "What should we do?"

Patsy opened the door to the bank. "Nothing right now. But when I mentioned it to Deva, she said one of the girls who works on the weekends for her is taking classes there, and she offered to watch out for Mel."

"That's good." With someone watching her back, Mel should be okay. Claire stepped through the door and went straight to Graham's office. He saw her coming and waved them in. Poor guy. With a glass office, he couldn't hide from anyone.

He set aside the stack of papers he'd been studying. "Good morning, Claire. Patsy. What can I do for you?"

"We don't want to take up much of your time, Graham, but we're a little concerned about Lacey—when she returns to work."

He frowned. "Sit down and tell me what you mean."

After she voiced her concern, Graham agreed and said he'd discreetly pass the word. Satisfied she'd helped a tiny bit, she smiled, and they took their leave.

If only her own trouble could be alleviated as easily. She had to find a way to get one of those tests without anyone knowing.

Xander stood at the table and studied the land parcels and plat maps Newlander brought him. He did okay on this assignment. For a redneck, anyway. Xander would've preferred to get them a couple of days ago, though. He pushed the top one aside and frowned at the second one. "Where'd you find these?"

"Online. Anyone can order them. Cost me, though."

Was he expecting reimbursement? He should be glad Xander's associates hadn't eliminated him from this venture. He pointed to the property lines map. "The property that backs up to Riley's belongs to a Haleigh Evans. You know her?" The purchase was recent, but for the right money, she might sell. Make a windfall profit. No husband listed.

Newlander shook his head. "I know who she is, but that's all. Looks like that young doctor has his eye on her." He snickered.

"You keep your mind off women and on this business." Xander stabbed a finger on the map.

The next two properties listed out-of-state owners. He circled them. One had owned the land since ninety-five. The other was newer—2013. He highlighted the listings he wanted Newlander to look into.

"Are there any properties for sale in this town?"

"Two." Newlander pointed to their location. "They don't come up often and are snapped up when they do."

Xander drilled his gaze into the redneck. Make him understand that failure was not an option.

Sweat popped out on Newlander's brow.

Good.

Chapter 17

Lacey tried to open her eyes. The right one fluttered. The pain was less than before. But what happened to her? Her left eye wouldn't open at all. She raised her hand to feel what held it shut, but something—someone?—gently lowered her fingers.

"Don't touch it, sweet stuff."

Jake. She managed to raise her one unfettered eyelid. Light blinded her, and she shut it. Try again. She lifted the lid, slowly this time to get used to the light.

"Wha … what happened?"

Days of growth darkened the stubble on Jake's face, but he looked wonderful to her. How long had she been here? And where was here? The sting of antiseptic smell twanged her nose. A hospital. Right. But where?

Jake glanced at someone outside her line of sight. Another hand touched hers, the one Jake held.

"Lacey, I'm Dr. Martin. You had a pretty bad accident."

Accident? She didn't have a car accident. Did she? Had she forgotten?

"You underwent fairly extensive surgery to stabilize your injuries. How's your pain level right now?"

Her lips twitched. "Painful." How bad *were* her injuries?

Jake snickered.

"Is she always this sarcastic?"

"Definitely. In fact, I'm encouraged." Jake squeezed her hand.

"Water." Her thoughts were starting to make sense, but her throat remained like the Mojave Desert.

A straw touched her lips. She sucked wonderful cold water.

LIFE IN CHAPEL SPRINGS

"Just a little to start, babe."

"So good."

Dr. Martin ducked back into sight. "How about on a scale of one to ten, Lacey."

She licked her lips. At least she still had lips. "If ten … is run over by a freight train … then eight."

A pen scritched. She hoped that meant a pain pill and not a knockout shot. She hated those. "Can I have another drink? My throat hurts."

"That's from the intubation. It'll be sore for a few days."

"Is that why my neck is stiff?"

"Partly." He patted her hand. "You suffered major trauma when you were hurt."

"What happened to me?"

Jake bent and kissed her lips. Were her lips and one eye the only things not bandaged?

"I'll be right back."

Where was he going? The doctor left with him. What was wrong? Why wouldn't they tell her what happened? Her pulse pounded, making her head hurt. A nurse appeared and raised her bed a little.

"That's nice. I was getting tired of that stain on the ceiling." She hoped her face wouldn't be like the ceiling. Not that she'd ever been pretty. Not even her baby pictures were cute. She wasn't ugly—simply plain, a little homely. Growing up in the shadow of Lydia, the pretty sister, Lacey had become used to it. It made people focus their attention on Lydia, and that was good.

The nurse snorted, making Lacey smile. It didn't hurt. Wonderful. She turned her head a bit. Yvonne, her name tag said.

"Yvonne, may I have some more water?"

"Yes, but go slowly. You've had nothing by mouth for eight days. Your stomach may rebel, and we don't want that."

Eight days? "I think I'll be okay. It didn't even get mad at the last drink."

Yvonne chuckled and handed her a glass with about an inch of water in it. "The doctor said you could go to a lower dose on your pain meds."

"Good. I want to enjoy your pampering."

Yvonne fluffed her pillow and straightened her bedding. Her quilt was on the foot of her bed. Jake brought her quilt? Her heart did a little flip. He loved her just right. She rubbed her toe over the stitching.

The nurse pulled it up to her shoulders. "Beautiful handiwork. It must mean a lot."

"Yes." Only Lacey didn't know why. She'd always had the quilt but no memory of receiving it. Who gave it to her or who made it was a mystery. But that didn't stop her from cherishing its handmade softness.

Jake came back in the room.

Yvonne moved toward the door. "I'll be back with your meds in fifteen minutes." She scooted out and left them alone.

Jake sat on the side of her bed. "How bad do you hurt, sweet stuff? Honestly."

"Nothing like the first time I woke up. I don't know when that was, but the pain owned me then. Now, it hurts like a bad migraine, but it doesn't define me."

"Good. Dr. Martin said they'll do the reconstruction surgery on Thursday."

Reconstruction? Her heart took off at a gallop again. She grasped his hand and gave his fingers a squeeze. "Time to quit evading my question. What exactly happened to me?"

His thumb rubbed soft circles on her skin. "One of the spotlights slid off the truss. Something broke, I think. Anyway, you looked up just as it landed on you, and thank God you did. Otherwise, I'd have been a widower."

"But what happened to my face?"

"Your cheekbones were crushed, your nose was broken. One eye socket was shattered, and you have a hairline fracture in your jaw, near the front."

"Oh." Each fracture let itself be known. Maybe she shouldn't have minimized the pain to the doctor.

"Yeah." Jake's eyes glistened.

"Do you think I'll have a lot of scarring? What did the doctor say?" She was sure that was what he told him when they were out of the room.

He scooted close and gathered her gently into his arms. "You know that won't matter to me, don't you?"

She did know that. He loved her even though she was plain. But could he stand to look at her if she was badly scarred? Worse, what if her face was frozen in some grotesque expression? People would stare. She couldn't stand that. Plain was one thing, but a freak ...

"Sweet stuff, I have to check in at the restaurant. I'll be back before dinner, though." He reached for the nightstand. "I put your cell phone in the drawer here, so you can call me if you want me to come sooner." Jake rubbed his thumb across her lips. "I love you," he whispered. "I couldn't bear it if I lost you." His kiss, while soft so not to hurt her, held passion.

Tears burned her eyes. "I love you too. I don't know what I ever did to deserve you, but I'm so glad you love me."

Maybe God did know she was there.

Nurse Yvonne came in with Lacey's meds right after Jake left. Blast, they made her sleepy too. She gave in and let the pain pill do its work. Maybe later, she'd unpack the idea God actually knew her.

Her door opened, and Claire peeked in, a big smile on her face and a wrapped package in her hands. Lacey couldn't help the smile tugging at her lips. She adored funny Claire. She eased her shoulders up on her pillow. "Come on in. I need some company."

Dressed in turquoise overalls, Claire pulled the chair up close to the bed. "I'm glad you're awake, but I hope you aren't hurting too bad. I brought you something to make you smile." She placed the box on Lacey's bed.

Lacey moved it onto her lap. The box was heavier than she expected. "I had a pain cocktail at dinner. They're going to do the reconstruction surgery tomorrow." She tugged at the ribbon. "I'm nervous."

"I can imagine. Did the doctor say anything about your face?"

"Nothing other than I still have one. Sort of." The ribbon pulled away, and Lacey lifted the lid. Inside, nestled in tissue was— "It's a girlfriend for Frankie Frog!" Lacey lifted the cute little whimsy frog vase from its nest. "She's adorable, Claire. I love her pink ribbon." It sat on top of her head, slightly askew.

"I named her Fancy." Claire set the vase on the bedside table, gathered the tissue and stuffed it in the box, setting that on the floor. "Now, what have you been doing besides healing and lounging around?"

A knot of gratitude rose in Lacey's throat. Claire wouldn't allow her to wallow in self-pity. "Noodling some new ideas for plays."

Claire wiggled her eyebrows. "Want to brainstorm them?"

Lacey would love that, and it would get her mind off her face. *Please don't let me be scarred.* She wasn't sure God would answer. After all, He didn't stop the accident from happening.

She and Claire tossed around several ideas. For someone who

didn't write, Claire had wonderful suggestions. Several sparked Lacey's imagination. She grabbed her phone and jotted them down, then emailed them to herself. After Claire left, she continued to plot the new play. Finally, she set her phone aside and lowered her bed a bit. Her thoughts grew fuzzy and her unfettered eye closed. Claire's visit had been good for her.

Shortly after Claire left, the doctor and Jake walked in together. The doctor waited while Jake kissed her.

"Now, I'm going to remove your bandages, Lacey. I want to make sure you're ready for the surgery tomorrow." He held a pair of scissors and snipped the last of the bandages, gently unwinding the gauze from her head.

In spite of the room's cool temperature, her heart pounded and her palms grew sweaty. Then the air hit her face. She opened her right eye. It worked. She blinked and the skin—or was it her muscles?—pulled tight. She lifted her fingers, but the doctor stopped her hand.

"Not yet, Lacey." He probed her cheekbones. "Does that hurt?"

It did. "Considering my face was squashed, I expect some pain. Is that bad?"

"No, it's normal." He smiled. "And it was more than squashed." He reiterated her injuries. "With that kind of trauma, you can expect it to hurt some for a few months." He probed several moments longer. She winced when his fingers touched her nose. "We put some plates there to support the reconstruction. But right now, you're still very swollen. You wouldn't recognize yourself."

What she wanted to know no one mentioned. They tiptoed around that gorilla. She swallowed nervously. "Doctor, am I badly scarred?"

He leaned back and appraised her. "Yes, right now you are. But I do very good work, Lacey. After I do your reconstruction, and after the swelling goes down, you'll be fine." He glanced at Jake, who stood smiling across the room. "You're in the middle of it right now."

So what did all that mean? Was she scarred or not? "Can I see?"

"Soon enough. Even after I do your reconstruction, you need to realize you're going to look different. I want you to talk with another doctor first."

That didn't sound good. "What do you mean 'different'? Different like a zebra? Do I have stripes?"

Jake snorted. She couldn't wrinkle her nose. It hurt. She glared at him. Anything to keep back the tears. Her face was scarred. She knew it. No matter how good the doctor was, how could it be avoided? Her whole face had been torn up and broken.

Chapter 18

"Come on in, Mel." Claire stepped back to let her in. "What's up?" She had dark circles under her eyes, and her brow wrinkled. Could it be about that boy?

"I ... uh, are 'Lissa and Megan here? I need to talk with them."

So she was right. This *was* about the boy. "Sure. Go on into the family room."

She called up the stairs for the girls. When Melissa came down, Claire stopped her in the hall. "Mel's worried about something. Will you tell me if it's something I should let Ellie know about?"

"Momma, you know I won't betray a confidence, but let's wait and see before you turn it into a mountain." 'Lissa scooted into the family room.

Cheeky girl. Claire kept one ear tuned to their voices as she poured glasses of sweet tea for them. If she timed it right, she might hear more.

She carried the tea into the girls. "Here you go."

As 'Lissa reached for her glass, Megan shouted from upstairs, "Are y'all coming up or what? And bring me some sweet tea, please."

'Lissa beckoned to Mel. "Come on. Let's get her a glass and go up to her room."

Claire gave her daughter the stink eye and her own glass of tea for Megan. The girls disappeared up the stairs in a cloud of giggles.

Van Gogh's ear! Now she'd have to wait until after dinner to find out. She sauntered back into the kitchen and absently wiped the countertop. Mel had never dropped by before to talk to the twins. Then again, she'd talked to 'Lissa in The Painted Loon while they worked. Boy stuff. That's what bothered her. Why would Mel need to talk with the twins about boys? What great wisdom did they have at their age? Why wasn't Mel asking her? Claire stopped wiping the counter and smirked. The same reason the twins talked with their peers instead of her and Joel.

She grabbed her tote and shouted up the stairs, "I'm leaving for the gallery. Your dad left dinner instructions on the fridge. Y'all are in charge." She didn't wait for an answer.

Claire stood at the kitchen sink, washing the last of the pans from supper, while Megan and Melissa dried. "So, what did Mel need to talk to y'all about?"

The girls exchanged glances and Megan nodded to her sister. 'Lissa set down her towel and sat at the banquette. "Some boy at school has been following her."

Exactly what Mel told Nicole. "How long has he been doing that? Does he talk to her?"

Megan shook her head. "That's kind of what bothers her. She said it started about two weeks ago, but he hasn't said anything to her."

The hairs on the back of Claire's neck stood to attention. "You know she told Nicole about this too?"

"Yes." 'Lissa raised a hand to stop Claire's tirade. "Easy, Momma. She's never seen him outside of school. But when she leaves class or goes to the library, he's always there."

"Has she tried to talk to him?"

"Once." Megan joined her sister at the banquette. Shiloh plodded into the kitchen and laid his big head on her lap to get his ears scratched.

"What happened? Did he say anything?"

The girls exchanged another glance. Something was definitely wrong.

"No. She said he pretended not to hear her and left."

Claire joined them at the table. "That's not normal behavior." She pulled the now-soggy napkin from beneath 'Lissa's glass and wiped the wet ring it left. "Why did she come to you instead of reporting him?"

"She wanted to see if we'd experienced anything like that," 'Lissa said.

"You didn't, did you?" They never told her about any stalkers. The word jumped out at Claire. "Do you suppose he's stalking her? If so, we need to contact the campus police."

"We never had stalkers, Momma." Megan twisted her hair through her fingers.

"But we knew a girl who did," 'Lissa said. "Remember Laurie, Meg? The boy was a foreign student and didn't speak English yet, so he never spoke to her."

Megan stopped twisting and tossed her hair over her shoulder. "I remember. But he wasn't a real stalker. Not like what happened to Samantha, who—" She glanced at Claire.

She didn't like the sound of that. "Who what?"

"She was raped."

Claire had always heard the saying "blood ran cold," and right then, hers did. She shivered. "What did you two tell Mel to do?"

"Be careful. Always stay with another person." 'Lissa gulped the last of her tea. "We don't know that this guy is a stalker, Momma. He could be unsure of himself but have a crush on her. We gave Mel our best advice." She slid out of the banquette. "I'm going to bed." Megan followed her twin upstairs after kissing Claire goodnight.

She stayed at the table. Being careful wasn't enough. It hadn't helped that Samantha. Claire couldn't sit on this and not do anything. Mel had a special place in her heart. She pulled out her phone to call Ellie, her finger hovering over the call icon. If Mel were home … Claire put her phone away. She'd see Ellie tomorrow.

The next morning, Claire pushed open the door to Dee's 'n' Doughs. She spied her friends at their favorite table by the window. They had one week left to enjoy the table—and the peace—until Spring Break and the hordes once again descended on the town. This year, though, they were ready for them with plenty of housing. She grabbed a cup of tea on her way to the table.

"Morning, Claire," Ellie said, moving her chair a bit to the right.

She returned the greetings and watched as the librarian took a bite of Dee's special gooey bun. How did she stay so tiny eating those all the time? She must have drooled watching Ellie because Patsy handed her a napkin.

"Thanks." Claire wiped her mouth. "Ellie, we have an issue." She explained what she'd learned from the twins. "I had a feeling Mel might not have told you about it."

"No, she didn't." Ellie's frown deepened.

Patsy pushed the cream pitcher to Claire. "I wouldn't worry about her not telling you. She doesn't want you concerned."

Claire snorted. "When will they learn we aren't stupid?"

"When they reach twenty-five," JoAnn said. "That's when ours realized we still had brains instead of grits in our heads."

"The point is …" Claire started to pour cream into her tea, then stopped. It would upset her stomach. She pushed the pitcher aside. "What are we going to do about this? We can't sit here and do nothing."

Ellie nodded once, then stopped, her eyes growing wide. "Say, you don't suppose her father hired someone to follow her, do you? I started the adoption process, and maybe he found out about her being in college."

"No way," Carin said. "From what all y'all have told me, he doesn't have the money to hire a mosquito hawk."

Ellie relaxed. "That's true. I think we need to let the campus police know. Or Sheriff Taylor."

"He'd laugh at us and say we're exaggerating things. No, we need …" Claire took a sip of tea, searching for a— "I've got it! We'll do it ourselves. That way, if it's all innocent, the police haven't been brought in." And Claire wouldn't be embarrassed for being the one who thought it up. Felix would love that. He'd make a big stink out of it. "We could all take turns. Mel won't even notice us if we're careful. Ow. What?" Claire rubbed her arm and turned to Patsy who'd flicked her.

"She'll see you and be mortified."

Claire smirked. She had Pat-a-cake here. "Not if we use some of the theater's paraphernalia. We can make ourselves unrecognizable. And quit rolling your eyes. It's a good idea."

"Claire has a good point," Ellie said. "Mel wouldn't expect to see us, so if we took turns, disguised ourselves as students, and stayed back, she'd never notice us. I think it's a great plan. Who wants to take the first watch? Claire? Will you?"

"Sure. I'll need her schedule of classes. Then I'll get Kelly—wait, where is Kelly?"

"At the hospital seeing Lacey." JoAnn pulled out a small spiral notebook and a pen. "If we're going to do this, we need a real plan. How do we hide? If Claire starts crouching behind trash cans, the campus police will arrest her."

What did JoAnn think she was? An idiot? "I know that. I'm going to carry a book. There are lots of places to sit and read while watching."

JoAnn patted her hand. "I know you're not a half-wit, Claire. You don't always think, though. Now, we can trade off. I'll take the second watch."

"I have an idea," Carin said. "Why don't we drill a hole in the book, big enough to see through but not too big to be noticed?"

Ellie cringed. "But the book would be ruined then."

"Better the book than Mel." Claire shuddered at what could happen.

Chapter 19

Jake walked beside her, holding her trembling hand as the orderly wheeled her to the operating room. "Don't be afraid, sweet stuff. I checked this dude out, and he's one of the best in the South."

"I don' wanna scaaar." Her words slurred from the shot they'd given her. Did she say what she wanted? Did he understand?

Jake bent down and kissed her cheek, then disappeared. She turned around to find him, and they were swimming in a pond beneath a waterfall at Enota.

"Lacey? Come on. Wake up now."

She didn't want to leave the lake, but someone called her name. Where was she? Her nose said the hospital. Wait, they were supposed to do her surgery. Was it so bad, they couldn't even reconstruct her?

"Come on, Lacey. Open your eyes. You need to wake up now."

No. If she did, she'd see a face like Frankenstein's monster.

"Sweet stuff, come on. Wake up."

"Is she always this hard to wake up?"

But they were supposed to do her surgery … weren't they? She needed to be asleep. She didn't want—

"Come on, babe. They finished your surgery and need you to wake up now."

She opened one eye. "Wa—" Dry. Her throat was dry. She'd been here before. An ice chip hit her lips and she sucked it in. "Thank you." Her words came out in a whisper, but she managed them. She opened her eye again and looked past Jake to the pale green walls. This wasn't her room. "Where am I?"

"You're in recovery, Lacey. I'm Dr. Martin."

She eyed him. "I remember you."

"You can open both eyes now, you know. The other one isn't bandaged."

She could? It wasn't? Well, how about that. It opened. She blinked. Her eyes didn't work together. She saw two doctors. Wait. Not two. One was Jake. When did he become her doctor?

"Lacey? Are you all right?"

She blinked. "Yes, but Jake … how'd you get to be a doctor?"

He chuckled. "I borrowed the chef's coat to come in here. No germs from the operating room."

Chef's coat? This was getting weird. "Can I go back to sleep now?"

"Go ahead. You'll wake up back in your room."

She didn't know if that was Dr. Martin or the orderly or Jake. Didn't matter. She was going to sleep and getting out of this dream.

"Well, I found nothing." Claire plopped her prosthetic nose on the table in Dee's 'n' Doughs. "No boy. Nobody remotely resembling a stalker. Talk about boring. JoAnn can take the next watch because I have five more pieces to make for this art tour."

Patsy picked the nose up, giggling. "You wore this? Really? And it didn't fall off?"

"Nope. It stayed on. When she passed me, Mel never took a second glance. Shoot, I didn't recognize myself. Just in case, I took a quick check in the mirror to make sure the nose was still in place, though." Claire laughed. "Fortunately, it kept me from smelling Dane's backpack. He must have kept his gym shoes in there. Ick."

Patsy swatted her. "Come on. Tell us every detail."

Claire raised one corner of her upper lip. "I can tell you I wished one of y'all was with me. Then I wouldn't have felt so out of place. My stomach churned, and my nose itched beneath the fake one. I was so afraid I'd forget and scratch and take a chunk out of it."

Ellie slapped her hand over her mouth, giggling. "I can see you doing that too."

Claire crossed her eyes at Ellie. "Well, I didn't. I kept my wits about me. After all, it was all for Mel's safety. The hardest part was finding the building. I sat on the first bench I came to and pulled out her schedule. I needed to go to the science building. However,"—Claire gave her BFF the stink eye—"Patsy forgot to put the map in the backpack."

That signaled Pat-a-cake's turn to clap her hand over her mouth. "Oh, I'm so sorry!" A giggle snuck out. "What did you do?"

"I tossed that smelly bag over my shoulder and headed to what looked to be the center of campus. A young man sat on the ground beneath a tree, so I asked him. To my embarrassment, he pointed over my shoulder." She grimaced. "Yep, there it was. Right behind me. If I'd've looked to my right instead of at the boy, I'd have seen the rather large sign on the side of the building that read Science. I was mortified. I thought my nose might melt off from the heat in my face."

"Okay, yes. You were embarrassed." Ellie leaned forward. "Now what happened? Did you see the kid who's been following her?"

"No. I had about an hour before she changed classes, so instead of trying to guess which exit to position myself near, I chose to risk standing across the hall from the classroom." She smirked at Ellie. "I pulled out our doctored book and raised it to hide behind." Claire grinned at Carin. "I moved my finger and checked how the hole worked. Perfect, as we hoped. So, I'm standing there, when the door burst open and the kids poured out like sweet tea at a picnic. I never even heard a bell."

Patsy opened a packet of sugar and added it to her coffee. "I don't think they use those anymore, at least not in college. The clocks buzz or something. I remember one of the kids mentioning that."

"Whatever. Anyway, suddenly Mel walked out, glancing over her shoulder. I raised the book real fast and peered through the hole. Mel walked past, never knowing it was me. I waited until a few more kids went by, then I fell in step behind them."

She took a sip of tea, and all her friends leaned closer.

"Then what?" Ellie asked. "Get on with it."

Funny, telling them was more fun than the actual surveillance. "Well, one by one, the students all wandered to different paths. Mel glanced over her shoulder once, and I dove behind a tree. Then she crossed the grass to the library. I wasn't sure if I'd need a pass or something to get in, but a young man held the door open for me, so I thanked him and scooted inside. He went up the stairs. I looked for Mel. Finding her took some time. The girl wasn't at any of the large tables. Finally, I spotted her in an overstuffed chair that faced the library doors. I slid into an aisle and found a seat at a table, where I could pretend to read and watch her."

She paused to snitch a pinch of Patsy's bagel, then wash it down with more tea. She considered another bite, but Patsy moved it away.

Before she could snatch it back, Ellie grabbed her hand.

"What happened? Did you ever find the boy?"

Claire sighed. "No. But I can tell you, wearing a wig is no fun. My scalp itched under that thing. I prayed it wouldn't move. I ended up pulling out a pencil and slid it beneath the wig for a good scratch. At least that was easier to take care of than my poor nose. That thing continued to plague me the entire time." She glanced at Kelly. "How do actors manage when they're onstage and get an itch?"

Kelly deadpanned. "They ignore it."

"And that's why I won't act. Anyway, the inactivity of sitting there made me sleepy. Or it could have been the weight of the nose pulling my eyelids down. Whatever, I blinked and looked up. Mel was leaving the library. I gathered that stinky backpack and the book and went after her. The same young man held the door open for me. I thanked him again." Claire shrugged. "He grunted and walked away. I followed Mel and saw her safely into class, the only one she had left."

Ellie's shoulders drooped. "Shoot. I was hoping we could get this solved fast." She consulted her list. "So who has the next watch?"

JoAnn wiggled her fingers at Ellie. "I do."

"Good. You can have this." Claire held out the prosthetic nose, a little lopsided now.

"No, thanks." JoAnn wrinkled hers. "Kelly and I will figure out another disguise for me."

Claire nodded and dropped the nose into an empty to-go cup. "I'll leave y'all then. I need to put *my* nose to the grindstone." She snatched the prosthesis out of the cup. "Maybe I'll keep this. Might come in handy." Like if she ever broke her nose, or it could cover Lacey's nose if it were badly scarred. Jake said her surgeon was good, but until her bandages came off, they wouldn't know for sure.

"Hey, isn't Lacey supposed to get her bandages off soon?"

JoAnn tapped her phone. "Two more days."

Chapter 20

D r. Martin slowly unwound the bandages, snipping here and there. Lacey resisted the urge to cringe. He peered closely at every part of her face like she was a new Maserati he intended to purchase. From the open door, rubber soles squeaked against polished floors in the hallway, going about their normal routine. She kept her gaze centered on his forehead. If she looked into his eyes, she might see something she didn't want to. The only problem was his frown came and went.

Finally, he leaned back and glanced at Jake. "What do you think?"

Jake smiled. "I think I love my wife, and I'm thankful to still have her."

Oh no! Lacey's heart pounded. Her fears had come true.

"I want Lacey to make an appointment with Dr. Jacobs after she's released. I think I gave you his card, right?"

Jake nodded. "You did."

"Good." He wrapped his stethoscope around his neck. "Lacey, I'll see you once more before you go home, then in my office in two weeks. I think you can go home tomorrow." Dr. Martin shook Jake's hand, then patted Lacey's shoulder. The hospital's intercom paged him, and he walked out of her room. In the hallway, he conferred with a nurse. Had he prearranged that to escape?

She stared at her lap, refusing to make eye contact with Jake. She didn't want to talk with whoever Dr. Jacobs was. Probably some shrink who would blather on about psychoses and junk. She could handle this fine. By herself. The same way she handled everything. By not caring. Except, she did care. She didn't want to look like Frankenstein's monster.

She raised her chin. The hallway was empty, and Jake leaned against the wall, staring at her. "What do you see? Give it to me straight, Jake. Don't try to fool me."

"Sweet stuff, when have I ever fooled you?"

"Okay, that wasn't fair. I'm sorry. But—" Lacey raised her hands and touched her face, probing her nose and cheeks with her fingers. "I don't feel like ... me."

"You look like you."

She held his gaze. "Do I? I don't have bad scars? I mean, I was never pretty, but I don't want to be hideous, Jake." The tears fell, stinging as they slid down her poor face.

The bed squeaked and Jake took her in his arms. "Baby, you're not. I promise you, that's not even a remote possibility."

"Why do you love me?"

With her head on his chest, his chuckle rumbled against her ear. "That's easy. You're beautiful. You're always happy. You're funny. You make me happy."

She sniffled. "That describes an Irish setter. And I'm not beautiful. I'm plain. Always have been. Always will be, unless ... unless I'm, I'm ... oh, crud. It hurts to cry."

"Baby, you've never been worried about your appearance. Besides, you didn't need to. Those who know you see the inside—the real you."

"But if I'm all scarred, they'll—" She choked on her words. Who had the patience to look past scars to *find* the real her?

"Enough, Lacey. You're not scarred." He crossed the room and pulled a hand mirror from her overnight bag. He brought it to her, setting it on her lap. "Now, remember, your face is swollen. A lot."

The mirror lay there, taunting her. She wanted to see. Needed to get it over with, but fear held her back. Her heart beat a rapid-fire staccato, its pulse throbbing in her throat. Adrenaline shot through her stomach, making her queasy. Her breathing roared in her ears. Like a news station's alert ribbon at the bottom of the TV screen, words from her past marched across her mind's eye: "You're a dirty, ugly little toad."

She couldn't do it. A single fat tear slipped down her cheek and splashed onto the mirror.

Brushing away the wetness, Jake held it up. "Look in it, sweet stuff."

Lacey slowly raised her eyes. A stranger stared back at her. Someone with a fat face she didn't recognize. Someone whose giant face was red and black and blue. The whole thing. Her face was hideous. "This isn't some kind of … of early April Fool's joke, is it?" Her voice cracked.

"Baby, it's all right."

No, it wasn't all right. He'd lied to her. Lacey burst into tears. Her nightmare had come true.

She was a freak.

Lacey pulled two gel ice packs from the freezer and carried them to the sofa in the living room. With the volume turned low, the television droned in the background. The initial shock of cold hurt her bones, but the doctor promised the ice packs would help reduce the swelling. She'd been home for five days and still didn't see much of any difference. She looked like the Pillsbury Doughboy with stitches—her face still black and blue and purple, with a touch of green and yellow where some of the bruising had faded. She actually looked more like Jabba the Hutt or Chucky, the doll from that horror movie.

The doctor may have thought he did good work, but she could see the stitches. Some had dissolved already, and Jake told her once the swelling went down, all the scars would be in her face's natural creases. She didn't believe that for a minute. She was a freak. A fat freak.

The bone-chilling pain receded and the cold numbed her skin. Lydia would be over soon with her lunch—and look at her with pity. Lacey loved her sister but hated the pity. It turned her into an object. One with a hideous face.

"Lacey? I'm here." Lydia sailed into the living room, bearing a bag from Dee's 'n' Doughs. Ever efficient, she removed a paper plate, plastic fork and knife, and a napkin. "I brought you a pimento cheese sandwich."

"Thanks." Her sister meant well, and Lacey appreciated that, but it was Lydia who loved pimento cheese. Lacey hated it. The spread always reminded her of her aunt and uncle who made the cheese sandwiches for supper several times a week. They never bothered to remember that she despised them.

Lydia wouldn't leave until she ate some of it.

"Share with me?"

Her sister split the sandwich, handed her half, and avoided looking at her for more than a second. Lacey took a bite. "Not bad." This was better than most she'd had. Maybe it was the texture more than the taste that bothered her. She put her sandwich back on the plate. What she really wanted was to be alone. Not stared at. Not to be a freak. She leaned back and closed her eyes.

"Is the pain still bad?"

Paper rustled. "It's tolerable, but the meds make me sleepy."

"I'll make you a cup of tea and bring it in here before I go. I wrapped your sandwich so it would stay fresh."

"Thanks, I appreciate it."

Her sister's cool hand touched her cheek. "Oh, sugar, I'm so sorry this happened to you."

Lacey couldn't think of a proper answer. What could she say? She hated that it happened to her instead of someone else? She did. It's okay? It wasn't. Don't worry. She'd be fine? She wouldn't. Instead, she opted to say nothing. Lydia sighed and her footsteps disappeared into the kitchen. The water turned on and then off. Lacey let her mind go blank and listened to herself breathe.

A few minutes later, Lydia returned. "Here's your tea, honey," she whispered.

Lacey pretended to be asleep.

Chapter 21

Claire rubbed night cream onto her face and checked for wrinkles. "Oh no, there's a new line." Why couldn't someone find a way to stop them? She applied more cream to that area. The hum of water flowing through the pipes stopped.

Joel stepped from the shower. "What are you doing, mapping them?"

"Not really. But they're hard to miss."

He wrapped a towel around his waist and came up behind her. His face appeared in the mirror as he leaned over her shoulder and squinted. "Nope. Gorgeous as ever, and babe, your wrinkles are all laugh lines. Every one of them adds a sign of joy to your face."

She locked eyes with his reflection. "You're going blind, but I love you."

He laughed and finished drying off. They were climbing into bed when the phone rang. Who could it be at this hour? It was after eleven. Joel reached over and answered it.

"Hello? Sure, hold on a second." He handed her the phone. "It's Tillie."

"What could she want that couldn't wait until morning?"

"Dunno. I didn't ask her."

Claire crossed her eyes at him and took the phone. "Hey, Tillie. What's up?"

"Esther has pulled up the floorboards in her back bedroom and is digging in the crawl space. That's what's up."

Claire glanced at Joel. He gestured that he wanted to hear what Tillie said, so she put the phone between them. "Did you say Esther has pulled up the bedroom floorboards and is digging in the crawl space?"

"That's exactly what I said. The woman thinks she's going to find gold."

Joel's eyes widened and he groaned. "That's why all those holes are being found in the woods. Gold fever."

"Shh. Tillie, what do you want me to do?"

"Well, I guess there's nothing you can do tonight, but I'm worried about her. If she digs too much, her house could fall down. Couldn't it?"

Claire raised an eyebrow at Joel.

He shook his head. "Not unless she messed with the foundation pilings."

"Tillie, I doubt she'll dig that much."

"I don't know, Claire. That woman is determined to strike it rich. She could use the money, you know."

"You're a good friend to worry about her, but why at this time of night?"

"I just came from her house. We were having a nice game of Scrabble when she suddenly swept all the tiles off the board and ushered me to the door. I was shocked, I can tell you. She's never done anything like that. Being a good friend, I wanted to make sure she was all right. I went around to the back door, which she hadn't locked yet. That clued me in that something was really awry. I heard strange noises from the back bedroom, and I ran to save her from whoever or whatever was attacking her."

A chorus of green tree frogs trilled as Tillie stopped to draw a breath. Now was Claire's chance to cut this short.

"I—"

"Well, I scared her witless, but she finally told me what she was doing. Claire, I'm worried. Talk to her, please?"

Me? "Don't worry so much, Tillie. She'll get tired of digging with little or no results. Everyone does. We'll go see her tomorrow."

"Well, if you think so, all right. Thank you, Claire. You're a good friend too."

She clicked the phone off and handed it back to Joel. "Esther is the last person I would have suspected of catching gold fever. She seems so solid, unmovable. Level-headed."

Joel pulled the covers up. "Gold has a way of turning the most staid of people into proprietary lunatics."

Voices competed in the lunchtime conversation derby at Dee's 'n' Doughs. Claire wadded her napkin and put it on top of the remains of her sandwich. "It sounds like depression. I can't say that I blame her." Poor Lacey.

Unshed tears swam in Lydia's eyes. "I don't blame her either, but I'm worried. She hasn't gone to the psychologist her doctor recommended."

"Somehow, I can't see Lacey lying on a shrink's couch. We'll come up with something to make her laugh to pull her out of this." Claire rested her elbows on the table and cupped her chin. "Put on your thinking caps, ladies." It did her good to worry about someone else instead of her own nagging problem.

Hazel and her husband smiled and waved at her as they took their tray, piled with trash, to the receptacle. Claire wiggled her fingers at them. She couldn't imagine the bearded, motorcycle-riding Oscar throwing his trash anywhere other than in the street, but he dutifully followed Hazel, and when she held open the lid, he dropped in their trash.

Ellie's brows dipped. "I think it's going to take some time. I saw her yesterday when I took her lunch over. She's so swollen that she doesn't look like the Lacey I know."

Hazel's swollen? Oh, Lacey. Claire returned her attention to her friends.

"According to Jake, she won't look the same as before even after the swelling goes down. The doctor altered her nose and had to reconstruct cheekbones for her out of some material," Carin said. "My fear is the Lacey we all knew and loved may be lost."

Lost? Claire frowned. "What do you mean?"

"I think I know what Carin's saying." Lydia leaned forward. "Lacey always hid behind her looks."

"But she's homely. Ouch!" She glared at Patsy, then grimaced. "Okay, that was a tacky statement. I'm sorry."

Lydia shook her head. "No need to be. It's the truth. Lacey is as plain as porridge, as our mama used to say. Lacey will tell you she's learned to be okay with that. In some crazy way, it all ties into something that makes her afraid. I'm not positive what that something is. Sometimes I think it was that Lacey never knew our daddy but still felt abandoned by him. But I don't know why that would make her afraid."

Carin tilted her head to one side. "I thought your uncle was a father figure to her."

"No. He and our aunt were deaf and only spoke in sign language, which we both learned as kids. Lacey was good at it, but Uncle Troy was … bitter, to say the least. He was the only one to do all the farm chores after Daddy left. Taking care of Mama while raising Lacey and me left no money for hired help. No wonder he resented us. Lacey was barely eight when I left the farm. She quit talking a few years before that, though. According to Auntie's letters, after I left, she became more timid than a bunny rabbit." Lydia sighed and rested her chin on her hand. "My worry is how this new face will affect her."

Tillie Payne sniffed. "I took lunch to her—what was it? The day after she got home. I took her a couple of books too. A new one arrived, an obscure one Lacey had loved as a child. Not easy to find, I can tell you. I looked everywhere. Finally, I called a—"

She'd babble all day if someone didn't stop her. "Tillie, what were you going to tell us about Lacey?" Claire smiled to take any sting out of her words.

Tillie startled and looked blank. "Oh, right. Well, before I left, I made a comment about how it appears her doctor did a good job. She all but told me to mind my own business. Can you imagine that?"

Claire exchanged a glance with Lydia. That didn't sound like Lacey, but then— "She's bound to be changed some. You can't undergo a trauma like she did without change. But I can't for the life of me imagine Lacey bein' rude."

"I never said she was rude." Tillie backpedaled. "But she was adamant about not talking about her face. Especially for one who,"— she looked at Lydia—"according to you, hides behind her looks. Hiding behind plain makes no sense."

Sure it did. "Yes, it does." Claire gazed at her friends. Lydia had classic good looks. Patsy had that fresh, girl-next-door pretty. Even Tillie, though aged, was still attractive. "When you can't do anything about how you look, it can become a wall to hide behind. I remember a girl in my art history class in college. She was breathtakingly beautiful. She was also withdrawn, and we all thought she was a snob. Turned out she had no confidence in her artistic ability."

"Why was that?" Patsy asked, reaching for the sugar container.

"Her dad told her she couldn't draw worth a hill of beans. She was four at the time. It goes to show you how a caustic remark can damage a child. Because of that, she didn't take any art classes until college. It doesn't matter what a person looks like. Looks can still be a defense mechanism."

Carin put her hand over Lydia's. "I think we need to all agree to pray diligently for Lacey. I saw what prayer did with my sisters."

"Carin's right. That's exactly what we need to do." Claire needed to do that for herself too. Why didn't she go to God with her problem to start with? *Because you have to relinquish control.* Oh. Right. Claire busied herself with brushing crumbs from the tablecloth.

Tillie put both hands on the table and leaned forward. "Did Claire tell you about Esther?"

Patsy shook her head. "What about her?"

"She's caught gold fever, that's what. She's gone and dug up the crawl space beneath her house. She has a gigantic pile of dirt in her back bedroom."

What? Tillie hadn't told her that part. Maybe Esther had gone over the edge. "Oh dear. I wonder if we should do something."

"That's not all," Tillie said as if Claire hadn't said anything. "She called me early this morning and told me ..." Tillie opened her eyes wide. "She dug up a chunk of quartz with gold in it."

Claire shrugged. "We've all found that at one time or another. Esther is still new around here. I'll go talk some sense into her."

Patsy picked up her wrapped leftover sandwich and nudged Claire. "I've got to go too. We both have last-minute details to see to for the shower tomorrow."

"Yikes! I need to wrap my presents still and—" Claire ticked off a slew of items in her head and glanced at Patsy. "I'll have to talk to Esther later. Have you seen the cake Dee's making for them?"

"I did and it's perfect." She turned to the others. "Instead of a regular sheet cake, Dee made it longer and narrower, and somehow recreated photos in icing of the kids growing up."

Claire's eyes misted. The twins getting married made her see her friends in a new light. Tillie's wrinkles had wrinkles. When had that happened? Patsy had several rogue gray hairs that refused to hold color. Lydia had a few crow's feet around her eyes, not to mention the ones Claire saw in her own mirror. Only Carin was too young to show much change yet. Claire always saw her friends as they used to be.

Thinking of Lacey, maybe that wasn't such a bad thing.

Chapter 22

Claire turned the Closed sign and shut the gallery door. Her stomach grumbled with increasing displeasure, not to mention volume, at being late for supper. Was a national art tour really worth all this? She wasn't trying to get rich. Then again, maybe it was a good idea. The twins' wedding cost a bundle, and they weren't being extravagant.

She turned to face the lake. Peace descended. Next to her, Patsy stood on the boardwalk with her face to the setting sun. "We've been inside so much getting ready for our tour that I'd forgotten how good the sun feels on my face."

"You have been inside too long if this weak sunlight feels—" At the end of the block by Happy's Hobbies, Felix stood talking to someone. Judging by his gestures, it wasn't a friendly chat. Her peace went poof.

"Can you see who Felix is talking to?"

Patsy turned and squinted. "No. He's not taller than Felix, so I can't tell."

Claire stepped off the boardwalk and into the street to see past Felix. "Van Gogh's ear! You aren't going to believe this. It's Howie, and Felix is the color of my new fuchsia. What do you think we should do?"

"Go home?" Patsy turned around.

Claire grabbed her arm. "No way. We need to stand with Felix on this. Come on." What she thought she'd be able to do, she wasn't sure, but the mayor needed help. If he was willing to sacrifice money for the benefit of the town, the least she could do was help him. She pulled her BFF along with her. Nobody turned belligerent when sweet Patsy was around.

As they drew closer, Howie's voice rose. "We can make this happen, Riley. You can't stop us."

"Oh yes I can. It's up to me and the town council to give the permits."

"Not for mineral rights development. The state has—" His gaze locked with Claire's and he stopped. "What do you want, Claire? This is a private conversation between the mayor and me."

"Not so fast, Newlander. She's on the town council and has an interest in this conversation." Felix turned to her. "Newlander here is telling me he's bought up all the mineral rights in town. Now he wants to buy the land."

Over her decaying body. Wait. He hadn't bought *their* mineral rights. She also knew Nathan and Patsy hadn't sold. He was lying. "Who's your backer, Howie? You don't have the money to buy all this."

"You don't know squat, Claire."

He was right. She didn't. Not really. But she'd bet her latest turkey vase he didn't know that for sure. Granny hadn't left him much. She gave more of her estate to the town. Claire studied Howie. That was another reason he was angry at Chapel Springs.

She sniffed. "I know enough to know you have to have backers. Have you told them what happened last time you battled the town?" She hit a nerve.

Howie's face turned a gorgeous shade of purple. "You stay out of my business, or so help me." He balled his hands into fists.

Felix stepped between them. "Back off, Newlander."

Patsy stood shoulder to shoulder with Claire.

Howie threw up his hands. "I don't understand you. Here you could have enough money to retire to Florida or somewhere in Europe. Yet you choose to remain here in this ..." His hand swept to include the beautiful lake at his back. "This ... this ... hamlet."

She took in the lake, trying to see it from his perspective. No good. Nothing but beauty met her eye. "That's what you never understood, Howie. You never saw the charm of this place. I don't need your money. I have more than enough, thank you. Go away and leave us in peace."

"I'm not going anywhere. Y'all are sitting on top of my investment, and I plan to get it out from under you. We can do it nice like and all make some money, or I can get tough." He turned and leaped onto the passing tram, not waiting for it to stop.

"What do you suppose he means by get tough?" Claire glanced at Felix. "There isn't any way he can steal our land, is there?"

"No. People would have to sell to him. I checked this out thoroughly. Now if it were gas or oil beneath us, that would be different. He could maybe get the state to declare eminent domain, saying it benefits everyone. But neither quartz nor gold is under that clause."

Patsy frowned. "Why is he so bent on destroying Chapel Springs?"

Felix shook his head and stuffed his hands into his pockets. "I don't know. I'm not sure destruction is his aim. It's more like he feels the town owes him for some reason. Maybe he was depending on getting his granny's land and a large sum of money he *thought* was there. He couldn't have inherited more than twenty thousand from her estate. When she left the land to Chapel Springs, she included enough money to cover taxes for years to come."

"I think it's sad," Patsy said.

Claire looked at her. "What is?"

"The way Howie expects good fortune to land in his lap instead of having the satisfaction of a good day's work."

Felix stared at the retreating tram. "How'd he get like that, anyway?"

Patsy nudged her. "Do you remember when we were freshmen? Howie was a junior. He tried to get on the varsity teams in every sport. Then he tried out for the debate team. No matter what he attempted, he either wasn't tall enough, big enough, strong enough, or he didn't want to do what was required."

Felix slapped his ball cap on his head. "I remember Newlander as the laziest kid in school. His daddy demanded he try out for sports, but Howie hated anything that made him exert any energy."

Claire folded her arms. "Granny blamed her daughter-in-law. But I don't know if we can ever know for sure why. He's going to bear watching closely, no matter what the reason. Has Faye contacted the last of the landowners? We must keep them from selling to him."

Claire adjusted the centerpieces of peonies and tulips Patsy brought in from her garden. She tweaked first one, then another. "These are beautiful, Pat-a-cake. I've never seen so many gorgeous blooms. How did you do it?"

Her BFF chuckled. "I threatened them."

"Well, whatever you did, the girls will be wowed by them. And Dee's cake will probably make them cry." Claire grinned at that. Megan hated for anyone to see her cry. "Did you get your paintings wrapped?"

"Late last night. I finally decided there was no way to disguise them."

"The girls would've been disappointed to think they wouldn't get one from you."

Patsy trimmed the end from the last tulip and placed it in the vase with its sisters. "Dane found the perfect wedding gift for Meg."

"What is it?"

"He hasn't told me. He said he'd wait until it arrived and show it to me."

"Arrived? Where did he get it?"

"North Carolina. He's been going over there every couple of weeks lately."

"And you have no idea why? I'd jerk a knot in his tail until he told me."

"Can't do that. He's a man now with the right to keep a secret."

Humph. How come they had to grow up? "So how did he find whatever-this-is in North Carolina?"

"Internet."

Really? "He trusts that?"

"You're kidding, right?" Patsy nipped a brown-tipped leaf off a stem.

"Uh, no. I've always bought stuff locally. How do you know who has your credit card number then?"

"Nathan keeps a close watch on it. We've ordered stuff for the gallery online before. That's never bothered you."

Claire waved away a mosquito dive-bombing her ear. "No, but I know who I'm ordering *from*."

"Girlfriend, you need to come into the twenty-first century. People go online and buy anything anytime, night or day. Things you can't find in stores."

What if— "What if somebody came on the computer after you, and say you'd bought a gift for them? Could they find out what you ordered?"

"They could, but that's an easy fix. You erase the history, and they can't tell where you've looked."

Whoa, she'd have to look into that. Maybe she could get a pregnancy test online. "All this technology makes me glad our kids are grown. The things I've heard kids can get into. Poor Charlie and Sandi. Our worries were pretty easy, weren't they?"

"They were." Patsy craned her neck. "And here come the first of our guests."

Claire called up the stairs on her way to the door. "Girls? Your guests are starting to arrive." Giggles and the clatter of footsteps made her eyes watery with memories of her twins as little girls. She turned to Patsy. "I need to stop the memories from emerging today, or I'll be a mess. Is my eyeliner still okay? I used a waterproof one."

Patsy examined her. "You're lovely. No smudges. If it makes you feel any better, I'm going through the same memories."

Of course she was. Claire's heart swelled with love for her best friend. Between them, they had eight kids and shared their love with all. She gave Pat-a-cake a quick hug before opening the door. Adrianna stood on the doorstep.

Claire screeched and pulled her eldest daughter into her arms. "What a surprise! I didn't think you'd be coming for the shower." Unable to stop it, she boohooed. Good thing she'd used that waterproof mascara. "Oh, sugar, I've missed you something fierce!"

Adrianna laughed. "I took a long weekend, Momma. I've missed you too. And I needed to see how you're faring. Think you can handle another wedding?" She held out her hand. A beautiful square-cut diamond surrounded by baguettes encircled her third finger. Andrew had finally proposed.

Claire squealed again and hugged her daughter. Patsy stood by, teary eyed. Claire pulled back to give her BFF her turn. Patsy gathered Adrianna into her arms. "I always knew you'd marry a preacher."

The twins arrived downstairs, and more squeals filled the air. Claire and Patsy stood in the doorway, watching the girls.

Claire nudged her. "I'm not sure poor Joel will survive all the weddings, but at least Adrianna's will be the last we're responsible for financially. Now, only your Deva is left. Any hints there?"

Patsy shook her head. "For some reason, I think Deva has chosen to remain single." A small frown creased her between her brows. "I'm not sure why."

"I wouldn't worry. She's only twenty-three, a baby still." Claire opened the door to the next arrivals coming up the walk. Alexis, Brandy, and Cora, the twins' ABC-trio friends arrived. These girls had a band and hoped to one day make it to Nashville. *Wait till they see Adrianna.*

Claire turned door duty over to Deva, who had been in the kitchen working, and retreated into the living room to make sure the games and prizes were ready.

She turned and an arm snaked around her, giving her a hug. "Ginny, sugar, how are you?"

"How do you always know it's me?"

"You've been doing it since you were six." Claire returned the hug. "How are you? Catch me up on what's been happening in your life."

"Not much. I had a lovely walk through the woods coming here. I saw Shiloh out there, rooting around a tree. I brought him home and put him in the backyard."

"Thank you, sweetie. He jumps that fence whenever he feels like a romp. I don't know why we bother. I'd better have Joel clean him up before someone lets him in." Claire found Joel in the basement tying fishing flies and told him about Shiloh. "Please make sure his paws aren't all muddy."

After all the guests had arrived, they went into the living room to play a game. Deva passed out paper and pencils. She instructed them to fill in a wedding acrostic by writing down everything they could think of that pertained to a wedding. Claire chewed the corner of her lip, writing as fast as she could. She never was good at games.

Shiloh lumbered into the room, his damp paws testimony to Joel cleaning them. He interrupted the game by grabbing all the girls' attention. But when he spotted Adrianna, he wiggled all over, whining and trying to climb into her lap. He'd always considered her "his" kid. He'd watched over her, and Charlie for that matter, from the day they got him as a puppy. Adrianna gave him a good loving, which included a lot of ear rubbing and chest scratching.

After a minute, Megan helped her big sister by pulling Shiloh off her. Claire laughed when the mastiff continued around the room to each person for his share of attention. Finally, he settled down at Adrianna's feet.

After the games were played—Brandy, Ginny, and Lydia were the winners—Claire and Patsy called the girls into the dining room for cake. The twins hadn't seen the photo cake yet. Dee had reproduced four special events in the girls' lives.

'Lissa pointed to the third photo. "Do you remember that?" She linked arms with her twin.

Megan kissed her sister's cheek. "I do. First time we'd been separated, and I was terrified."

Claire thought of her twin sister, CeeCee. She'd missed her every day since she'd died too young at fifteen. Her girls were blessed beyond measure to fulfill their dream of a double wedding. Megan and Melissa posed for pictures with the cake, pointing at certain parts of it and being silly. The bridesmaids photobombed them. Then they cut slices of the cake, and everyone took theirs back into the living room. After a few minutes, Megan put her plate down, and the girls opened gifts. Great-aunt Lola would have loved to see this moment. She never knew the twins, but she was a sucker for weddings. She had enough of them. Claire smiled over some fond memories of her flamboyant great-aunt.

The word *caterer* cut into her musing. "What about the caterer?"

"Belinda, tell Momma what you heard." Megan's voice shook. This couldn't be good.

"My cousin in Pineridge hired Twila's Wedding Catering for her reception, which was last week."

The same caterer. An inkling of dread prickled Claire's scalp. "How was the food?"

"They never showed up. We called, but the phone had been disconnected. My poor cousin had no wedding dinner and worse … no wedding cake."

Claire started hyperventilating. She sat next to 'Lissa.

Megan wailed. "What are we going to do?"

'Lissa, ever the calm one, handed Claire a paper bag to breathe into. "We have time to find another, Meg. And Dee is doing our cake."

"It's not going to be easy this time of year," Adrianna said. "Too many weddings. You'll have to move fast."

"I'll jump on it tomorrow." Why couldn't things go smoothly?

Amid giggles and oohs over the gifts, Adrianna took the ribbons and bows from the twins after they opened each package. She carefully wove them through holes she'd made in a paper plate, making "bouquets" for her sisters to use at the wedding rehearsal. Mel sat beside Adrianna, helping her.

Claire joined JoAnn and Ellie, standing in the doorway. She could watch the twins and still ask about Mel without her protégé hearing. "How has the surveillance of stalker-boy been going?"

Ellie shook her head. "He hasn't done anything. He only follows her."

"He doesn't seem to fit the M.O. of a stalker. He looks like any other engineering student," JoAnn said. "Last week, he smiled at me." She shrugged. "I'm off the team now. Somehow, he knew who I was."

That added another pickle to the pot. "And has Mel said anything more?"

Once again, Ellie shook her head. "I think she quit worrying about him."

Not good. Claire shivered. "That's when a stalker can attack—when her defenses are down."

Chapter 23

Lacey shuffled through Springs Park. She was not looking forward to this. Her stomach turned over at the thought of going back to work. That's why she'd left so early and avoided the tram. She wanted to get into the bank and hide in her office before the other employees arrived. No matter what Jake or any of her friends said, she felt like a freak. Some of her coworkers had even called to see when she was coming back to work. Said they couldn't wait to see her. Right. They wanted to examine her face—stare like Uncle Troy—and talk about her.

Lacey crossed Park Avenue and went behind Carin's house and the others on her curve of Pine Drive. Her shoes would be damp, but it brought her right out at the bank. And avoided a lot of people. She hadn't gone to Dee's 'n' Doughs today and hated to have missed her friends. She wanted her old life back. People may have overlooked her, but that was okay. She didn't mind. She preferred that to being an oddity.

Lacey passed her I.D. over the access card reader mounted next to the bank's door. A light turned green and the door unlatched. Inside, she punched her code into the alarm pad, disarming it. She quickly crossed the lobby without turning on the lights and shut herself in her office. There, she dropped her purse in a corner. She had a job to do before anyone else arrived.

Once she rolled her chair to a corner, she heaved and shoved the desk bit by bit until it faced the far wall, still giving her room to move around it. There. Perfect. The credenza was next. It needed to be behind her. Filled, it was too heavy to move alone. She quickly removed its contents, then using leverage, shoved it to its new place and replaced everything. Good thing she was always organized. Everything went back in place in ten minutes. Now when someone came into her office, the first thing they would see was her back. She smiled. The whole exercise took less than forty-five minutes.

She opened the thermos she'd brought and poured a cup of coffee. Much better than the bank's coffee, and she avoided the break room. She glanced at the time on her computer. The employees should be pouring in about now. Her stomach lurched. Why was she subjecting herself to this? Mrs. Chester's elfish face rose in her mind. Right. Lacey liked the bank's customers. But there were others who could help them as competently as she did.

She reached for a stack of loan applications and sorted through them, one pile for good credit and one for questionable. A moment later, her door opened. Her shoulders tightened.

"Hey, welcome back." Rhonda from legal walked around the front of her desk and bent down, staring at Lacey. "Wow. It really looks good, Lace."

Lace? Lacey raised her chin, but Rhonda was too busy scrutinizing her face to meet her eyes. In Lacey's mind's eye, Rhonda disappeared, and in her place was Uncle Troy, staring at her. Always staring. Lacey dropped her chin and hunched over her work. Would Rhonda get the hint?

"See you later. Want to have lunch?"

Why would a face make a difference? Nobody from here had ever asked her to go to lunch. Lacey shook her head. "Can't. Too much to catch up on."

"Okay, but if you change your mind, we're going to the Pasta Bowl. Eleven thirty."

She nodded but didn't say anything.

Rhonda didn't close the door, and one of the tellers walked in. Lacey didn't even know her. "Hey, I want to see your face. Did it hurt? How does it feel to be pretty now?"

I belong in a sideshow. She didn't say anything but turned away. After a moment, the girl left. Tears stung the back of Lacey's eyes. She pressed on the bridge of her nose. Ouch. Her nose was still tender. How ironic.

Not ten minutes later, two girls from customer service came in, giggling. They wanted to ask her opinion on whether one of them should date a guy from commercial loans. Lacey didn't look up. They'd lost their minds. She pointed to the door and they left in a huff. Before the accident, she could work in peace. Now, she couldn't read two sentences without an interruption.

Not five minutes later, her door opened again. This time, it was Barbara Roche, the mortgage officer. Lacey couldn't ignore her.

"Good morning, Barbara."

"I see you rearranged your office." She pulled a chair up to Lacey's desk. "I'd like your opinion on these loan apps." She pushed two legal folders toward Lacey, but her eyes were on Lacey's face. Like Rhonda, Barbara examined every part of it.

Lacey's skin puckered like ants were crawling all over her. Uncle Troy had examined her like that too. She knew if left alone with him— she shuddered. She learned to stay out until suppertime. Then she went to bed, placing a chair in front of the door and wedging it under the doorknob.

But this was now. Lacey stiffened her spine. "What's the problem with them?"

"Graham said you know the applicant personally." Barbara reached out her hand.

Don't touch me. Lacey leaned against the back of her chair.

Barbara's hand paused. "Does it still hurt?"

Could she lie and say yes, it hurt like the devil? "No."

The mortgage officer launched forward and pushed back Lacey's hair.

"What are you doing?" Lacey jerked back.

Barbara shrugged. "I wanted to see if there was much scarring. I'm thinking of get—"

Lacey jumped up. "Get out. Just go. Please." She didn't wait to see if Barbara had gone but grabbed her purse and went to Graham's office. She'd had it. "Graham?" She poked her head in the door.

"Come on in, Lacey. What can I do for you?"

She pulled her I.D. card from her lanyard and handed it to him. "I quit. I was right. I can't work here anymore." She turned to the door.

Graham rose and came toward her. "Lacey, wait. What happened?"

"I'm an aberration, Graham. My office has become the sideshow at the circus, and I'm the freak everyone wants to look at." She shuddered. "I can't do it."

Lacey strode from Graham's office and out of the bank. Once outside, she ran across the street, past Carin's house, through the park, and onto her front porch. She fumbled with her keys, unlocked the door, and stumbled inside. Dropping her purse on the floor, she fell on the couch as the sobs she'd held back now cascaded out of her.

She mourned the loss of her anonymity. She wept because people didn't see her before the accident. She wailed because now all they saw was her face but not *her*. She cried until she had no more tears. Her head ached. Her face ached. Her nose was stopped up and her cheeks were flushed.

She went to the bathroom and ran cold water over a washcloth, then held it to her face. She stared in the mirror. If she'd been born with this face, she might have liked it. But she didn't. She hated it. It had turned her into something everyone stared at. She stuck her tongue out at her reflection.

After some eye drops soothed her hot eyes, she went into the kitchen and made a cup of coffee. She felt like the Phantom of the Opera. Lacey hunched over her coffee and lurched to the table. She laughed at herself, but her laughter lacked real mirth. All this angst belonged in a play. Even that wouldn't work. Her plays may have humor in them, but there was no humor left in Lacey's life.

What did a woman do when she was glad to be alive but had lost herself?

Chapter 24

A flash of blue flitted past Lacey. She startled and screeched, one hand flying to her chest. The laundry basket dropped to the floor. It took a moment of staring wide-eyed at the mirror before her muscles went weak with recognition. A stranger wore her blue T-shirt. Leaning closer, she examined the face that was now hers. When would she feel like it *was* her mug?

She wrinkled her nose and crossed her eyes. "Go away."

Lacey missed her old kisser. Not that it was a great one, but she grew up with it, and it was comfortable. Non-competitive. She turned her head from one side to the other. This one … she wasn't sure about. Most of the puffiness was gone now, but even so, it scared her.

With the swelling down, the scars fell into the natural creases of her nose or into her hairline. Her new mask was attractive. Not movie-star gorgeous—no doctor could have turned what she had into that. Thank goodness. She squinted at her reflection. Nonetheless, this face was pretty. She turned away from the mirror as her heart wrenched with grief.

Jake had been bugging her to get out of the house more. For the first time in their marriage, he didn't understand. While she was thankful to still be here and able to love him, he had no idea what it was like to be a stranger to her own self. She had to deal with that along with the stares.

The other night at his restaurant had been horrible. Even though it had been late, some diners lingered as if they knew she'd come in. They gawked at her. Her worst fear had come true. Even though she wasn't scarred, she was still an oddity. They looked at her like she'd done this purposely. Like she was so vain and hated her old face so much that she got a new one.

She kicked the laundry back into the basket, schlepped it to the closet, and after putting it away, went to the kitchen for a cup of tea. The hot water swirled in her mug, lifting the teabag and making it spin. The steam floated up, and she leaned over the rim, watching the water gradually change from clear to dark.

Her change hadn't been gradual but sudden. Granted, the doctor had to do something. But why didn't they ask her opinion? Okay, they couldn't, but still. Why couldn't he have put her back together the way she was? Did he have to change her so much she no longer recognized her own image in the mirror?

The doorbell rang, startling her. She jumped and knocked the tea into the sink, breaking the cup. She left it, went to the door, and peeked through the sidelight. Carin stood on the porch.

"I know you're there, Lacey. Come on. Open up. It's just me."

She'd dodged everyone, even Carin, for the last six weeks. Either she had to become a total hermit, or she had to face them. *Ha! Good pun, Dawson.* She twisted the knob, opened the door, and then turned away.

Carin stormed into the house and put her hands on Lacey's shoulders.

"Okay, girl. Let me look at you."

Lacey took a deep breath and turned to face Carin. Get it over with. But if she stared—

Carin's eyes roamed every inch of her face. Like she was memorizing the landscape. Then she gave a nod and walked to the kitchen. Lacey stood for a moment, watching Carin's back retreat from sight. Well, at least she didn't make a big deal over the change. Huh. Finally, she followed her friend.

Carin had already poured water into a teapot. And thrown out the broken cup. She glanced up. "Do you know what you put me through these past weeks?"

"Put *you* through? What do you mean?"

"I thought we were good friends, Lacey." Carin dropped a teabag into each mug. "You're one of the few people who understand me. But you completely shut me out. I wanted to help you."

"I'm sorry. I …" She sat down at the table. Carin was her closest friend, but how could she understand when Lacey didn't understand it herself? "What do you see when you look at me?"

"A face that's different than it was. It's pretty." Her eyes grew soft.

"But I still see Lacey." She poured water over the tea bags, set the mugs on the table, and sat.

"I went with Jake to the restaurant. Everyone openly stared at me. I hated it."

"Why?"

"Because I feel like Quasimodo."

Carin frowned. "Why? I mean, why does staring make you feel like that?"

"If I wasn't some kind of weirdo, why would they stare?"

"Sugar, that makes no sense."

"It does to me." She wrapped her hands around the cup of tea Carin set before her. "Life is smoother, easier when people don't notice me."

"But I noticed you and we became friends."

"That was different." Lacey blew into her cup to cool the tea, then took a sip. Carin hadn't noticed her until Claire said she was a writer too.

"How was it different, Lacey? I saw you with the other ladies. I *noticed* you."

"But you didn't gawk at me." A shiver snaked up her back. "Uncle Troy used to stare at me. He was deaf and never spoke, but his eyes watched my every movement. He was creepy."

Carin's eyes grew wide. "Did he ... did—"

Jake had asked her the same question when they first started dating. He noticed how Uncle Troy's eyes never left her. "I don't think so, but somehow I knew he could at any moment."

"That's horrible. Did you ever tell anyone?"

"What could I have said? 'He looks at me?'"

"What about your aunt? Did she know?" Carin pulled off her long-sleeved shirt, exposing a coral tank top.

"She resented having to raise me, so I don't think she ever noticed. If she did, she didn't do anything about it."

Carin crossed her arms. "That stinks. Why did he hate you so much?" She draped the blouse over the chair back.

"I was the reason my father left, and nobody let me forget it."

"What could you have done to make your father leave?"

"I was born. Conceived, really. He left before I was born."

Carin leaned back in her chair. "You don't believe that, do you?"

"Not now, but as a child I did. Lydia hated me. She and her dad—our father—were close. So when I came along and he left, she blamed me.

Aunt Sylvia and Uncle Troy blamed me too. We lived on their farm with them. Dad shared the workload. When he left, it all fell on Uncle Troy's shoulders. That and caring for Mom, who sank into severe depression."

"That's hard for any kid to deal with."

"My sister had to help raise me until she married. When she left, I stayed in the background. It was easier."

Carin sipped her tea and added a spoonful of honey. "But now you're safe and married to a man who adores you. You shouldn't worry about people staring."

Lacey tapped her temple. "Up here, I know you're right. But except for you and the ladies at Dee's 'n' Doughs, getting noticed for my face is so disingenuous. I went into the bank last week trying to get back to work again. People kept stopping by my desk to talk. They never talked to me before. Now they stop to see the face. That's what I've become."

Lacey rose and set her cup in the sink. She pulled a dead leaf off the Boston fern hanging in the window, thankful Carin didn't say anything but let her ramble. "They'd stare and ask my opinion about stuff they never talked to me about in all the years I worked there."

Carin came up beside her. "Okay, that ticks me off."

Having a friend who had her back was nice. "What scares me is finding Jake staring at me."

"He's another subject altogether. Think of his side of it, Lace. The woman he married looks entirely different."

"Well, I'm not different. I'm still me." She grasped the edge of the counter.

"Calm down. I know that. So does Jake. Okay, think of it this way. If you bought a new painting, you'd look at it a lot until the newness wears off."

"It's not that easy. I know he loves me, but he never stared at me before."

"You probably didn't notice."

"No. He never has. Even when we dated." Another thing she loved about him. "He never stared *at* me. He looked *into* me. Does that make sense?"

"Yeah, it does. He loves you, not the shell that houses you. But is it so wrong for him to like what he sees now?"

"I feel like I've lost myself."

Carin gazed at her for a moment, then the left side of her mouth rose in a little smile. "Can I help you look?"

Carin was good for her, but as much as she tried, Lacey wasn't sure her friend actually understood. She didn't understand it herself. "I quit my job." Now she could write in the privacy of home, and no one would look at her.

"That's kind of drastic, isn't it? You know you can't stay inside all the time. What about groceries?"

"Lunn's delivers."

"Lacey, that's not healthy."

"Sure it is. Lunn's carries organic."

Carin glared at her. "You know what I mean. Listen, I want you and Jake to come over for dinner Monday night. And don't try to tell me Jake'll be working. I already talked to him."

She loved her friend, but this was coercion. "I don't—"

Carin balled her fists on her hips. "Lacey, you have to let your friends who love you see you. Look, I've asked Claire and Joel, and your sister and Graham. Besides, JJ misses seeing you and is worried."

Lacey adored JJ and didn't want him worried, but didn't anyone understand all she wanted was her old face back? No. They couldn't. Who in their right mind would want to be plain when they could be pretty? Only a crazy person.

Claire turned the key and started the car. "Did you confirm the appointment with this caterer?" They didn't need another wild goose chase. The last one they made an appointment with mixed up his schedule and wasn't available when they arrived.

Megan turned in the passenger seat. "I did. And 'Lissa called him too." She laughed. "He wouldn't dare risk the wrath of two brides." Megan scratched her neck.

"Did you bring the directions?" They were only going to Scarlet's Ferry, but Claire knew the little hamlet had several alleyways and roads that changed names. She needed explicit directions.

"Yes, Momma. I programmed the address into my phone. Siri will guide us." Megan's condescending tone held a note of teasing.

"Humph. I don't get lost that often."

It didn't take long to get to Scarlet's Ferry. Claire kept an eye on her rearview mirror for Trixie's car. Silly, of course, but after the last incident, Claire didn't trust that woman as far as she could toss her carcass. She wouldn't put it past her to encroach on their appointment.

Egad, she sounded paranoid.

They pulled up to a cute little bakery-slash-café—on a tiny street, almost an alley.

"Momma, do you have any antihistamine?" Megan scratched the back of her neck and her shoulder. "I'm itchy for some reason."

Claire dug a tablet out of her tote and gave it to Meg, who swallowed it dry. Then they got out of the car and faced the bakery. The white building was shaped—and decorated—like a square wedding cake. A balcony with tables and chairs ran around the top of the bottom "layer." The upper "layers" had smaller balconies that were decorated with pots of flowers. The sign on a post in the bricked patio read Top Tier Cakery & Café.

"If the food is as good as the décor, we hit the jackpot. How come he has an opening?"

"A cancellation," 'Lissa said. "The groom was called to active duty, so the couple eloped."

"A blessing upon them." Claire opened the door and was smacked in the nose by a delicious aroma of roasting meat and caramelized onions followed by burnt sugar. "Ooh, I hope that's for us to taste."

A gray-haired woman wearing a bright red apron greeted them. "You must be the Bennett party. Welcome to The Cakery. I'm Allegra, the baker. Zachary will be with you in a moment. He's putting the finishing touches on your plates. Please be seated."

Funny how Allegra left out the café part of the name. Claire wondered how the partnership flourished with that kind of rivalry. The baker—shouldn't she call herself a caker?—directed them to a table set for four. Claire raised an eyebrow at Megan, who had set up the tasting. "Who's joining us?"

"The chef is. He explains what's in each dish we try."

Claire didn't particularly like that idea. How could they be honest about the food if they didn't like it? She hung her raccoon tote over one spindle of the ladder-back chair, then sat in it. 'Lissa wandered over to the pastry display cases while Megan checked her email.

Five minutes later, the chef sailed into the room, followed by two teens carrying platters. They made a big display of placing them on folding stands, turning the trays to the right position as the chef directed.

"Welcome, my dears. I'm Chef Zachary. You are the most fortunate of ladies to have called when you did." He looked over his shoulder at

'Lissa. "Come, come, both brides must taste. Now this first dish is …" He spouted off a long French name, which set warning bells clanging in Claire's head. If it was good and made with normal food, he should make it understood. It had as fancy a name as those green beans—hairy cot vert or something.

Megan's phone rang. She gave him an apologetic shrug and answered it. While she talked, he plated their taste of the whatever-it-was. It looked like beef.

Megan's eyes grew large and her brows drew together. "Momma, Ginny has poison ivy. Says she thinks she got it from Shiloh." Meg scratched her neck again, and her eyes widened in dismay. "If he gave it to her, it was the day of the shower."

Chef drew back. "Who is Ginny?"

"One of our bridesmaids," Megan said, scratching her shoulder. "And if she has it, everyone at the shower may have it. Shiloh was all over everyone."

Chef Zachary took a step back as 'Lissa scratched her arm. "I'm highly allergic to poison ivy. If you have been in contact with this Ginny or that Shiloh,"—he grabbed their plates off the table—"I cannot do the wedding. Good evening." He twirled his hand in the air. His helpers lifted the platters from the stands and retreated to the kitchen, leaving Claire and the twins alone.

Claire blinked. "Now what?"

Megan scratched her forehead. "A trip to the pharmacy and a call to Uncle Vince. I've got poison ivy too."

'Lissa grinned. "At least I don't. I'm not allergic to it. And don't worry, Momma. We'll find someone to cater the wedding. If all else fails, Megan and I can make spaghetti."

Her twin looked at her in horror.

Chapter 25

Claire turned on the computer. Joel was in the shower, and if she hurried, she could find a test online and order it. The phone rang. Oh, for the love of Van Gogh. Her phone seemed to be ringing more and more lately. "Hello?"

"Claire, it's Esther Tully. I went over to Tillie's house to show her the nugget I found, and guess what? No, you'll never guess. I'll tell you. She's rented a machine and is jackhammering her basement."

"What?" That didn't compute. Sensible Tillie, who was so worried about Esther digging in her crawl space, has gold fever now? "Say that again."

"You heard me. I found another rock with gold in it. Now she thinks there's gold under her house too. Isn't that silly?"

Esther was territorial about the gold? It made sense, actually. Gold fever did that to people. They needed to nip this in the bud.

"Exactly how much gold have you found?"

"Why do you need to know?"

They both needed a good wake-up shake. "For your own good. I can promise you won't find the mother lode. That was mined out by the late 1800s. Yes, there's gold to be found, but to unearth more than small amounts, you'd have to dig down a couple of hundred feet or more. What would happen to your house if you did? And if you don't own the mineral rights to the surrounding property, how would you know you're not under their land?"

"Oh. I hadn't thought of that. But I found enough to buy a new space heater for my office in the back of my bookstore."

"I'm glad, Esther. But I think it's time to fill in your crawl space and stop digging. Your guest room has to have a mountain in it by now."

Her sigh blew through the phone. "I suppose you're right. It is getting pretty tight in there. Now, what should we do about Tillie?"

"Whatever you do, don't stare at Lacey." After Claire slid the gold hoop through her ear and fastened it, she went to the closet in search of her shoes. They weren't where they should have been. Where could they be? She exited the closet and scanned the bedroom.

Joel paused, threading his belt through the loops on his pants, and gawked. "What'll I do if she says something—look at the floor and not at her?"

"No, silly. Just don't look at her when she isn't talking. And believe me, I know it's hard." Ah, there was the left loafer, sticking out from behind the bathroom door. How'd it get there?

"Yeah, I guess if she'd been scarred, we'd try not to stare. I'd think she'd be happy to be pretty now."

Claire bent down and felt under the side of the bed for the other shoe. Bingo. She grabbed it before it could make a getaway. "You'd think so, but Carin told me Lacey feels like she lost herself or something like that." Claire slid on her shoe. "There. I'm ready. Anyway, be careful how you look at her. I'll go get Shiloh. Carin said to bring him over to play with Edgar."

Downstairs, Claire bagged a couple of towels for Shiloh's permanently wet chops and tossed in some wax-paper-wrapped treats for both dogs. Once the monster's leash was clipped on, she gave his chest a good rubbing. His favorite spot. Almost immediately, his back leg started thumping, and he twisted himself into a comma.

Joel descended the stairs. "Are you ready to go see Edgar?" The mastiff gaped a doggy grin at him and danced in excitement, vibrating the wood floors. Joel looked down. "I need to secure a few floorboards."

The nights were still cool, and Claire slid her arms into a light sweater as they walked to Carin's house. Funny how in the last few months, she'd begun to think of it as Carin's home and not Miss Cora Lee's anymore. But Carin had become an intricate part of their lives. Like Mel had.

"Have you noticed Mel's tattoo is getting lighter?"

"Can't say that I have. Slow down, Shiloh." Joel pulled on the lead. "But I haven't seen her since she started college."

"She's had three of several laser treatments. I can already see a difference."

"It'll seem strange not to see her with them. I'm used to her that way."

"Like we're used to Lacey looking a certain way."

"Huh. Hadn't thought of it like that." He stopped to let Shiloh investigate a tree.

"I'm trying to understand how she feels. Lacey, I mean. Carin told me how much she hates to be watched. She quit her job because of everyone staring at her."

Joel tugged on Shiloh's lead and they moved down the sidewalk. "Was it really that bad?"

"Lacey told Carin that people who never knew she existed came into her office to ask her advice. All they wanted was to stare at her. They didn't even hear what she said to them. I was surprised at how shallow a lot of them are."

"Chapel Springs people?"

Didn't he notice anything when he went to the bank? "No, mostly from Pineridge and Scarlet's Ferry."

"Ah, well, there you have it."

"What do you mean?"

"They're not Chapel Springs." Shiloh whined and pulled on the leash. "Ah, we're here."

Warm light spilled out of Carin's house, and through the windows, Lydia and Graham laughed at something. Lacey was seated on the sofa, scratching Edgar's ears. Joel handed the leash to Claire and reached for the doorbell. Carin opened the door before he could ring it.

Edgar bounded away from Lacey and woofed hello. Before Claire could unhook Shiloh's leash, the two took off running, yanking the lead behind Joel's knees before pulling it out of her hand. Joel went down on his backside as Edgar careened around the side of the sofa. Shiloh hit a scatter rug and skidded into the love seat trying to follow his pal.

Lydia laughed and pulled her feet up onto her chair. "I don't want those giants stepping on my toes."

Ryan grabbed Shiloh's dragging leash and stopped him. Joel reached over and unhooked it. The moment he was unfettered, Shiloh was off again in a gallop. Joel grinned at Ryan. "That's one way to break the ice at a party."

"Edgar! Shiloh! Out!" Carin pointed, and Edgar disappeared

through the large doggie door, with Shiloh hot on his heels. "They'll be back in an hour or so."

"I'm just thankful it hasn't rained. At least they won't be muddy," Joel said.

Claire took the leash from him and dropped it on top of her sweater. "Unless they go after the loons and end up in the lake." A good possibility.

A tray containing three frosty pitchers of sweet tea sat on the island beside glasses and a bucket of ice. The island made a natural divider between the great room and the kitchen. That was well thought out. Carin gestured to them. "Help yourselves. There's regular, peach, and raspberry sweet tea. Dinner will be about fifteen minutes." She crossed the kitchen and opened the oven, poking at something.

Claire sat next to Lacey. "Are the headaches gone now?" She took the glass of tea Joel handed her. "Thanks, honey."

Lacey didn't look up but turned her glass in her hands. "Pretty much."

Her voice was so soft Claire could hardly hear her, like when she first came to Chapel Springs. "I'm sorry, sugar, I didn't hear you."

Lacey raised her head and looked Claire in the eye. "They're pretty much gone." Then she dropped her chin again and picked at the napkin cradling her glass.

Oh, for the love of Van Gogh. For a moment there, Claire had thought Lacey had a spark of defiance, but it wilted and fled. She was worse than ever.

She caught Jake's eye and raised one eyebrow in question. His gaze slid to his wife, softened, then returned to Claire. He raised one shoulder. Poor man didn't know what to do either.

Instead of making Lacey feel like the eight-hundred-pound gorilla in the room, Claire punted. "I have a problem. The caterer we chose for the twins' wedding has gone out of business. We don't have a lot of time left to find another. Jake, do you know of any caterers?"

"A couple, but I doubt they'd be available at this late date. They book up months in advance."

Joel refilled his glass of peach tea from the pitcher on the island. "I offered, but Claire said as father of the brides, I can't."

She handed him her glass for a refill. "Raspberry, please, and you're right, you can't. Besides, you'll be a basket case of emotions that night. We'll figure something out. I hope."

"Why not look online?" Ryan asked. "You can find anything online.

Caterers, dog trainers." He and Joel laughed.

Another online champion. Was she the only one left in the last century? She slid onto a barstool. "But how do you know if they're any good?"

"Read the reviews," Lacey said.

Whoa, she actually joined the conversation. Granted it was almost whispered, but it was the first step. Claire crossed back to the sofa and sat beside her. Go slow. "So people review caterers? Not just books and art?"

Lacey kept her head down. "Yes. And restaurants and all kinds of services."

"Thanks. I'll go look online. And Lacey …" Claire waited until the chin lifted again. "When you're with us, sugar, there's no reason to be so withdrawn." A light bulb went off in Claire's head. "It hurts my feelings to think you don't trust me."

Lacey's chin snapped up. Her brow knit with concern.

Score!

"I'm sorry, Claire. I hadn't thought of that. I wish I could somehow explain it to everyone." Tears welled up in her eyes.

Uh-oh. *Backpedal!* "I—"

"I've lost myself. I don't know who I am anymore. And it fills my mind with bad memories. I'm sorry, I …" Lacey jumped up and hurried out the front door.

"My, my. That went well." Claire turned to Jake. "I'm sorry. I'd hoped to have her see how much we care about her—that she doesn't need to feel shy or frightened around us."

Jake shook his head and gave a sad little smile. "It's the strangest thing I've ever seen. Lacey was always shy, but not like this, and not around y'all. She needs to go see the psychologist her doctor recommended. I'm hoping she will."

"What if you took her on a trip?" Lydia hugged Jake. "Get away from what she's used to here." She handed Jake Lacey's sweater.

"You know, that's a good idea. I can take her up to Enota Retreat. It's only an hour away and she loves the falls there." He kissed Lydia's cheek, shook hands with the men, thanked Carin, and left to catch Lacey.

Lydia stood at the window. "She told me about our uncle after I left home. His eyes followed her everywhere. That would unnerve the strongest of people. He never touched her that I know of, but the fear was implanted just the same." She turned and crossed to the love seat.

"However, she's been gone from there since she graduated from high school." Lydia glanced at Claire, then Graham. "Why does it still bother her? I don't understand."

Graham shook his head. "I'm no psychologist, but I can almost imagine what it would be like to wake up as someone else."

Lacey was still Lacey. "She's not someone else. She only *looks* like someone else." Wait. That was the same thing. Sort of. Claire offered a grimace. "I guess it is kind of like that." She shook her head. "Lydia, didn't that doctor warn her?"

"I don't think so. I think he decided she'd be so happy to be pretty she wouldn't feel that way. The night she was hurt, after they stabilized her, he asked Jake if he had a photo of her. He gave him the one he carries of their wedding day and one taken a couple of years ago when they were in Belize."

"Why?" Ryan asked. "I mean, why did the doctor want a photo, not why Jake carried their wedding one."

"Well, I don't know. I guess to see what she looked like before the accident, so he'd know how to repair her face. Good grief. That makes her sound like a clock."

That wasn't so far off base. Claire shook her head. "But he didn't take time to find out what made her tick. Too bad there wasn't time to consult her before he made his decision. Why—"

Lydia held up her hand, stopping Claire. "He did what he thought best. Her cheekbones were crushed. He rebuilt them a little higher and made her nose a little smaller. Whether out of necessity or decision by inflated ego, we don't know. But she's not scarred, and she could have been." Lydia sighed. "I get frustrated with her. Jake's frustrated. I wish she'd—I don't know. Accept it and move on."

"But can she?" Claire shook her head. "It's almost like Lacey died and someone else took her place. Except it's Lacey. Talk about confusing."

"Let's pause this and eat." Carin gestured to the dining table.

Claire perused the platters. "It looks wonderful." She inhaled. "And it smells heavenly."

After the blessing had been asked, the food passed, and they were starting on seconds, Carin set down her fork. "Once for a character that had bariatric bypass surgery, I talked with a psychologist. He told me a large percentage of those who have the surgery and lose vast amounts of weight feel like they've lost themselves. They're still the *old* person inside, but on the outside, that person is no longer there." She glanced at

Lydia. "He said it really messes with the psyche unless they are mentally prepared for it."

Claire swallowed a bite of pasta. "And Lacey had no preparation. What can we do to help her?"

"Pray and encourage her to see that psychologist," Lydia said.

"I do every day." Carin went to the oven and withdrew a fresh loaf of crusty garlic bread. She cut it, then passed it to Ryan.

After munching a piece of the bread, Ryan sat back. "I received a phone call this afternoon from Newlander, asking if I wanted to sell." With his thumb and middle finger, he turned his water glass around and around. "I played along with him for a while. Said he wanted the mineral rights too. What I ferreted out was he has a friend who wants to live here."

Joel shook his head. "You didn't believe him, did you?"

Chapter 26

"Jake, I'm not sure I'm ready for this." Lacey removed the special ice pack the physical therapist had given her. It covered her whole face but left openings for her to speak and breathe. It helped to reduce the swelling. She'd breezed through the short time in physical therapy. Her facial muscles had returned to normal, and she scored the special cold mask.

"It's only the rehearsal, and you can sit in the back in the dark. You said you wanted to see how things were coming along."

Lacey placed the gel-filled mask on the arm of the recliner. "You're right, but I can't seem to raise the energy to go. I'm tired. I think I'll go to bed."

"No. You slept in this morning. Honey, I'm concerned you're getting depressed. The doctor warned me about depression."

"Can you blame me? I went from plain to monstrous in one hot minute."

Jake frowned. He pulled her into his arms. "Sweet stuff, you're not a monster. You're still the same lovely Lacey."

"I was plain Lacey before." Her words muffled against his chest.

"No." He put a finger beneath her chin and tipped her head up, looking into her eyes. "You've always been lovely to me." He raised his eyes and seemed to search for the words he wanted. She waited. "It's hard to explain. Yes, you look different, but to me, you look the same. Your inner loveliness has come out for everyone else to see."

She wasn't so sure she was lovely inside anymore. Sometimes her thoughts turned ugly, hateful. The other day at Lunn's, she ran into Mrs. Chester and almost snapped at her when she said she couldn't wait for her nephew to see the new Lacey. After she left, Lacey ran to her car, closed the door, and cried.

"Maybe we should hold a funeral for the old me." She regretted her words when Jake looked at her with a horrified expression. "I feel like I'm grieving for someone, and then I realize it's myself." She trembled. "Am I going crazy?" They'd lock her away if that happened.

"You're not going crazy, but if you would talk with the psychologist, I think he'd be able to help you. I'm guessing a lot of your feelings and fears are normal, but if he can help you get past them, wouldn't you want to see him?"

Would she? The thought of sitting—or would she have to lie on a couch? Her noodle legs almost folded. She was glad Jake's arms supported her. "I wouldn't have to lie down on a couch, would I?"

"No, that's TV stuff." He kissed her nose and cupped her cheek in his hand. "How about I go with you?"

Her knight in a chef's apron. "Would you? Then I could pretend I'm talking to you." And maybe the psychological therapy would go as quickly as the physical therapy. That wouldn't be too bad.

"I could and I will. There's something else. I made us reservations in New York. We're going for the weekend, and I bought tickets to see a play."

Jake's face held such hope. She sucked in her lower lip. While the idea of going to New York scared her silly, she could see a Broadway play. "Could we see an off-Broadway one too?" If hers ever had a chance, that's where it would play. There or off-off-Broadway.

"We can go to Poughkeepsie, if you want." Jake kissed her lips, then her chin, and finally her cheeks. "I promise, you'll have fun. Remember, nobody knows you there. They won't see any difference."

She saw what he was doing and loved him all the more for it. "Go ahead and call the psychologist. But make the appointment when you can go with me."

Lacey took a deep breath to quell her nerves and reached for the stage-door handle. A second breath for good luck, and she stepped inside the theater. No one was backstage yet. She tiptoed past the dressing rooms and down the hall leading to the lobby. From there, she could enter the house, sit in a back row, and observe. All without anyone knowing she was there.

She settled into an aisle seat. Down in the front of the modified orchestra pit, Kelly conversed with Eileen and Ellie. They were probably going over notes from the last rehearsal. Lacey had missed so much. Opening night was three weeks away, and she couldn't wait to see how they had progressed. A woman tapped Kelly's shoulder and pointed to the back of the theater. Right where Lacey sat. Oh no. She ducked. She didn't want to be seen. Who was it and why did she point at her?

Kelly called for quiet and then Alexa's voice—well, Ellie's voice as Alexa—cut through the silence. Lacey straightened in her seat and watched her story unfold on the stage. The magic of theater carried her out of herself and into another world. Alexa and Bonnie took on flesh, and Lacey suspended all disbelief, following the duo through their investigation.

"I'm so excited to see you here. How's it going?"

What? That wasn't in her script. Where did—wait the voice was beside her. When ... better question, who? Lacey turned and was nose-to-nose with a stranger. Her stomach flipped so hard and fast, it made her light-headed.

"Ooh, your face is so pretty, Lacey. How does it feel?" Fingers rose and closed in on her, drawing closer to her cheeks.

"Like Pinocchio." Heart pounding, Lacey scrambled to get away. She grabbed her keys and fled the theater, not stopping until she reached home. There, she collapsed in tears on the front porch. "God, how can you be so cruel? What have I ever done to deserve this?"

Claire pulled her chair up to the computer. She wasn't needed at the rehearsals since the set was finished, so she stayed home and Joel went alone. She had a mission. Tonight, she was going to find a caterer for the girls *and* one of those tests online. It only took a moment for the computer to come to life after she poked the power button, but she hated watching it do its gyrations bringing up all the programs. She went back to the kitchen for a cup of tea to pass the few minutes it took. They really needed a new computer.

While her tea brewed, she unloaded the dishwasher and then gave Shiloh the treat he was begging for. Enough time wasted. She grabbed a couple of cookies for herself, another treat for Shiloh along with her tea, and went back to the computer. Whirligigs flew in her stomach. Shiloh flopped down by her feet.

"You're not nervous. Why should I be?" The mastiff raised his head and watched her—or the canine cookie sitting on the edge of the desk. "You're no help." She handed the treat to him.

Her hesitation was ridiculous. After all, she ordered clay online all the time. Patsy would be ashamed of her. Claire straightened her shoulders and opened the search engine. The first order of business should be a caterer. There were several within a fifty-mile radius of Chapel Springs. She filled out each one's online scheduling and found one that had an opening for their wedding date. She booked it. His business had a German-sounding name, but as long as he made more than sauerkraut and schnitzels, well, they didn't have a lot of room to be choosy.

That done, she glanced over her shoulder and then typed "pregnancy test" in the search slot.

A bunch of listings came up. She clicked the first link. It wasn't somewhere to buy one but a site that explained the physiology of testing for pregnancy. That wasn't what she wanted. She tried several more before she gave up. What had she left out? Home. That was it. She went back to the top and typed "home pregnancy test" into the slot.

She peered at the screen. Who knew? All this time she could have bought one from Amazon? "Did you know they sold stuff other than books?" she asked Shiloh. Apparently, the rest of the world did. "I guess I need to get out from behind my pottery wheel for a while." Shiloh stopped crunching his cookie and doggy-grinned at her.

"Hey, I wonder if we can get your treats on here." She clicked the little magnifying glass and typed. "Wow, there are all kinds here and some good prices." Since she was there, she ordered two types of dog cookies. "You'll be a happy boy when these get delivered."

Back to business now that Shiloh was taken care of. She searched again for home pregnancy tests. Van Gogh's ear, there must have been twenty pages of listings. And several price ranges for each. Why was that? Had they been used and returned? Were they too old? Claire blew out a pent-up breath and started reading each one. By page seven, she was cross-eyed.

She needed a pad and a pencil. After digging through the drawer, she found a stub of a pencil and an envelope. They'd do. She went back to page one and listed the brand and price. Oh, wait. That last one was a bulk price. Now why would someone want them in bulk?

"Hey, babe. Whatcha doing?"

Claire screeched, and the pencil flew out of her hand. She hit the sleep icon and stuffed the envelope under her thigh. "You scared me! Don't sneak up on me like that."

Joel kissed her cheek. "Sorry. I called when I came in." He leaned down and ruffled Shiloh's ears. "So how come you didn't bark, boy?"

Claire remained in the chair, the envelope beneath her. "He was too busy eating his treat. Did you know you can buy doggie cookies online?"

Joel scratched the back of his head. "Nope. You know I hardly ever get on that thing." He pointed at the computer.

He was right. The kids usually did all the Internet surfing. Truth be told, she probably would have learned more about using it if they didn't have five kids who needed it for homework all the time.

"How was rehearsal?" She needed to get him out of the room so she could put the envelope in the trash. No, in her pocket. She needed it.

"Great. I know my lines, not that there are a lot of them. Kelly worked with me a little on the delivery. I'm going to make some tea. Want a cup?"

Thank You, Lord. "Yes, I'd love one. I'll shut this down and be right there." She slid the envelope in the drawer. No, the twins might find it. They were still using the computer instead of their phones for last-minute wedding decisions. The bathroom. That would work. She'd slip it into her makeup drawer.

The tap was so soft he barely heard it. He opened the door a crack. Newlander. He opened it all the way. "Come on in." He stuck his head out the door and peered into the darkness.

"Nobody followed me. I made sure." Howie pulled out a chair at the small table and sat.

Xander took the other chair, pushing the remains of his takeout dinner aside. "So what do you have for me?"

"I found a small house on the other side of the woods on Hill Street. The owner died and the daughter inherited it. But she lives in Seattle. I remember her. She hasn't been back here in over ten years. I'll bet she'll sell to you."

"You don't think she'll want to keep it as a rental property?" She'd be a sap if she didn't.

"I'll tell her rentals are slowing down."

This yahoo must have grits for brains. "Even a cursory search on the Internet will tell her otherwise. Find out the appraised value of the property. Offer fifty thousand over that. If the mineral rights are included, keep increasing it until she says yes."

His associates wanted gold, and gold they would get. No matter what.

Chapter 27

Claire pointed to an unusual-looking bun with a square shape and what appeared to be blueberry custard and apricot compote inside a pocket. The whole thing was topped with a lattice of golden brown flakey pastry. "What is it?"

Dee grinned. "Another of Trisha's heavenly experiments. We haven't named it yet. Ooh, you look itchy."

"Yeah. Shiloh gave a lot of the guests at the shower poison ivy. Including the twins. They thought they were immune to it, but no such luck. My only hope is that everyone is over it by the wedding and no new cases break out. I had no idea some could take as long as three weeks to break out."

"I didn't know that. I break out within two days."

"You will if you're already allergic to it. That's what happened to the twins. It took them a week. And I'll try one of Trisha's temptations."

Claire picked up the cup containing a tea bag, added water from the thermos pot, and carried it and her breakfast to a table by the window. She was early this morning. Calamine only worked so long, and unable to go back to sleep, she'd given up and made her way to Dee's 'n' Doughs.

She pulled out a pad and pencil to jot a list of what she needed to do today. At the top, she wrote "check with caterer." Beneath that, she added "test" and stuffed the note inside her tote.

The first bite of the confection confirmed that Trisha's new experiment would be a colossal success. After she'd downed half her tea, she felt human. Patsy waved at her through the window. Right after her, Ellie arrived. Dee's 'n' Doughs was coming alive as her friends showed up. Soon they all crowded around one table, coffee cups steaming, pastries compared and tasted, and life discussed. Claire loved this time of meeting with her friends. How did women who lived in big, cold cities get along without this?

Lydia pulled a small notebook from her pocket. "I need to report my findings. Yesterday was my day to play private detective." She grinned. "I've never had so much fun. I used a red wig Kelly fixed me up with, and you never would have recognized me. I wore dark sunglasses too."

Claire untangled a strand of hair from her earring. "So Mel didn't see you, but did you see anything of her stalker?"

Lydia shook her head. "I was so disappointed. Nobody looked remotely terrifying or threatening."

"Mel hasn't said much about it either," Ellie said. "I wonder if it's stopped."

"Until we know for sure, we don't dare relax our efforts. I told y'all what the twins said about that one girl getting raped." Claire checked her "Mel schedule" and frowned. "Patsy, you have tomorrow. Can you still do that?"

Her BFF grinned. "Absolutely. I can't let all y'all have all the fun." They discussed what Patsy should wear for her disguise. If Mel ever heard about all their subterfuge, she'd ... well, Claire wasn't sure what she'd do. Hopefully, she'd feel loved, not humiliated.

Carin strolled in a few minutes later with JJ. Why wasn't he in school? He ran over to see Claire while his mama ordered something for them.

"Hey, Miss Claire. Wanna see what I got? His name is Whiskers." He reached into his pocket and pulled out a white mouse. Uh-oh. Cute as it was, some of the ladies hated rodents.

Nancy Vaughn squealed and pushed her chair back. "Put that thing away!"

"Aw, he won't hurt you," JJ said. "Look at his whiskers wiggle." He thrust the mouse toward Nancy, earning another squeal. "His wiggly whiskers mean he likes you." He turned to Claire. "Mikey has Whiskers' brother." JJ put the mouse on his shoulder.

"Son, put your mouse back in your pocket before he jumps on someone." Carin winked at Claire. "He's having a special day off for a straight-A's report card."

JJ obeyed and then picked up the donut his mama set before him. He reminded Claire so much of her Wes when he was small. She always gave her kiddos a day off, too, for straight A's.

"Claire, is your brother-in-law dating that new widow in town?" Carin asked.

"Mmfopso." She swallowed the bite of pastry. "I hope so." Poor Vince had come home to Chapel Springs a couple years ago and gone into practice with Patsy's daddy, Doc Benson. His wife had run off with a hospital administrator. Caused a scandal and broke Vince's heart. "He deserves some happiness."

"I saw them over in Pineridge at an outdoor concert. He didn't even see me—if that tells you anything. He never took his eyes off Haleigh. They talked and laughed throughout the whole evening."

That made Claire's heart happy. Wait. Did that mean Carin had a date too? "Who did you—ow." Patsy kicked her ankle. "What was that for?" Patsy rolled her eyes and shook her head at Claire. Oh. She grimaced. It really wasn't any of her business. But ... she made a face at Patsy. "With the weddings, I guess I have romance on my mind."

Carin chuckled and ruffled JJ's hair. "This is my love."

"Aw, Mama." JJ's little face turned red.

Ellie screeched and pulled her legs up onto her chair, bumping the table and splashing coffee out of everyone's cup. Nancy jumped up, and like a wave at a baseball game, JoAnn and Patsy joined her. What in the world?

JJ frowned, then he leaped to his feet. "Don't anyone move. You'll step on him."

Him?

JJ dropped to the floor and scrambled between their legs. "Whiskers, come back!"

Oh dear. Claire leaned to the left but couldn't see the mouse anywhere. Carin pushed her chair back, mumbling something about a "bad idea." Nancy climbed on top her chair. Ellie held her sides, laughing. Dee dove for the door to the back where Trisha was working. No mouse was going to get inside her bakery. Technically, it already was, though.

The front door opened and Felix walked into the chaos. JoAnn used the open door to run outside. She stood at the window, though, watching the goings on inside and laughing. Felix pushed his ever-present baseball cap back onto his head and looked perplexed at all the commotion.

"Close the door, Mr. Mayor. Don't let Whiskers out." JJ dove under a chair, chasing his mouse's tail.

Felix obeyed and glared at Claire. What? Did he think it was her fault?

As JJ crawled forward, the chair moved with him like a turtle shell. Claire grabbed the chair's back and pulled it off him. He shot her a grateful glance, then disappeared under a woodland creature cloth, jostling the table. Claire grabbed her coffee cup before it fell over.

Cookie Halverson, a summer resident, dropped to her hands and knees and crawled around under the table with JJ. When Motorcycle Mama Hazel climbed on top of her chair, squealing, Claire lost it and laughed so hard that coffee shot out her nose and she had to cross her legs.

Patsy, whose boys had several mice, dove to help Cookie. "I'll herd him your way and you grab him."

"I've got him," Cookie hollered a moment later. She came up laughing and cradling Whiskers. "Just another adventurous day in Chapel Springs. Now I have a fun story to tell my third-grade students." She handed Whiskers to JJ.

JJ thanked Miss Cookie and slid his mouse into his pocket. Carin gathered her purse, their napkins, and the empty cups. "I think it's time we went home—all three of us. See y'all later."

Felix lumbered over to the coffee bar. After getting a cup and a donut, he joined them. "Dee hadn't ought to let kids bring their pets in the bakery. It's against the codes."

"Back off, Felix." Claire faced off with their mayor. "Dee didn't know he had the mouse in his pocket. She has a No Pets sign, but mice can't read." Everyone laughed except Felix. What was his problem? "What has you twitterpated this morning?"

"I heard that insurance company denied Lacey's claim."

"What?" Claire craned her neck looking for Lydia. She was at the coffee bar. "Lydia, why did the insurance company deny Lacey's claim? Did Trixie have a hand in it?"

"They said it was cosmetic surgery." Lydia joined their table. "Eileen told me Trixie was trying to touch Lacey's face last night at rehearsal."

"What? Why that—I ought to—" Claire jumped up.

Patsy pulled on Claire's arm. "Easy, girl, before you go bulldozing into trouble."

"We can't sit by and let Trixie manufacture something to keep from paying Lacey's medical bills."

"You're all worried over nothing," Ellie said.

Felix snapped his head around to her. "And what makes you think this is nothing?"

"Well, who in their right mind would think Lacey would have planned getting hurt that badly for a nose job?" Ellie sat back and folded her arms.

She had a point. Claire studied her. "But they could try to hold up payment for a long time. Besides, Felix said they already denied it."

"The doctor will resubmit it. And they wouldn't dare hold up payment. Not with this case."

Lydia's eyes twinkled. "I think I see where Ellie's going, Felix. It would become terrible publicity for them. Too many people witnessed the accident. And you can bank on Claire leading the charge to make it well known to the press."

Felix's right eyebrow went up. He was hopeful. If his left brow rose, he was getting cantankerous. "Ya think?"

"I've seen it before," Nancy said. "A few years ago, the insurance investigator was a young yahoo who wanted to ingratiate himself with his bosses."

Wait. Claire read all about that in the newspaper. "That's right, Felix. He alleged the victim and their insured client were in cahoots and were going to split the insurance money."

Nancy barked a laugh. "When the lawyer used that in court, the judge looked at him like he'd lost his last brain cell. He asked if the insurance company really expected the jury to believe a man would agree to being run over and lose his leg for money. The insurance company decided to settle out of court. But because of the publicity, they lost a lot of clients, not to mention the money."

"So you don't think they'll try to deny payin' a second time?"

Claire grinned and folded her arms. "Not if they're smart, they won't. Come on, Patsy. We have work to do."

Felix stood when they rose. "What are you doing?"

"I'm a potter, Felix. With an art show looming. What do you think I'm doing?"

"Oh. I thought you were gonna stop that Trixie."

"Believe me, she'll trip herself up."

Felix pulled on the bill of his baseball cap. "Let's hope she doesn't trip anyone else while she's at it." He turned around, then stopped. His brows dipped when he frowned. "Does your sister have co-insurance?"

"No." Lydia's voice was a whisper. No one said a word as the enormity of it sank in.

Felix popped his suspenders. "Her accident was on town property. Somehow, we'll make it right for them. I'm calling a council meeting. For tonight."

Boone tapped his gavel. Claire silently chuckled at his restraint, but there wasn't any reason to bang it with nobody but the council members here.

"The meeting is called to order. Felix, you called us here. What's up?"

"It occurred to me this afternoon that the Dawsons, Jake and Lacey, don't have co-insurance. Their part of the medical bills is pretty hefty. Since the accident happened on town property, I feel like we're responsible."

Who was this man? Certainly not their penny-pinching mayor? Claire leaned back in her chair, waiting to see what he had in mind.

Doc pursed his lips. "I think that's a fine idea, Felix. But that could be one large chunk of our treasury."

Felix nodded. "I know. That has me worried, but I want to be preemptive. Jake has the grounds to sue the town."

"He wouldn't do that." Claire leaned forward. "He loves this town."

"So does anyone have any ideas?" Boone asked.

Felix puffed his chest. Oh boy, another harebrained scheme of his. "I started thinking how the town pulled together for that fundraiser to revive Chapel Springs. Why couldn't we—"

Claire jumped out of her seat. "Brilliant! We'll do the same for Lacey and Jake." She threw her arms around Felix. "Sometimes, you really surprise us."

Felix pushed her away, his face red. "Get off me." He looked through squinted eyes. "Somebody'll think you're soft on me."

Laughing, Claire sat. Ellie stopped her note-taking. "We did an auction for the town. What should we do for this?"

No one said a word for a minute. Claire tossed and caught a couple of ideas but dropped them. "Wait! I've got it. One of Lacey's plays is being performed for our grand opening of the theater."

Ellie jumped in. "She's right. We could make it a charity event. Well, a fundraiser, anyway. Best to avoid the word *charity*."

"How will we advertise it?" Boone asked.

"We can call it a fundraiser. But"—Claire glanced at Doc—"do we want to let Lacey and Jake in on it? Give them some relief? Or do we keep it a secret?"

Doc pulled his glasses off and took his time wiping them. When he settled them back on his nose, he smiled. "I think we should let them know. We can tell them the town council is firm on it too. Like Felix said, the accident took place on town property." He stopped. "Wait a minute. We have liability insurance in case someone gets hurt on town property." He looked at Felix.

"We do," Felix said. "But I sure hate to use it if we can avoid it. It'll send our rates through the roof."

That wasn't good for Chapel Springs. Claire doodled on her notepad. After a moment, she stopped. "I think we have to let the Lakeside Players decide. After all, they'll be giving up a large amount of money."

Felix scowled. "They'd just better remember who owns the theater they perform in."

Chapter 28

Claire and Patsy hurried down the boardwalk to Sunspots. Nancy had called Claire about a new shipment of summer shorts and tops that had arrived that morning. She couldn't wait to see what had come in. Most of the clothes she carried were designer and one-of-a-kind, but they were the most comfortable clothes Claire owned.

"I hope she still has those cute walking shorts she told me about." Claire pulled open the door and stopped on the threshold. The place was packed with all her friends. She whispered to Patsy, "Looks like we weren't the only ones Nancy called. At least we can beat the tourists."

The hangers clacked on the racks as Claire shuffled through the tops. She grabbed a pretty teal tank top with a rolled white satin edging.

"Ooh, Claire, there's a gauze blouse in a lighter turquoise that would be divine with that tank," Nancy said. She whirled around. "I'll get it for you."

"Thanks. Well, hey, Ellie." Claire eyed the pile of colorful shorts in her arms. "Are those for you or Mel?"

Ellie smoothed her hand over a yellow pair on the top of the stack. "Both of us." She winked and headed toward the dressing rooms. Ellie winked? Becoming Mel's foster mother had transformed her and brought out a playful side Claire remembered from high school—before her mother became so crippled with arthritis and her personality gnarled as badly as her hands.

Patsy moved to the adjoining circular rack. "I feel like our caveman ancestors on a foraging adventure." She nodded toward Ellie's back retreating into the dressing area. "Moving out of her mother's house really changed our little librarian, didn't it?"

"Decidedly. And give Mel some of that credit too."

Claire had four tops, six pairs of shorts, and a bathing suit in her arms. "This is enough. I'm heading to the dressing rooms." She only had to wait a minute for one. She hung her bounty on the hooks and pulled off her jeans.

"Claire, is that you?" Ellie's voice floated from the next dressing room.

"It's me."

"I'm such a dolt. I forgot to tell you we discovered who Mel's stalker is. You're not going to believe this." She chuckled.

"Don't keep me in suspense." Claire stepped into a pair of shorts and pulled them up. Cute. She turned and looked at her backside. Not bad for an old preg—egads! She hadn't bought that test yet. Yanking off the shorts, she grabbed her jeans. Wait. What did— "Ellie, I'm sorry. What did you say?"

"Mel's stalker turns out to be a shy boy who kept trying to ask her out."

Claire exited the changing room. "How did y'all find that out?"

Ellie joined her and they walked to the register. "Mel finally had enough. She grabbed his arm so he couldn't flee and asked him why he'd been following her." Ellie giggled. "She said he turned fifty shades of red and blurted out would she go to dinner with him."

"And?" Claire set her clothes on the counter. "That's it, Nancy."

"And she said yes."

"Wait, is that smart? How can she be sure he's not a psycho?"

"Because he's Bobby Eisler's cousin, who lives in Pineridge."

"I didn't know Bobby had a cousin in Pineridge." Claire handed Nancy her credit card. "How about that. Well, I'm relieved, that's for sure. Nancy, I don't have time to try those all on. Can I return them if they don't fit?"

"Of course." Nancy ran her card.

Ellie set her purchases on the counter. "I'm relieved too. Mel went out with him last Friday night and said they have a lot in common. He's an engineering student, too, and she likes him."

"Claire, where are the twins registered?" JoAnn asked. "I'm so busy right now that I'd like to order their wedding presents online."

That online thing again. Claire told her and took her bag from Nancy. "Patsy, I'm running these home, then I'll see y'all back at the gallery. Bye, Ellie."

ANE MULLIGAN

Claire set herself a brisk pace. She wanted a few minutes to do what Wes said was "surfing the net." Honestly, her head was into her pottery too much.

"Silly woman." And she'd looked the tests up that one night before Joel almost caught her. She opened the front door, hurried upstairs, and dropped the clothes on the bed. Then she went into the upstairs den, which used to be Charlie's room. They'd turned it into a study for the kids after Charlie married. This time, she was going to buy that pregnancy test online. Right now and end this worry.

Claire sat at the desk and turned on the computer. Now, where did she find those others? Oh, right. She went on Amazon. She logged in and typed "home pregnancy test." Crossing her fingers made it hard to type, but she needed all the luck she could get. Van Gogh's ear, how to choose? Thinking logically would be best, although she wasn't known for her logic. But if she tossed out the lowest prices and the highest, she should be able to choose one.

Why was there such a difference in price? What difference could there be? After reading several, she decided to choose a mid-priced one. That was logical. She clicked on it. Did they come in a brown wrapper? Was the name of the company on the shipping label? If Lester Gordon knew what was inside, he'd tell Olympia, and she might tell Lydia. Claire paused. Before she clicked Place Order, she looked to see if it said how they were packaged. She couldn't find anything about that. Nope, no way she'd risk it. Not until she made a few inquires. Discreetly, of course. She closed the Internet and spent a few minutes reading emails. Nothing earth shaking there.

Wait. Maybe she could look at the reviews. She opened the Internet again, clicked onto Amazon, and—whoa. Advertisements for pregnancy tests appeared on the side of the page. She had to get rid of those. But how? Her heart raced. She didn't want Joel to see this. He'd ask why she'd been looking at those. Wouldn't he? Where was that history thing she heard Mel talk about? She searched the toolbar. There it was. She clicked on it and cleared the history. Hopefully, those ads would disappear.

She opened Amazon again, and an ad for a home pregnancy test appeared. It might as well have been in neon green. Look up something else. Maybe that would help. She spent the next fifteen minutes looking up everything from frying pans to bathrobes. Finally, the ads changed. *Thank You, Lord.* But she still needed to get a test. The library! They had computers there. At the library, she could order it, and no one would be the wiser. She could also read the reviews and see if she could research how they came packaged.

Claire pulled her phone out of her pocket and called Patsy. "Hey, I have to stop at the library before I come back." Cheese Louise, she had way too much to do. Her inventory list for the tour leered at her. "I'll only be twenty minutes." She should be able to get it done by then.

My shadow moved across the room, following me as I explored my "new" house. It continued to follow me through the sunroom, past the den door, and into the kitchen, where I slid the knife into the dishwasher. I glanced down at my feet, from whence my shadow sprawled across the floor, its head ending near the window overlooking the cul-de-sac. That window made keeping track of their comings and goings easier. How convenient.

No one had suspected a thing the day I moved in. The neighbors welcomed me with a casserole and banana pudding. I didn't tell them I despised banana pudding, but I memorized the name of the giver while it swirled down into the garbage disposal.

I memorized a lot of names and trivia about my neighbors, but only the ones whom I had grievance against. The others were of no consequence. I flicked my fingers against my shoulder in a dismissive gesture and turned from the window. There were chores to be done. Unpacking of boxes, filled with new things. Everything I owned was new, as new as I was.

A silent chuckle spurred me on as I mounted the stairs of this, my new house. Its former owners had been kidnapped. Murdered by their kidnappers, so the police supposed. No bodies had been found, though. No suspects arrested. The neighbors who had welcomed me so eagerly now eagerly told me terrifying tidbits, watching to see if moving into that house frightened me. I let them think what they wanted, that I didn't know anything being from somewhere far away.

If they only knew.

My laughter rang out in the stairwell, echoing in the hallway above. I would bide my time. Let the past titillation die down before I struck.

Again.

I paused as I passed the hallway mirror. Stretching forth my hand, my fingers rested on the mirror's surface, touching my reflection's cheek. A lovely face with high cheekbones, eyes no longer hooded, the nose patrician now. An open face. Honest. Innocent. The laughter bubbled up on its own once again. I winked at my reflection.

"If they only knew."

"Knew what?"

"Jake!" Lacey screeched, jumping. "You frightened me." She bent over to retrieve her dropped pen. "Don't sneak up on me like that."

He kissed her neck and picked up her notebook. Reading, he frowned. "Babe, this is dark. Not at all like your normal writing." He stared at her. "You okay?"

"I'm fine. It's therapeutic. I'm working out my inner angst. Don't look at me like that. This is the kind of thing a psychologist would encourage me to do. Write my feelings."

"But they're so dark, Lacey. This is—"

"Is what?"

"Really creepy."

"Good. That's what a good murder mystery should be."

"But yours are usually funny."

"Well, the new me is moving into a new way of writing." She turned back to her desk. "It's about a woman who killed her husband and then disappeared. The police think both the husband and wife were kidnapped."

Jake's face turned from horrified to contemplative. Good.

"So, what do you think?"

"Why do the cops think they were kidnapped?"

It did her heart good when Jake expressed interest in her plays. It bolstered her courage to try something new, something like this. "She left a ransom note, made from cut-out letters from magazines and newspapers. They never found the husband's body, and she left town. She's had facial reconstruction in Mexico. And she's now come back and bought her old house. I plan to have her murder a couple of the neighbors before they catch up with her."

"That could work. What did she do with the husband's body, though?"

Lacey turned sideways in her chair and rested one arm on its back. "Either an old well out back or—what?"

"The well would be the first place the cops would check."

"Even with the ransom note?"

"Yeah, probably. If they knew the well was there."

"And if they didn't?"

"What do you mean?" Jake crossed the floor to the refrigerator and opened it, peering inside.

"She could have had a patio with a fire pit built over it, so neighborhood kids couldn't fall into it. It would be easy enough for her to move the portable fire pit, lift a few pavers and toss his body down into the well. Then she could replace the pavers and the fire pit, and Bob's your uncle. No body."

"Hmm," Jake mumbled around a bite of peach cobbler.

That looked good. She stood and stretched. "I think I'll have some." She pulled the cobbler out of the fridge. "Do you think people will like it?"

Jake sat at the table. "If you add in some of your humor."

"That's a given if I use Alexa as the P.I. It's natural, organic with her. But I've never done a really creepy villain, and I want to."

"I think it can work. What I read gave me the chills."

Chapter 29

By the noise coming from the bank's community room, Claire was late. She opened the door to a room filled to capacity. Every chair was taken, and several men stood against the back wall. She hurried to her place at the council table. Felix glared at her. She held her hands up in a couldn't-help-it gesture. A stack of papers lay in the center of the table. She withdrew a set and read.

Boone banged the gavel. "Let's get this meeting going. Since this was a special called meeting, we'll dispense with reading the minutes of the last meeting."

Really? Did that mean if she called a special meeting each month, they could quit reading the minutes altogether? Yeah, right. In her dreams.

"The mayor asked for this meeting, so go ahead, Felix."

He pulled the table microphone closer. "I've had several calls in the last two days. Newlander is pushing people to sell him their property. We all know Howie doesn't have that kind of money or credit. What we don't know is who's backing him. The three mineral rights he managed to get were purchased in his name."

Doc crumpled the paper in his hand. "That scalawag either won the lottery, or he's found deep pockets. What I can't understand is why they've let his name alone appear on the titles. What's to keep him honest with them?"

"Maybe it's the mafia."

Claire jerked her head up to see who said it. Hazel Jones's hubby, Oscar, stood in the third row. What were they doing here? They didn't own land. "What makes you say that?"

"My old lady and I bought that little cottage on Hill Street, uh, the—what"—he turned to Hazel—"what was their name?"

"Walmsley."

"Yeah, the Walmsleys. Anyway, I paid $125,950 for it, and this bozo is offering me one-sixty for both the property and the mineral rights."

"Don't do it."

"You're getting hornswoggled."

"When Newlander's involved, you're sure to be scammed."

"You're an idiot if you do."

Boone banged his gavel until everyone quieted.

"I ain't sellin' to that scum. Hazel and I have ridden our bike all over these United States. We've finally decided to retire here. We like it. But what I was about to say is it's gotta be drug money or mafia having deep enough pockets to do that all over the village."

Retire? From what? She didn't know he had a job. What did he do? She looked at Seth. He shook with silent laughter. She frowned at him.

"What?" she mouthed.

He wrote something on a scrap of paper and passed it down to her. Nancy read it before she passed it to Claire, her eyes growing wide and her lips stretching into a huge grin.

Claire took the slip from her and read, "Pastor to motorcycle clubs." Her jaw dropped. She looked up at Oscar with new appreciation, then glared at Seth for not telling her this before.

"But even if you don't, others might sell. We have to stop them."

Who said that? She wished people would stand up if they were going to speak. Boone banged his gavel. He liked that thing entirely too much. Although, in this case, it was probably warranted.

When the room quieted, Doc wore a pensive expression. Keeping his elbow on the table, he lifted his hand. "Do you think his backer is the same man who backed the hotel?"

Claire startled. "Mr. Shoulders?"

Felix frowned. "I don't know. We never did get his name."

"Mayor?" Jacqueline Ford stood.

"Ma'am?"

She waited for the microphone Tom Fowler brought to her. "I've been researching this story. Your Mr. Shoulders is actually Elliott T. Burke, a racketeer, and is currently serving time."

Doc thanked her. "So we know Howie's backer isn't him. Who do you suppose it is?"

Glen Tabor raised his hand.

"Glen has the floor, and Warren, would you set up a speaker's mic?"

Glen waited for Warren to set the microphone in the middle of the aisle. When he finished, Glen stepped in front of the stand. "Mr. Mayor, Mr. Chairman, council members, right now, it doesn't matter who the backer is. After the last meeting, I had a talk with Nathan Kowalski."

Claire snapped her head to Patsy. Did she know about this? But Patsy sat staring slack-jawed at Nathan, so apparently she didn't.

"After a remark made by Claire, I asked Nathan to tell me who the investors were on that hotel business. He did. And I did some investigating on my own. I concur with Ms. Ford. The point is not who is backing Howie. We need an idea of how to put an end to this business. Permanently."

Time was slipping away. The library had been a bust. Teenagers had every computer staked out. Claire left the gallery early so she could have time to find that blasted test online, but Megan came home and needed the computer "right away!" Claire's hands trembled as she poured Joel a cup of coffee and tea for herself. She had to get that test. If she wasn't really pregnant and had ca— No. Until she knew for sure, she wouldn't project any what-ifs. Pregnant was bad enough.

She carried their cups to the table. "It's a new blend from Dee." She didn't tell him coffee made her nauseous lately.

Joel pushed the cup away. "You know I can't drink coffee after dinner. It'll keep me awake."

She pushed it back. "It's decaf. Try it." She held her breath until he sipped, waiting for the inevitable surprised look. There it was. "Now, give me your script, and I'll help you with your lines." His scene was short, so they went through the scene several times. It gave her time to calm down.

"I needed the help. Thanks."

"You know them perfectly. You'll do great."

"You should change your mind about taking a part sometime, sweetheart. You read with such animation. You'd be wonderful."

She shuddered. Okay, maybe she exaggerated it to make a point. "No way. I'd freeze. Did you call that catering company Jake referred to us?"

Joel chuckled. "And you accuse Dee Lindstrom of changing the subject fast? Yes, I did and no, they can't."

"What are we going to do? The girls don't want German food. I canceled that one. There are only a few weeks left until the weddings."

Joel patted her hand. "It'll all work out." He rose. "Come on, we need to get over to the theater." He carried their cups to the sink.

Claire picked up her tote waiting by the front door and glanced up the stairs where Megan tapped away on the computer. She heaved a sigh and checked to see if her glasses were in the new tote. It had so many pockets she could tuck all kinds of things in it. "They may be lost forever, though."

"Want to cut through the woods?" Joel took her hand. "And what are you mumbling about?"

"No woods. There's a bumper crop of poison ivy this year. Patsy walked out there the other day and is now sporting a case of it. And I was just hoping my glasses are in this." She tapped her hand on the tote, then waved at Earl Appling, who was mowing his front yard. "We need to bathe Shiloh every time he comes in from the woods until the cold kills it off."

When they arrived at the theater, Joel went to the stage and Claire went down to the scene shop. Patsy was already there, repainting a flat. She looked up when the door opened.

"Hand me that red paint can, please."

After Claire grabbed it, she examined her BFF's face, covered in calamine lotion. "How are you feeling?"

"Itchy, but Dad gave me a new medicine that seems to be helping. It's not as bad as it was an hour ago."

"The twins warned the rest of their bridesmaids to be extra careful. We've had five out of the eight come down with it."

"I swear it's sneaking in through the screen door. I wasn't out in the woods."

Uh-oh. "Did you happen to see Shiloh out there and pet him?"

Patsy stopped painting and peered up at her. "I did." She wrinkled her nose.

"I'm going to have to chain him up or lock him in the house until this is over. We can't spray for it. That would kill everything else." Or could they? Maybe she could find that out online too. She smiled. That would give her a good excuse to be on the computer. If their dog was the cause of so many poison ivy outbreaks, she should be part of finding a cure. Or at least a preventative.

After pulling out her reading glasses, Claire hung her tote on a hook. "What am I doing?"

Patsy pointed to a clipboard hanging over the workbench. "It's on there. I think you're doing the backgrounds. I'm painting on wallpaper."

"Painting on wallpaper? Why would you do that?"

"It's not *on* wallpaper. I'm painting the flowers to make it *look* like wallpaper." Patsy pulled a small bucket of green paint closer.

Claire planted her hands on her hips. "That's silly. Why not wallpaper them?"

"Costs too much."

Claire turned at the sound of Lester Gordon's voice. "Did you ever think of asking for a donation? People sometimes order special paper, then don't like it and return it. You can get those for a buck a roll."

Lester leaned back on his heels. "I didn't know that."

Patsy shook her paintbrush at him. "That would save a lot of time. Do you want me to keep going?" She had three flowers covering a two-foot section.

"No. Let's see if we can find actual wallpaper." He pulled out his phone. "I'll call Pat Holcomb." He searched through his contacts. "Wait. Do they carry wallpaper at The Tool Box?"

Claire slipped a painting shirt over her clothes. "Yes, but ask for Cherry. Pat won't have anything to do with it." She checked the change of color written on the flats in pencil and found the matching paint bucket and a paint tray. It didn't take more than five minutes to roll the paint onto each flat. She glanced down the line. Eleven more to go.

With her roller filled with paint, Claire made a "w" pattern on the wall, and then filled it in, covering the flat. She needed to remember to find Jake after rehearsal and tell him about the fundraiser for Lacey's medical bills. The whole troupe was enthusiastic about it. If she didn't see him tonight, she'd call him in the morning. Her roller stopped mid-swipe. Email. She'd email Jake and use that as another excuse to get on the computer, then go online and buy the blasted pregnancy test. If she hurried and finished painting, she could get home before Joel.

"Claire?"

"Joel? Are you finished already?"

"Yep. You about ready?"

She dropped her paintbrush into a can of water. What was that saying about the best-laid plans?

"Coming."

Chapter 30

Felix was in front of Claire, hurrying as fast as his legs could carry his rotundness toward Chapel Springs Boat Launch. When would Wes get the new sign made? The new name was Bennett & Son: Boat Launch and Storage. If Wes wasn't going to continue his education, she at least wanted to see his name in neon. Truth be told, her son was in his element here. His ideas and business sense had increased sales too. Her muse played through several designs for the sign as she and Felix climbed the stairs.

The mayor stopped outside Joel's office door, stood with his hands on where his hips should be, and caught his breath from the exertion. "Joel needs an elevator in here." The red receded from his face somewhat.

"What couldn't wait until tonight?"

"We need some of your Wes's strategic thinking to stop Howie."

Really? Her Wes? Felix was getting smarter. She reached for the door handle. "Let's go get him. And Joel."

When Wes joined them in the office, Felix brought them up to speed. "So far, residents have refused Howie's offers to buy them out."

"That's good, right?" Claire glanced at Wes. "We don't want them to sell to him."

Felix nodded. "It is, but this business has sparked gold fever all over town. Pat Holcomb told me a few have been in to buy new shovels and gold pans."

"As long as they dig on their own land," Joel said, "it's not a problem that I can see."

Felix shifted his weight, making the chair creak in protest. "What they do on their own land isn't our concern, but the streams are. Some of these gold-happy clowns are using suction dredges."

"What are those?" Claire looked to Wes and Joel.

Joel raised his shoulders, but Wes frowned. "They're like an underwater vacuum cleaner. They suck up gravel and dirt into a sluice box that catches any gold and dumps the other material back into the river."

She didn't see a problem, except for making the stream muddy. "So why's that bad?"

Felix leaned forward. "It's a problem for anything living on the bottom. Fish eggs and river insects don't stand a chance. They get sucked up and killed by the machine, and those that don't are smothered in the stirred-up sediment."

Joel blanched. "That could be a real problem for fishing. The lake is the major draw for tourists. Several species of fish use the streams to spawn. Can we put a ban on those machines?"

Felix looked unsure. "The council could. This has the potential to become a dire problem if people use dredges. But I can foresee resistance."

Claire's blood pressure rose ten percent. "Who from? Not residents, surely?"

"I don't know, Ma. When gold's involved, people go squirrely. They panic and want their gold fast and before anyone else gets to it."

Like Tillie and Esther.

Felix slumped. "I wish I'd never uncovered that quartz or said anything about it." He slapped his ball cap against the arm of the chair.

"You couldn't have known Howie would come back again, Felix," Joel said.

"If not him, then someone else. Gold affects the brains of people."

But apparently not their mayor. Claire's heart warmed.

"At the meeting the other night, Glen said we need an idea to stop this." Joel ran the back of his fingers along his chin. "Anybody have one?"

"Not me. You, Claire?"

"I'm working on one." She'd have it, too, if the blasted pregnancy tests didn't keep getting in the way of her thoughts.

"Wes, what do you think?" The mayor waited.

"The first order of business should be a moratorium on any dredging. Get that done as soon as possible. That will slow down Howie and his investors. Dredging is the cheaper and easier way to prospect."

Felix rose. "I'll call an emergency meeting tonight. Wes, will you come with that info on what those machines do?"

"Sure." Wes turned to the office computer and began tapping on the keyboard. "And I'll work on a plan to stop Howie and whoever his money man is."

Maybe she could use *this* as an excuse to get on the computer at home. Except she had to work at the gallery. Oh, fiddle.

Claire opened the door to the community room. Not too many people had heard about the emergency council meeting. The room held only a handful of non-council members. She was next to the last one to arrive and hurried to the table.

Doc entered the room as she took her seat. "Sorry to hold you up. Cooper was having a bit of an episode, and I had to have Patsy come stay with her."

Alzheimer's was a horrible disease. It broke Claire's heart to see her best friend's mother, Cooper, suffer from it. The whole family suffered. It amazed her how they all kept their sense of humor about it. Cooper said some artists paint insanity, and she was going to paint Alzheimer's … if she could *remember* how it felt. She said she couldn't wait to see what it looked like. Cooper made them all laugh, but it was bittersweet.

Boone raised his gavel but thought better of it and set it down. Thank goodness. "Let's get this meeting started. It has been brought to the council's attention that some people are using dredging machines to prospect in the streams. A moratorium has been proposed. Any discussion?"

Felix raised his hand. "Wes Bennett has some good information on what dredging does to the aquatic life in the streams. Wes, will you please tell the council what you told me?"

Her son rose and approached the council. He handed everyone a sheet of paper filled with facts. Claire beamed at the other members and winked at Costy. One look told her that her daughter-in-law was popping with pride.

She looked over the paper she received. He'd used bullet points and had the data backed up by the source. He could have been a lawyer. Too bad he didn't finish college, but he was happy working with his dad at the marina. Actually, he'd nearly taken over the business. Joel went fishing most days.

Boone read the paper, then looked up. "If we allow people to continue to use these things, it could spell disaster for the fish. Not to mention the aquatic insects that the fish eat. Can I have a motion on the moratorium?"

"I object to this. It's against my first amendment rights!"

The voice came from the back of the room. Who was it? Claire stretched her neck to see. A ragged-looking man with an unkempt beard stood up.

"How can this be against your first amendment rights? It's not a free speech issue."

"It's my right to pursue happiness."

Boone snickered. "That's in the Declaration of Independence, not the Constitution."

"Well, it shoulda been. You're still invading my rights."

Doc stood. "How do you figure that? The first amendment is about freedom of speech, of the press, and the right to assemble."

Scraggly-beard raised his hand, his index finger pointing to the ceiling. "And that's what I'm doin'. I'm assembling on the side of the stream."

Tom Flower rose. "Where do you live? I don't recognize you."

Scraggly-beard hitched his overalls and cast his eyes around the room. Was he looking for an ally? Finally, he faced the council. "I live in Young Harris."

Tom smiled. "I thought so. You have no say here." He sat down after Scraggly-beard skulked out the door. "I move we set a moratorium on dredging."

Nancy Vaughn seconded the motion, and they all voted in favor. At least that was taken care of. But would it stop Howie's consortium? Not everyone in the room seemed happy about the decision. That new man, what was his name? Barlow something. No, Barlow was his last name. What was his problem? As if he felt her staring, he turned, smiled at her, and then left. She'd have to mention him to Joel. See if he'd met him. Hadn't she heard he bought a place in town? He should be happy about this.

Claire caught up with Wes and Costy. "Have you come up with an idea to stop Howie?"

"As a matter of fact, Ma,"—Wes drew Costy under his arm—"my dear wife came up with it."

And this was the same girl who once wanted to take Wes back to Colombia. Claire beamed at her. "Tell me quick."

Costy leaned in and told Claire the most wonderful idea. It could work! She put her hands on the sweet girl's shoulders and kissed her forehead, making Costy giggle.

"You are brilliant, my dear. And your English is improving dramatically. Now don't tell anyone yet. I'll bring your Papa Joel and the mayor in on it. I think you may have saved Chapel Springs."

The yammer of the voices competing with one another for attention assaulted Xander's ears as he waited to pay for his breakfast at Dee's 'n' Doughs. If this weren't so important, he'd wrap up his food and go across the street to a bench overlooking the lake. Instead, he took his coffee and a bear claw to a table near the ladies. He should get an extra cut of the gold for this.

He'd met most of the chatterbox ladies now. The painter smiled at him, but to his benefit, they basically ignored him. The Bennett woman talked about the moratorium they'd passed on dredging last night. That had the potential to set him back a bit, but it wouldn't stop him. Actually, it could help if he worked it right. When the local yokels couldn't dredge for gold, and panning took too long, they'd give up. Sell to him. It could work, as long as he convinced them to accept the futility of it. So far, no one had connected him with Newlander, and he could continue to do the dirty work.

The ladies' conversation turned to some art tour, then the theater. Amazing. They could switch subjects without losing a beat. How they managed to keep up with each other, he didn't know, but they were definitely a bunch of busybodies. Some kid named Mel had been followed. Too bad nobody asked him. If anyone knew how to spot a tail, it was Xander. Sounded like it was old news, though, so he dismissed it.

The lady who owned the gift store, somebody Appling, caught him watching them. He smiled and emptied a sugar packet in his coffee. Dang. He hated sweet coffee and nearly gagged when he took a mouthful. She turned her attention back to her friends. He'd wait a minute, then get a refill, dumping this in the Coke dispenser overflow.

These rednecks were so slow to trust a newcomer, even one who bought a house in town. He'd worn clothes that looked like theirs. He fished. He spent money in their shops. How could he gain—

"Costy came up with an idea that will stop Howie cold."

"What is it?"

Yeah, that's what he wanted to know.

He couldn't hear anymore. The Bennett woman leaned in and whispered.

"That's brilliant."

"It could work."

"I'm in. If Warren gives me any guff, I'll do it myself."

Do what?

Wait. He didn't need to worry. Xander broke off a chunk of the bear claw and bit into it. Almond paste and sweet icing coated his tongue. Nothing to worry about. Nobody could stop him. After all, money talks.

Chapter 31

Tonight was Jake's early night off. Lacey opened the fridge door. Other than some tavern ham, a couple of eggs, and a loaf of bread, there wasn't much to make supper. She didn't have the energy to go all the way to the Piggly Wiggly in Pineridge. Lunn's would have to do. But could she get in and out of there without any fuss?

Dark glasses. Of course.

Lacey hurried upstairs to her bedroom and rummaged through her top dresser drawer. Somewhere in its depths, she had a pair of oversized sunglasses. Sliding her hand beneath a stack of silky scarves, her fingers hit pay dirt. With the sunglasses in place, they hid the top half of her face. She might be able to pull this off with the aid of one of Jake's ball caps. No, not a ball cap, but a straw hat. She could tuck her hair up beneath it. Then she could easily be one of the tourists.

Inside Lunn's Market, Lacey kept a light grip on the buggy handle, pushing it lazily down an aisle. Tangy citrus wafted from the produce section, where a teenager was offering samples of freshly squeezed lemonade. Residents shopped with purpose, but tourists took more time finding what they wanted, not knowing the layout of the store. Frank Lunn told Jake he sold more to vacationers since they shopped on impulse. It made enough sense for her to adopt it as part of her disguise. She tossed a bag of marshmallows into her buggy, along with a chocolate bar and graham crackers. That looked like vacation fare.

At the butcher's counter, although the pork chops looked tempting, she selected two thick steaks. Glen Tabor had outfitted each of the cottages on Cottage Row with barbecue grills, so her choice added to her camouflage. And steaks called for corn on the cob, so she headed toward the produce bins. She shucked the corn, tossing the husks and silk into a trashcan provided for that purpose. That was nice of Frank to do that for shoppers.

Soft music played in the background—an oldies station with tunes that inspired her to wander. She perused the lettuce and decided to add a salad to their dinner. Maybe she'd buy some popsicles since kids liked those and most of the tourists had families with them.

"Lacey?"

As she looked up, a woman's hand pulled off her dark glasses. The giant diamond came close to Lacey's eye. She flinched.

"I thought that was you. My, my, you're so pretty." The strawberry blonde searched every inch of her face. "You must be so pleased."

Frozen in place, Lacey's mind whirled. Who was this woman? She'd seen her before but didn't know her. But she sure was pushy and flat-out rude.

Lacey held out her hand. "May I have my glasses back?"

The woman shrugged and laid them in her palm. "Why are you hiding behind them? I'd think you'd want to flaunt that face."

Flaunt it? She didn't want it in the first place. Before she could stop her, the strawberry blonde touched her cheekbone, pushing with two fingers. "Wow, it doesn't feel stiff or wooden."

"What?" Lacey jerked away.

"Well, you had plastic surgery. I've never known anyone who's had it, well, not personally. I thought it would feel like plastic."

"Who are you?"

"You don't remember? You're not trying to claim amnesia, are you? That won't fly, you know."

"Should I? Remember, I mean."

She heaved a dramatic sigh.

Trixie. She'd been given a walk-on part and had no idea of subtlety on stage. Apparently, not in real life either. She was also from the insurance company.

"I remember you now. Has going to the grocery store suddenly become a crime?" Lacey whirled, left her grocery buggy and its contents in the aisle, and ran out of Lunn's.

"She touched my cheek like I was ... was something she considered buying." Lacey shuddered and buried her face in Jake's shoulder. She'd run to his office in The Rib Cage and flung herself into his arms.

Jake tightened his hold. "Felix warned me about her. What I can't understand is why they gave her a part in the play."

Lacey drew a stuttering breath and wiped her eyes. "Claire said it's better to keep your enemy in sight. That and Trixie has always wanted to act."

"So, make her obligated and she won't betray you." Jake's mouth quirked into a half grin. "Not a bad idea."

"But she did and she watches me all the time too. I'm sick of being stared at. I wish ..." Lacey wilted against his chest. "I wish I could turn back the clock and take a big step sideways so the light hit the floor."

He ran his hand over her head, smoothing her hair. "But we can't, so we go forward. I think we need to get away for a couple of days. I'll tell my managers, and we'll go over to Enota Retreat. Would you like that?"

He always knew. Even before she did. "It's exactly what I need. Go where no one knows me."

It didn't take long for Jake to make arrangements with his managers and for her to throw some shorts and T-shirts into a suitcase for them. Her shoulders lost their tightness as soon as they drove out of Chapel Springs. That was sad. She loved this little town. Trees passed in a blur as she gazed out the window. She glanced at Jake, but his concentration was on navigating a tight curve. Her fears weren't fair to him. She really needed to pull up her big-girl panties, as Claire would say. The problem with that was she didn't know how. Years of fear led to her shyness.

"Why do you suppose I get so tongue-tied when people talk to me?"

Jake glanced at her for a heartbeat, then turned his attention back to the road. "I've thought about that. I think when Lydia married, and you were left alone with your aunt and uncle, there wasn't anyone to talk with. The house was a silent one, and farm animals don't make good conversationalists."

She smiled and leaned back against the headrest. "If I spoke out loud, it sounded scary in all that silence. Maybe you're right." But there was more. Something else that made her fearful of being noticed. As much as she tried to think of what that was, she hadn't found the answer. Maybe she should talk to Lydia about it. She might remember something from their childhood. She'd give anything to not be so timid.

When they arrived at Enota, they quickly settled into their cabin, and a few minutes later, they set out for the waterfall. Hiking to the falls released any stress that still clung to Lacey. It always erased her cares. They'd discovered the mountain retreat quite by accident while on one of those one-hundred-mile-yard-sale weekends. They returned whenever they needed a quick getaway.

Lacey followed Jake up the trail. When they reached the falls, she chose their favorite flat rock to sit on and watched the cascading water. Another couple rested on a smaller boulder a few feet away. The brunette smiled at Lacey but then didn't pay any undue attention to her. She was just another face—a normal one. What would it be like to live like that?

She turned her eyes back on the water, listening as it thundered over the falls. It drowned out the voices that usually haunted her. Her eyelids grew heavy, and she closed her eyes. A memory rose to the surface from her subconscious. The water cascading over the falls became pounding rain. Lacey opened her eyes and glanced at Jake, but his were closed. She let him relax while she unpacked the memory.

A storm had moved in fast that afternoon. Lightning struck close to where the big kids played. She had followed them, hoping to be included in their game, but they wouldn't let a five-year-old play. When the storm hit, they scattered, looking for shelter. Rain turned to hail and hurt as it pelted her. The big kids had disappeared—to where she didn't know, but this kind of storm meant tornado. The church across the street. She ran and yanked open the door. A tall, frowning man told her she couldn't stay, she wasn't clean, and he pushed her out. As lightning struck all around her, she ran for home. When she arrived, she threw herself into her uncle's arms.

Lacey began to shake. A whimper escaped her lips as the rest of the memory rose. One she'd completely forgotten.

Jake sat up and reached for her. "Tell me, sweet stuff. What is it?"

"I remember what happened. I've told you about the storm when I was a kid and how they threw me out of the church. What I hadn't remembered was what happened when I got home." She shuddered. "I ran to Uncle Troy, thinking he would keep me safe. Instead ... instead ... he ..."

Jake held her tight.

She took a breath. "He touched where he shouldn't have. I felt dirty and violated. For the first time ever, he tried to talk. I couldn't understand the guttural sounds, and he frightened me. He turned angry and threw me on the bed. As he pulled his belt out, I thought I was going to get a spanking. What he had in mind was worse. Thankfully, Aunt Sylvia came in to put away the laundry and caught him."

Jake tightened his arms. "Shh, you don't have to say anymore. Was it after that when he started staring at you so much?"

"Yes. I was terrified of him, but I didn't really know why. Just that he was bad. I guess the trauma of their anger and my fear made me block it. As I grew up, Auntie made sure I was never alone with him, but I knew she resented me. I'm sure now that was the reason for her resentment, more than having to raise me."

"I think forgetting and your aunt were God's protection."

She pulled out of his arms. "Why did He let it happen to begin with?"

"We all suffer evil in this world, Lacey. It's part of the fall from grace. But God promised to always be with us and help us through it."

Jake leaned back and closed his eyes. She knew he was praying for her. He did that a lot. He loved God. She never could understand that. Her image of God was so different from his. She believed in God, but not the same one Jake did. The God she knew was an angry one, one that played favorites and didn't answer her prayers.

What about Jake?

Lacey glanced at her husband. Was he a prayer that God answered? She hadn't realized she prayed for a husband. He just found her at school.

I knew what you needed when I formed you in your mother's womb.

Jake was exactly what she needed. He loved her no matter what she looked like. He loved the real her. The inside of her.

And I love you with an everlasting love. I will never leave you nor forsake you.

A fissure opened in her heart, releasing her fears. And she knew it was true—God loved her. Did anything else matter? She laid back and stared at the sky. Knowing that was such a new feeling, she wasn't sure what to do with it.

Her heart whispered, "Thank You," and a still small voice inside told her God heard.

Back in the cabin, Lacey stretched out in front of the fireplace. Jake lay beside her. He rose on one elbow and smiled. She reached up and brushed his hair off his forehead, her heart full of love for this man. He leaned down and kissed her.

"What's going on in that sweet head of yours?"

She loved how he never said "pretty" but always "sweet." Even before the accident. "This getaway was inspired."

"Why's that?"

Lacey locked her gaze with his, searching. "I realized when I was a little older that when Uncle Troy stared at me the way he did, I panicked and was unable to breathe. I felt if I wasn't good enough for God to protect, then who could I ever turn to?"

Jake took her hands. "Sweet stuff, you realize the fallacy in that way of thinking, don't you?"

"I do, but I hadn't actually connected the two until now. Somehow, the attention and the storm and what Uncle Troy did all turned into the same thing. Attention was something to be feared. I believed if I was quiet, I became invisible."

The fissure opened wider. The time had come to make peace with the change. Lacey rose and went into the bathroom. She'd lost the plain face she was born with, and in its place was one that was pretty. What made it that way? She examined her reflection, turning her head to the left and then to the right. Her cheekbones were higher, her nose smaller. It did fit her face better. Maybe she'd gotten used to it, but it was okay.

She walked back to the front room and sat beside her husband. "I think God gave me you to show me what He's like. You've loved me from the start and never put any conditions on your love." She leaned closer, snuggling against him. Then she kissed him.

When she broke the kiss, Jake looked deep into her eyes for a long moment. "I think I just got my wife back."

She couldn't help but smile. He looked so happy. "I think I'd still like to go see that psychologist to make sure I'm okay. You'll come with me, won't you?"

"I'd go to the bottom of the ocean with you. I'd go to the moon with you. I'd go to the—"

She tossed a pillow at him. "The psychologist will be enough."

Chapter 32

Claire threw the covers off as soon as Joel closed the front door. He was fishing this morning with Nathan, and they wanted to get to Henderson Island before the sun rose. She grabbed her robe and headed to the computer. She'd tried the library the other day, but once again, kids had claimed all the computers. She'd been foiled at every turn.

Armed with coffee, she pushed the power button. Once the Internet came up, she went to an online pharmacy, found the pregnancy tests, and ordered two. She filled in all her shipping address information, choosing the gallery. No one there would bother about it. And if they did, well, she'd figure out what to say then. She completed the billing information, gave them her credit card, then clicked Complete Order.

A new window came up. She squinted at the screen. Were they nuts? They wanted her to tell all her friends on Facebook she ordered her pregnancy test from their company? No way. She closed the page.

Wait. She forgot to print her receipt. After reopening the site, she searched for her order but couldn't find it. Oh, for the love of Van Gogh. It didn't even save her login information. She had to start all over again. This time, when it asked her to post to Facebook, she closed the window, not the whole page. Now she clicked Place Order. What? They wanted her to tell her friends on Twitter? But she wasn't on Twitter. This was ridiculous. She blew a strand of hair out of her eyes.

Another new window popped open. Why was it thanking her? Oh no! She didn't post that to Facebook, did she? Or one of the kids' tweeter things? Her heart raced. How could she check? And if she did, what could she do about it? Lord, have mercy!

History. Megan showed her how to erase the history. She searched in the settings. Where's the history thingy in the settings? Her hands shook. Wait. Megan said *Internet* history. Claire brought back up the browser. There it was right in front of her eyes. She clicked, then it wanted to know how much history. How was she supposed to know that? What were her options? Today. Today and yesterday. All history. What were cookies? Who did this stuff for the gallery's computer? The worst part was she couldn't ask anyone without being questioned.

She clicked all. The computer started having convulsions or something. A timer turned over, spilling its sand into the other side. Did that mean—the computer blinked and went black. Uh-oh. What had she done to it? Was this what they called a crash? Or had she told the world about buying a pregnancy test? She groaned and pushed the power key. Nothing.

"Forget it, Shiloh. I'm not waiting to find out. I'm going to Dee's 'n' Doughs. Wrangling this computer made me hungry. And yes, I'll bring you a cookie." Silly dog knew Dee's name meant cookies.

"Morning, Dee. I'll take a ... a blueberry bagel today. With strawberry cream cheese. And coffee."

"I'm glad to see your stomach is better." Dee handed her a paper plate and a coffee mug.

Claire stared at her. Her tummy *was* better. What did that mean? That she was further along than she thought? Or she wasn't pregnant and had actually had a stomach bug?

Claire grimaced. "Huh, thanks." She took the bagel and cream cheese, filled the mug from the selection on the bar, and headed to her favorite table.

She hooked her foot around the chair leg and pulled it out while she set her plate and mug down. With a sigh, she lowered herself into the chair. What was going on with her body? She stuck her knife into the cream cheese, slathered her bagel, and took a bite. Oh, heavenly. Wouldn't it be wonderful if heaven were paved in cream cheese?

What in the name of Van Gogh was Tillie Payne doing carrying a shovel down Sandy Shores Drive? She thought Esther had talked her out of this gold hunting. Claire jumped up and ran outside. Tillie went straight into The Tome Tomb. Oh dear. Was she going to start digging beneath the bookstore? A lot of strange things were happening in

Chapel Springs lately. The woods being dug up, Tillie jackhammering her basement, Esther digging up her crawl space. Gold fever was highly contagious.

She shook her head and turned back into the bakery. She needed more caffeine. Halfway through her second cup, Dee joined her, and then Patsy arrived, dropping her sketchpad on the table. Dee poured a cup of coffee for her.

"Have we decided when we are holding the fundraiser for Lacey?" Patsy asked.

Claire pinched off a piece of bagel. "Opening night. That's usually the best attended."

The bells on the door jingled as a new customer entered. Dee rose. "Have you told Jake yet?"

"Yes. He was touched and very relieved." Claire waved at Hazel, who waved back on her way to the pastry counter. Dee went to wait on her.

"Claire, what's wrong?" Patsy's question came from the west side of nowhere.

"Uh, what do you mean?"

"Don't put me off, girlfriend. You haven't been yourself for a while now. You're forgetful, and your mind is always off somewhere else. You're almost acting like you did when you were preg—" Patsy's eyes grew wide and her mouth dropped open. "You're not—are you?"

The jig was up. Claire blew out the breath she'd been semi-holding for the last two months. "I don't know. I finally ordered a home test online. At least I hope I managed to order it. What a fiasco."

"I don't know why I didn't put two and two together before this." Patsy frowned. "But why didn't you go to the drug store and buy one?"

"Really? You have to ask that? Why do you think?"

"Oh. Right. Well, there's Pineridge."

"Let me tell you about Pineridge."

By the time Claire finished, Patsy was wiping her eyes from laughing. "I'm sorry. It isn't funny, but oh my goodness. The condom aisle?"

"Yeah. And, of course, I had to keep Trixie quiet. Anyway, I'm waiting for the test to arrive. Patsy, what am I going to do if I am pregnant?"

Patsy's eyes grew soft. "You know I'll help you."

"Right. That will be two of us holding canes while pushing a pram."

"Oh, stop. It isn't that bad. Why, Nathan's mom was forty-nine when he was born."

Claire hadn't heard that before. "She was?" She never seemed that old when Claire was a kid. Maybe she could do this. Right. Like she had a choice. She *did* have a choice. No, she didn't. She couldn't. She'd never be able to live with herself if she did that.

"Yes. By the time we married, she was seventy, but she still had a young attitude."

"Well, I'm still holding out for it not to be true." But if it weren't, what was wrong with her?

"When is your test arriving?"

"If I managed to actually order it, tomorrow. I paid for overnight delivery." They wouldn't put that on Facebook too, would they? "Oooooooh, please no."

Patsy put her hand on Claire's arm. "What's wrong?"

"I'm hoping I didn't click the wrong thing and announce to Facebook and the world what I was buying from that online pharmacy."

Patsy had the audacity to laugh. She clapped her hand over her mouth. "I'm sorry, Claire, but you manage to order our supplies online from the gallery's computer. I don't understand how you can be so inept—I take that back. I can understand in this case. Nerves and frustration don't help when navigating the Internet."

"Ya think?"

"Tell you what." Patsy pulled out her cell phone. "Let's make sure." She tapped a few times and turned her phone for Claire to see. "You're safe. Not a mention of buying anything online or anywhere else for that matter."

Thank You, Lord. "That's a huge relief. More for the twins than me. Everyone would think it was for one of them, and they'd be mortified. Oh no!"

"What's wrong now?"

"What will the kids think if I *am* pregnant? They'll be so embarrassed."

"No way, Claire. The kids will welcome the new baby."

"What new baby?" Dee pulled her chair out and rejoined them.

Yikes! Had Dee heard anything before that? "Any new baby in our family is welcome." Claire tried to smile. "I can't wait to see our Wes become a daddy. He is so good with Micah and Aela."

"Oh, is Costy expecting?"

"No, not that we know of, anyway. I was, uh, thinking ahead."

Kelly entered the bakery along with Carin and JoAnn. Thank goodness. Now, maybe the talk could turn to the theater.

"Kelly, how are rehearsals going? Since we finished painting the set,

I haven't seen or heard anything."

"They're going great. Ellie and Eileen may have a long-time commitment here. They are brilliant in their roles. Your Joel is perfect for his part too. I always suspected he could act."

"I've wondered about that. What made you think he could?" She thought her Joel could do anything, but then she loved him. What had Kelly seen that made her ask him? Claire poured another cup of coffee from the pot Dee left on the table for them.

"He's animated when he expresses himself."

Her Joel? "Why haven't I seen that?"

Kelly snickered. "A spouse is always the last one to notice it. And most men aren't animated around home. That's where you relax and let down."

"I guess. So, you're really okay with giving up the ticket money to Lacey and Jake on opening night?"

"Why wouldn't I be? We'd do it for any member."

"Speaking of any member, look who's here." Patsy pointed to the door, where Lydia and Lacey stepped inside. Lydia waved, then her sister grinned and waved.

Lacey grinned? Claire stared at Patsy. "I can't believe what my eyes just saw? Can you?"

Patsy shook her head. "I ... I don't know what to think of that. She normally ducks her head. Could it be ...?"

Something was definitely different. Lacey stood tall instead of hunched over. And her smile was open and friendly. Lydia arrived at the table first.

With a glance over her shoulder to see if Lacey was close, Claire pounced. "Lydia, what happened?"

"A miracle, that's what. Shh."

Lacey pulled a chair out and joined them. She settled in and then gave them the most glorious smile and a small shrug. "I've been set free." Then she picked up her coffee cup and took a sip.

And? "Don't stop there, girlfriend. What happened? Ouch! Doggone it, Patsy." Claire rubbed her kicked ankle. "My question wasn't tacky."

"No, but your timing is suspect. You might let Lacey tell us what and when she wants. And *if* she wants."

Lacey's soft laughter took the sting out of Patsy's rebuke. Still, Claire wrinkled her nose at her BFF.

Lacey folded her hands and rested her chin on them. "Jake took me to Enota Retreat over the weekend. I finally remembered what happened to me as a child that made me so afraid of being noticed." She lowered her hands to her lap. "I ... I also discovered the depth of God's love for me and what that means. I feel like I've been let out of prison."

Claire picked up her napkin and dabbed her eyes. She wasn't the only one by the looks of it. Swallowing the lump in her throat, she picked up her cup. Coffee might help.

"Lacey, I wasn't sure that was you. How are you?" A redhead stopped by the table. Her face was familiar. Where did Claire know her from?

"Hey, Ashley. I'm fine. You?"

Lacey's formality was strange, after her revelation. Why? Oh, right. Red worked at the bank. She was a teller, a rather self-obsessed girl if Claire remembered right. Wasn't she the one who was so rude to Lacey? This should be interesting.

"I'm fine as frog's hair split in two. *I* got your old job."

"Did you? That's nice." Lacey dipped her chin and stared at her plate.

She wasn't regretting leaving the bank, was she? Claire's eyes ping-ponged between the two.

"Sure did. Do you have any tips for me?"

Ooh, Red was a bold little tart. Claire glanced at Patsy, who pressed her lips tightly into a thin line. Claire cleared her throat to cover her laugh. Her BFF clearly was not impressed.

"Nothing in particular. Just use your head and be discreet." Lacey raised her chin and looked Red straight in the eye. "Remember, these are people you're dealing with, not anonymous applicants. They're neighbors—honest, ethical, and hardworking. If you keep that in mind, you'll make wise decisions."

Red wasn't expecting that. She blinked and stared at Lacey. "Uh, thanks." She walked away without another word.

Lacey watched her go.

"I'll bet she makes the bank a pleasant place to work." Claire slid her legs to the side and wagged a finger at Patsy. "Ha. Moved before you could get me."

Lacey turned back to the table. "She didn't even know I existed until I returned after the accident. Then she saw me as competition. Why, I don't know. I never even spoke to the men. And I'm married. Doesn't that exclude me from competition?"

Claire snorted. "Not in some women's minds. But why they're so ugly about it, I can't figure out."

Patsy patted her hand. "That's because you love everyone, Claire. You're confident and sure of yourself."

She was? "I am? I don't feel sure of myself." Then again, maybe she did, or rather she was sure of the One in whom she placed her confidence.

Chapter 33

"Claire, there's a package here for you. It's from Amazon. Since when do you buy stuff on Amazon?" Nicole's voice carried into the workroom.

Claire's stomach flipped. Patsy's head popped out from behind her easel, locking eyes with her. The test. She leaped up and hurried to the gallery.

"Thanks." She took the package and retreated to the back with as much nonchalance as she could manage.

"Okay, girlfriend, it's here." Claire ripped open the box.

"Well, go use one."

"Now?" Here?

"Why not? You're anxious to know."

She wasn't so sure she was. Yes, she was. Claire grabbed both boxes and slipped into the bathroom. Good thing she drank two cups of coffee this morning. After choosing which box to open, she pulled out the directions and read them.

"Uh, Patsy?" Claire called through the closed door.

"You okay in there?"

"Do you have any hints on how to go about this without … uh, well you know, peeing on my hand? Hey, quit laughing. This is—" A giggle snerked out her nose. She corralled it. "This is serious. I can't find out any results if I can't aim. What do I do?"

"I never used one. And I'm not a grandmother. You are. Call Sandi. Oh. No, you can't do that. Well, my friend, you're on your own on this one. I'm not coming in and holding it for you." At that, Patsy erupted into uncontrolled laughter.

"Humph. Some help you are." Claire stared at the stick. Finally, she positioned it carefully and proceeded to do what she came in to do. Then she checked her watch.

Patsy knocked on the door. At least Claire hoped it was Patsy. "Yes?"

"Did you manage it?"

"Yes. Now I'm waiting." A couple of minutes later, Claire stared at the test stick. The line was a blue minus sign. She checked the instructions sheet again. A plus sign meant pregnant and the minus was negative. She wasn't pregnant. Her arms went limp. *Thank goodness.* It would be so embarrassing to have her grandchildren older than her youngest child. Of course, Joel would have liked all the backslapping for still being so studly. She snorted.

But what if it was wrong? She'd heard stories. She grabbed the other box and managed to do another test.

"What are you doing in there?"

"Making sure the first one was right." Drumming her fingers on the box, she waited. Then the answer appeared, faded at first, then clear.

Oh no. What did two pink lines mean? Her breaths came fast. Did that mean twins? She grabbed the box out of the wastebasket. Oh. She sat down on the lid of the commode. One line was positive and two lines were negative—not twins.

Negative! Relief made her knees weak for a moment. Then she whistled "Zip-a-Dee-Doo-Dah" and exited the bathroom. Okay, she missed a few notes, but who cared? All was well in her world.

Patsy stood waiting beside her easel. "I gather that means negative."

Claire did a victory dance. Wait. Her feet stopped mid-step. If she wasn't pregnant, something else was wrong with her. Visions of her twin sister, wasted with cancer, rose. Her hands started shaking.

"Claire? What is it, honey?"

She stared at her best friend. "If ..." Her voice came out in a strangled whisper. "If I'm not pregnant, then what's wrong?"

Patsy's thoughts must have gone to CeeCee too, because fear filled her eyes. Like a robot, Claire pulled out her phone, and keeping her eyes on her best friend for grounding, she called her gynecologist.

"Hey, Elaine. I need an appointment with Dr. Anderson."

"It's not time for your annual checkup, Claire. What's wrong?"

"Uh ..." She didn't know what to say. "Nothing I can pinpoint, but I think I'd best see Dr. Anderson or Dr. Jordan." Claire could hear Elaine tapping the keys on her keyboard. She turned from Patsy, who was tapping her on the shoulder.

"I can get you in on Tuesday, July nineteenth, at eleven forty-five."

Two and a half months? If it were cancer, it might gallop all through her by then. "There's nothing sooner?"

"Not unless it's an emergency, Claire. Is it?"

Yes. "No. I don't think so." *Yes, I do.* "I'll keep the July one. But please, if you get a cancellation, call me. I'll take any day, any time."

"Are you sure you're all right?"

No. Mom died of cervical cancer and so did CeeCee. Claire had always been proactive about her exams, and so far nothing had ever shown up. Had her luck run out? She inhaled, hoping she drew in some fortitude with the air.

"Yes, I'm sure. See you then." *If I live that long.*

Patsy wrapped her arms around Claire. "Let's not jump to conclusions. Let's wait. And pray. God's got this, honey."

Right. Where was her faith? She searched Patsy's eyes. Her BFF was afraid. But she was trusting God. Claire could do no less. *Hold me, Lord.*

"What will I do about Joel? He's no pushover." Especially this new Joel. Claire hung her head and shook it slowly. In the revival of her marriage, she never took into consideration what would happen when Joel asked how she felt. "I'll never be able to hide this from him if he asks. How can I avoid him for the next ten weeks?"

"Tell him, Claire. He's your other half, and wouldn't you want to know if your roles were reversed?"

She would. "I'll tell him. Tonight."

"Claire, where do you keep your eyebrow pencils?" Joel stood in the kitchen doorway. She paused her knife. Tonight was her night to fix supper, which consisted of a salad with meat left over from last night.

"In my makeup drawer. Why?"

"Kelly wants to do a makeup check tonight."

"Don't they usually save that for dress rehearsal?"

"I don't know." He turned and left the kitchen.

Huh. Joel putting on makeup for any reason would be about as far off type as one cou—makeup drawer! She'd slipped that envelope in there. The envelope with the names of the pregnancy tes—

"Claire? What's this?" Joel was back in the doorway again. This time, he held a used envelope in his hand and wore a bumfuzzled expression.

She set down the knife. "Uh, well, it's something I need to talk to you about."

His eyes narrowed. "One of the twins isn't ...?"

"No. It's not theirs."

He cocked his head to the right. "Then whose?"

Her stomach flip-flopped. *It's now or never.* Come to think of it, never would be nice. She glanced up at him. But he'd changed so much in the past year, it wouldn't be fair to leave him out. Maybe he'd think it was funny. Would he?

"Honey?"

"It's mine."

"Yours?" Now his head cocked to the left.

She set the knife down and wiped her hands. "Come sit down a minute."

Understanding dawned on his face. "You're ...?" His eyebrows rose and with them, the corners of his mouth.

She'd been right. He thought it would be great. After sitting beside him at the banquette, she shook her head. "No, I'm not. I finally took the test and I'm not."

His shoulders slumped a bit. "Were you relieved?"

"What do you think? We'd have grandchildren older than our youngest child. Think about that."

Joel chuckled a bit. "Yeah, I guess. So what made you think you were pregnant?"

Take a deep breath and let it out slowly. "I'm two months late. I started trying to get a test over three weeks ago." She went on to tell him the whole story about getting the tests. At least she could get him laughing before delivering the punch line. As she expected, he cracked up and plucked a napkin from the holder to mop his eyes.

"I can see it, all right. You standing in front of the condoms?" He hooted and howled all over again. "Hard candies?" He cracked up again.

"It wasn't *that* funny. I was embarrassed." She couldn't help a smile, though.

Joel settled down. "I know, babe. But you have to admit you do keep life hopping."

"To your enjoyment." She gave him as cheeky a grin as she could muster.

Before she could tell him the rest, his face drained of color. Something clicked in that brain of his. "Claire? You said you're late, though. Did you call the doctor to find out why?"

"I did, but they can't see me for ten weeks."

"What? With your family history, they let you wait?"

"I didn't want to tell them I thought I was pregnant."

"Whoa, whoa. Wait a minute. Back up. You said you took the test and you aren't. When did you call the doctor?"

"Right after I knew the test results."

"And you didn't tell them it was an emergency? Honey, what were you thinking?"

"Uh, I wasn't. I mean, I don't know. Maybe subconsciously, I don't want to know?" She laid her head on his shoulder, and he put his arm around her and held her close.

"We're not letting this lie for ten weeks. I'm calling Doc."

"But what about Dr. Anderson?"

"She should have pushed to get you in now." Joel sat up and pulled out his cell phone. He tapped in Doc's speed dial number. "Doc, Joel. Hey. Claire is two months late, and she took a test that says she isn't pregnant. Yes. Two of them. I want her seen by you. Now. Now? Well, sure. We'll be right there. Thanks." He clicked off, and some of the color returned to his face. "We're going to Doc's now."

"Without your supper?"

"I can eat anytime, but I want to be sure it's with you—not alone." He took her hand, and they walked to Doc's office behind Patsy's house. Doc met them at the door. Why was it every doctor's office—no matter where—smelled like antiseptic? Of course, they had to keep things sterile, but couldn't they use something that smelled better?

"I'm having trouble with Francine Anderson not seeing you right away." He turned and started toward his office.

Claire reached out and caught his arm. "To be fair, I said it wasn't an emergency."

Doc stopped and glared at her. "Not an emergency? With your family history?"

Exactly what Joel said, and said as if she were a five-year-old again, caught with her hand inside his doctor bag. He'd shouted at her and Patsy then, and he came close to shouting at her now. "I know. I'm scared."

"Well, you should be. No, you shouldn't." Doc held her close. He'd always been like a second father to her. "Come on. I want to get some blood and run some tests. We'll start there."

"What kind of tests?" Joel followed them into the exam room.

"First, I'm going to do a complete blood count, and with it a CA-125 screening." He wrapped a rubber strap around her upper arm. "Make a fist." After tapping the veins on the inside of her elbow, he picked up the syringe. Claire shifted her eyes to Joel until Doc had all the blood he needed. There were several vials.

"Did you leave me any?"

Doc chuckled. "Enough." He slipped a cotton ball in the crook of her arm and bent it upward. "Hold there for a minute." When he finished labeling the vials and put a bandage on her arm, he motioned them into his office.

"I'm calling Dr. Anderson and scheduling you for an immediate pap smear and a transvaginal ultrasound. If those and the blood tests are negative, then most likely we're looking at menopause. Have you experienced any hot flashes or night sweats?"

She was too young for menopause. "I don't think so." Claire glanced at Joel. "Have you noticed any?"

"Nope."

Doc went through a list of symptoms, but she hadn't experienced any of them. Her stomach flipped back on its earlier flop. "Is that good? Or bad?" Her voice shook.

"It isn't good or bad, Claire. It may simply be a case of 'that's you.' Every woman experiences menopause differently. Let's get these tests done and see what we're dealing with. If it's cervical cancer and we've caught it early, which should be the case, there's every reason to believe you'll beat it. You've always been proactive about getting your checkups." With that, he picked up the phone and called her gynecologist.

Claire was going to have to take the receptionist, Elaine, a peace offering since she told her it wasn't an emergency. When he hung up, he handed Claire a slip of paper with a time on it.

"What day is this?"

"Tomorrow."

Chapter 34

Lacey's fingers flew over her keyboard. That creepy character she'd developed to get out her angst was so psychotic she'd be a wonderful foil for Alexa. It also stretched Lacey as a writer. Carin said that was important. "Always keep growing," she'd said. So far, Lacey's plays had been what they called cozy mysteries. But this one moved a step further. She'd added the psycho factor.

She read over what she'd just written. The scene revealed Alexa's quirky humor while examining a dead body. If it made even her shiver, audiences should love it. She stretched the kinks out of her back. Lights shone through the front window, and Jake's car pulled into the driveway. Eight thirty. Why was he home so early?

Closing her laptop, she went to meet Jake at the door. "Hey, how come you're home so early?"

He held up an airline folder.

He hadn't said anything about a trip. "Are you going somewhere?"

"*We* are. New York. It's all planned and booked. We leave in the morning. We have tickets to a Broadway show tomorrow night and an off-Broadway one the next night."

She threw her arms around his neck and squeezed. At the same time, she squealed. Then she drew back and grabbed the folder. "What are we going to see?"

"*Jersey Boys* on Broadway at the August Wilson Theatre and *The Fantasticks* off-Broadway at The Snapple Theater Center. It's a whirlwind trip, but I want you to get a feel for New York." He pulled the tickets from his jacket pocket. "And we're staying at the Muse Hotel."

"The Muse? Really? That's funny."

Jake wrapped her in his arms. "I want the best for you, and I thought the name was pretty funny, considering. Then I found out it's an upscale hotel. Sweet stuff, you're on your way."

Lacey leaned back and eyed him. Did he really think she was good enough to have a play performed up there? Honestly? Or was it only because he loved her? Probably the latter, but right now that didn't matter. She was going to see a play on Broadway. And one off-Broadway.

Lacey took Jake's hand as they stepped off the plane and into the Jetway. Stale hot air greeted them until they exited the tunnel. They hurried through the airport and went straight outside to the longest line of waiting taxicabs she'd ever seen. Jake hailed one like a pro.

"Short visit, bud?" the cabbie asked Jake as he stowed their single bag in the trunk.

"Just taking in a couple of shows."

"We have the best. Where're ya staying?"

"The Muse."

The cabbie didn't blink an eye but nodded and closed their door. He shot into traffic. Lacey craned her neck to see everything. How did anyone drive in this craziness?

"First time in New York?"

"How'd you guess?" Jake took her hand in his.

"By the little lady's reaction to the traffic."

Jake didn't seem bothered by it, so she relaxed. "Does everyone drive in this?"

"Naw. Most New Yorkers take the subway or cabs. Lots don't even own cars."

Then most of them were used to this wild traffic. If she and Jake came here often—

Horns blared, tires screeched, and the cab swerved. The cabby shook his fist out the window and shouted a curse on the other driver's firstborn.

Lacey gasped.

"Sorry about that, ma'am. He shouldn'ta oughta be stopping there."

She smothered a giggle and shared a grin with Jake.

The cabbie kept up a running monologue of the places of interest they passed. Flushing Meadows where the US Open Tennis Championships were played, then they crossed under a river and came out in Manhattan. She wasn't sure about that tunnel. If it sprung a leak, they could all drown under there. She shivered.

"Look," Jake whispered. "That's Park Avenue. Looks a lot different than the Park Avenue in Chapel Springs, doesn't it?"

About as different as chalk and cheese.

"We're coming up on Times Square. Your hotel is half a block from there and smack in the center of the theater district." He pulled up to the hotel front entrance, and a valet jumped to their assistance. The cabbie handed Jake their bag. "You and the pretty lady have a good time here." He smiled at the tip Jake palmed him.

Inside, the lobby was opulent. The air bore a barest hint of citrus. Lacey slid behind Jake as they approached check-in. All around her, everything shouted, "Money, money, money!" She glanced down at her slacks. When she raised her eyes, the desk clerk smiled with frank amusement.

She leaned closer to Lacey and whispered, "You're fine. Most of these people are here to impress someone. You enjoy your visit. Forget everyone but your husband."

Lacey planned to do that. Jake squeezed her hand, picked up the key the clerk laid on the counter, and they headed up to their room. There were four people in the elevator, but no one paid them any attention. No one said, "Hello." Not even an "Up your nose." Frankly, it was weird. By the eighth floor, the others had exited and she could breathe again.

In the room, they quickly unpacked and hung up their clothes.

Jake pulled out the map the concierge had given him. "What do you want to see first?"

"I'd like to walk past some of the theaters, then see Times Square. Oh, and then Central Park."

"Do you want to take in the Empire State Building?" Jake changed his T-shirt for a collared golf shirt.

"Not really. I mean, maybe sometime, but not today." She went into the bathroom to freshen up and brush her hair. She applied a bit of the special makeup to the scars on the side of her nose. They were fading, but they hadn't disappeared completely yet.

When she came out, Jake was by the door, ready to leave. The elevator ride down was a repeat of the earlier one, with a few more people. Someone stepped on her toe and said, "Sorry," without even turning around to see on whose toes they'd trod. In Chapel Springs, she'd have received a profuse apology and a hug. Didn't anyone here take time to see other people?

Out on the sidewalk, the spring weather was beautiful, although with all the traffic, instead of blossoms, the air smelled of exhaust fumes. They strolled hand in hand. The map Jake held showed forty theaters within walking distance of their hotel. It made her giddy. The theaters she especially wanted to see were the Neil Simon and the Eugene O'Neill. The Neil Simon Theatre was on West Fifty-Second Street across from the August Wilson Theatre, where they would see *Jersey Boys* tonight. She could wait on that one.

Jake held her hand as they walked to Seventh Avenue and turned right. "Look to your left, sweet stuff. That's Times Square."

Lacey turned in a circle and took it all in. Too bad if she looked like a tourist. She *was* one and loving every minute. They cut over to Broadway and then turned left on West Forty-Ninth. She saw the theater sign with the playwright's name as soon as they turned the corner. As they approached the theater, Lacey stopped. She lifted her face to that iconic name on the marquee, soaking in all the Eugene O'Neill she could.

"An American legend."

The heavily accented voice came from behind Lacey. She couldn't decide if it held respect or something else. Turning, she faced a beautiful woman, not much younger than herself.

She smiled. "His works have been an inspiration to me."

The brunette held out her hand. "You are a playwright, then?"

Jake introduced them. "My wife's plays have been produced in Georgia, and she's been signed by an agent here in New York."

While she loved his pride in her, it still embarrassed her to have him tell people.

"That is wonderful. I am only an actress. In Madrid, not here. I am in awe of your ability to write plays for others to perform." She nodded, shook their hands, and slipped inside the theater.

Jake watched her until she disappeared. "I'm sure I've seen her picture somewhere." He slapped his hand against his thigh. "I have. In a movie magazine. That was O'Neill's granddaughter."

The plays had been eye opening for Lacey. She almost believed she was good enough for off-Broadway. It wouldn't take a lot to push her over into the belief column either. On Saturday, they explored restaurants.

The food was divine. They ate in three Jake had researched and met two of the chef-owners. One of them, to Jake's surprise, actually knew of Chapel Springs and had eaten in The Rib Cage. Chef sat at their table for a few minutes.

"I was impressed. What do you use for your dry rub? And how long do you leave the ribs in the smoker?"

She laughed when Jake turned several shades of red. They talked food for twenty minutes before the chef excused himself. When Jake tried to pay the bill, there wasn't one. He gave the waiter a hefty tip and left his card with a note that he'd like to return the favor, should Chef find himself in Chapel Springs again.

Saturday night's play, the off-Broadway one, was also a musical, and it set Lacey to thinking. What would one of her mysteries look like as a musical? She and Jake had laughed over that. Somehow, neither of them could envision Ellie or Eileen dancing. Next time they came, she'd like to see a non-musical to get an idea of how her plays would resonate with audiences up here.

Sunday morning, Lacey leaned back in her seat on the plane. It had been a whirlwind trip. New York City was wonderful. It seemed no one ever slept. Noise and lights were a twenty-four-hour thing, and energy flowed nonstop. It wore her out. She closed her eyes.

Jake's hand squeezed hers. "Feeling frazzled?"

"I don't know how people do that all the time." Her eyes popped open, and she rolled her head to see him. "I loved it, but I'll be glad to get home. Actually, I'm anxious to get home."

Her thinking shifted while they were in the City That Never Sleeps. People there didn't stare at her, but they didn't see her either. They looked through her or around her. Only two of those she'd interacted with saw her, O'Neill's granddaughter and the woman at the hotel desk when they'd checked in.

"We packed a lot into two days. Close your eyes and rest. We'll be in Charlotte soon enough."

Chapter 35

Xander opened the front door. Newlander. Just what he wanted with his morning coffee. He quickly peered up and down Cottage Row. Lucky for the hayseed, no one was about yet. He grabbed the man's arm and pulled him inside.

He sniffed the air. "Any more of that coffee?"

Xander ignored his question. He wasn't about to make this social. "I thought I told you not to come during the day."

"I figured you'd want to know this."

"What could be so important you would jeopardize people knowing we're in this together?"

Newlander shifted from his left foot to his right and back again. "Those three houses that were on the market have all suddenly come off. There's nothing for sale here."

"What happened?" Xander sat at the table and motioned for the redneck to sit too.

"A big town meeting the other night. I'm guessing they're trying to stop us." He snickered. "They can't do that. I bought us the mineral rights to three properties so far."

No jury in the world would convict him if he shot the dummy right now. "Three. Good, Howie. But have they sold their land to you?"

"No. They say they're not going to either."

"How are you going to persuade them?"

Howie brightened. "I can use force? Or fire?"

Xander closed his eyes. Three years. That would be the most he'd get, he was sure of it. "No. Get to the absentee landowners. Make *them* an offer they can't refuse. And meanwhile, find me a house to buy. It's imperative."

The hick was halfway out the door when he turned around. "Hey, you could buy my house."

"Your house?"

"Well, my granny's. It's down by the lake too. I'd make you a good price. I don't want to live there once we're done here."

And he was actually thinking about this, why? "By rights, you should give it to me,"—he held up his hand at the dimwit's protest—"but we need to keep our association as separate as we can. Go ahead and list it. Then let me know when it's up. I'll call the agent then. And you better not try to fleece me. I'll get an appraisal."

The people here stymied Xander. They acted all friendly and welcoming, as long as you were a tourist. They wanted his money well enough, but they seemed to keep him at a distance. Why? He rose. A trip to that bakery was in order. Maybe he'd overhear something. He perused the bookcase for a likely looking title to take with him.

Bookcase.

Books.

All the book people he'd ever met were chatty, not that he knew that many. His brother-in-law was. Dude could talk the balls off a Christmas tree. There were two bookstores in Chapel Springs. *And* a small library. No, not the library. He'd met the librarian. She was too shrewd. Some people, no matter how hard you tried, couldn't be charmed.

He'd go first to the one by the bait shop—The Happy Hooker. He shook his head and couldn't stop the grin that stretched his lips. What a name. When he came into town, he almost drove off the road when he first saw it. He wandered out his back door and turned right. In two minutes, the sign came into his view: Leave the World Behind. That's what this town had done. He pushed the door open.

"May I help you?" The voice's owner was tall and angular and as skinny as a hockey stick. Xander stood six-foot-two in his stocking feet, and this woman looked him in the eye.

"I'm new in town and ..." What would open her up? "I'd like a book on the history of Chapel Springs." Yeah, that sounded good.

"I thought I hadn't met you." She held out her hand. "Esther Tully. I'm new myself. Only been here a year."

Her handshake was strong, which surprised him for some reason. "How long before a person is no longer considered a newcomer?"

Her laughter was deep and booming. "A lifetime, I reckon. However, the people are friendly and welcoming if you live here."

He hadn't experienced that. Were they onto him?

"So, you want a book on our history. Follow me. We have three. One was written by one of the town's first settlers, Miss Cora Lee Rice. She's passed on now, but she came as a child with her parents." Esther tapped her temple with her forefinger. "She died at ninety-three and was sharp as a tack right up to the end. The other was written by Doc Benson's grandfather." She leaned close, a conspirator. "Some interesting contradictions between their renditions."

Xander perked up. *Easy, boy.* Don't arouse her suspicion. "Really? What kind?"

Esther beamed. "Several. But the one that raised a ruckus back in the seventies was over water rights." She stopped and bent down to reach a book on a low shelf.

"Water rights in the 1970s?"

"Eighteen-seventies. Old Celia Newlander's daddy and Doc's grandpappy tussled over naming the creek that fed the area for years."

Newlander? That was a bit of news he'd tuck away in case he could use it. "Who won?"

She handed him the book. "Chapter fifty-three. Now ..." She ran her finger along the spines of several books on the next shelf up from where she took the one he held. "Ah, here we are." The book almost launched itself into her hands.

What just happened?

"You saw it?"

He wasn't sure what he saw or if he really did. "Uh ..."

"Doesn't matter. Books are alive, y'know. Authors pour their souls into their work. A good book will breathe its life into a reader." She looked around. "When the right person comes along, the book will nearly leap off the shelf. I'm guessing this one is meant for you." She handed the slim green volume to him. "Go over there." She pointed to the coffee shop on the other side of the space. "Take a look. You can pay me when you've decided."

Xander settled in with a cup of coffee and two donuts. He opened the first book, but the second one kept distracting him. It was nuts. That Esther was a little wacky too. Still, that second book might have some interesting information for him. And it was by one of Newlander's grand-somebodies. That was a promising coincidence. He set down the first book, and the second one settled into his hands. It felt good.

Good grief, this place was rubbing off on him. Well, he came here to learn about the locals, and the book held some background information. Read it he would. He turned the first page.

When he turned the last page, he believed Esther. This book, or what was in it, unraveled several threads of his belief system. It kind of freaked him out. Was it because he'd met the descendants of this first Benson and Newlander? And why had this last Newlander gone against his ancestor's way of life?

A better question, what was Xander going to do?

Chapter 36

"Felix, get your backside over to our house fast. And call me as soon as you get this." Claire tapped the end icon on her phone. She paced the kitchen while Joel deglazed a pan. The aroma of orange marmalade in the glaze started her mouth watering. "You'd better put another chicken breast in there in case Felix gets my—" Her phone quacked. "That's Felix." She swiped the answer bar. "Can you come over now? We'll feed you. Good. See you in five. No, I'll tell you when you get here."

Joel poured the sauce into a dish he'd warmed and set it aside. He tossed three chicken breasts into the hot pan, adding butter and shaking it to keep them from sticking. "Now, what have you discovered?"

She hopped up onto the kitchen counter. "You know that new man who's staying at the cottages? The one who said he was buying a house here?"

"Yeah, I saw him in Dee's 'n' Doughs the other day. What about him?"

"He's the money man, and he's buying Howie's house."

Joel stopped shaking the pan. "What? Are you sure about this?"

The doorbell rang.

Claire pushed off the counter. "Hold that thought. That'll be Felix." She hurried to open the door. "Come on in. Dinner's almost ready, and I'll fill you in while we eat."

Felix rubbed his hands together. "I'll listen to you sing for one of Joel's meals."

She gave Felix the stink eye, then laughed. He probably would.

"Better be careful or she might. And thanks," Joel said as they stepped into the kitchen. "Grab a seat."

As soon as their meal was before them and Joel had said the blessing, the men dove in. Claire took a bite, then laid her fork down.

"Felix, that new fellow in town, Xander Barlow, is not a tourist. He's Howie's money man."

Felix gaped. Thank goodness he'd swallowed already. "How'd you come up with that?"

"I don't know why, but from the first day I met him, I didn't trust him. Maybe because he and Howie both showed up around the same time. Xander isn't a fisherman or a sunbather. So I asked Nathan to have his P.I. look into it." Claire cut another bite of chicken and popped it into her mouth. "This is really good, honey."

Joel fidgeted. "Thanks. Now, tell Felix about the house."

"What house?"

Claire swallowed. "Howie's. Barlow's buying it."

"How'd you find that out?" Felix took a drink of water. "And Claire's right about the chicken, Joel. It's real tasty."

Joel winked at Claire and nodded his thanks to Felix.

"You've met Haleigh Evans, the woman who lives behind you, right? She bought her house not long ago?"

Chewing, Felix only nodded.

"She's been looking for one for a colleague. There were two on the market, and then a day later, they were both pulled from the listings."

Felix blushed.

Claire stared at him. "So you know something about that?"

"Yeah, both are owned by the same investor. Apparently, Howie had asked him to sell to him privately. But Smith is one savvy businessman. He called me, saying he figured if Howie had asked him, Smith could put it on the market himself and cause a bidding war. I told him what was driving Howie's bid and convinced him not to sell. At least not to Howie and not right now." He took another bite, chewing with gusto and gesturing for the potatoes.

Joel passed them to Felix. "Good job, Mayor." He followed the potatoes with the gravy.

After Felix filled his plate with seconds on both, he scooped a forkful, then stopped halfway to his mouth. "How do you know it's this Barlow buying Howie's old house?"

"Two reasons. First, someone—Haleigh now concludes it was Barlow or Howie—called and asked if she wanted to sell her house. He offered her fifty thousand over what she paid for it."

Felix's eyes bulged. "That's serious money."

"It's suspicious money, according to Haleigh. It would have to be cash. The normal investor wants to use as much of the bank's money as possible, keeping their assets liquid—unless"—she waited until she had their full attention—"they were laundering money."

"That's a serious accusation." Joel motioned to his coffee cup.

She reached over to the kitchen counter, picked up the coffee carafe, and handed it to him. "It is, but it's most likely the truth." Claire added cream and a half-teaspoon of sugar to her coffee and took a sip. More sugar would be better, but this would do. "I ask you, who offers fifty-K over the assessed value when the owner isn't selling? Someone who has to have the property and a quick closing."

Felix pulled his napkin from his shirtfront where he'd tucked it. "Why didn't Haleigh take the offer?"

Had he lost his marbles? Claire had the insane desire to look beneath the table to see. "Felix, Haleigh loves it here. And … she's met Vince." Claire glanced at Joel. "I think they're falling in love. She doesn't want to move."

"And"—Joel tilted his chair back—"there aren't any other houses on the market right now."

Claire kept one wary eye on Joel's chair. One of these days, he'd fall over or break her chairs. Sure, he'd never actually fallen in twenty-nine years of marriage, but one of these days—

"So what's the other reason she suspects Barlow?" Felix asked.

"Since the rental market here is hopping, and the absentee landlords use realtors to handle the rentals and property management, Haleigh decided that was the perfect summer job. She took the classes and passed her state exams. I forget who she's working for, but she was looking over the listings for her colleague and found Howie's."

While he chewed, Felix motioned for Claire to pass the rolls. She pushed the platter across the table. "Anyway, Haleigh called Howie to see if she could show it to her colleague, and he said he'd sold it. But she couldn't find anything that supported his statement. So she dug a bit deeper, having been at the council meetings."

Felix put half his roll back on his plate. He stared at her and Joel. "What are we going to do? If this Haleigh woman is right, we're up against some serious money. I don't know how we can hold Chapel Springs together. I'm afraid we've lost."

Were those tears in his eyes? Their mayor might be her biggest thorn-in-the-side, but they had the same love and regard for home. For Chapel Springs. Her heart thrilled that she held the answer. She glanced at Joel and grinned. "You tell him."

Joel smiled back, making a big deal over wiping his mouth and hands. When he laid his napkin down, poor Felix was at the edge of his seat.

"Our sweet daughter-in-law, Costy, told us about something that happened in her village once when a drug cartel tried to take over."

Claire fairly wiggled with delight. Belief they could win dawned in Felix's eyes.

Claire winked at Nancy and Ellie over Boone's constraint with the gavel tonight. It fit the hastily called secret meeting. Some secret. Everyone in town with the exception of Howie and Xander had been personally called. She scanned the audience. Nathan and Patsy sat in the front row, lending support.

Boone's gavel came down a second time. "Let's get this meeting under way. Mayor, you want to tell us why we're here?"

Felix turned to Claire. He seemed to wrestle with something. He wasn't backing out, was he?

"I think Claire Bennett should tell you about it. It came from her family. Claire?" With that, Felix took his seat, leaving Claire flabbergasted. He never gave up the opportunity to shine.

After a moment, she stood. "Thank you, Felix. You're right, it was our daughter-in-law, Costy, who came up with the idea. It seems that in her family's little village, a drug cartel once tried to take over. Though they weren't dealing with mineral rights, we are going to do what they did, or at least something similar. Joel is best at this kind of thing. Honey?"

Joel rolled a large chalkboard out. "We laid out everyone according to the street you live on. It's a well-known fact that my wife and Patsy Kowalski are joined at the heart, so we will start this." Joel put an *x* next to Nathan's name and handed him a certified bank check. "We have bought the Kowalskis' mineral rights."

"What?"

"How does that work?" Pastor Seth asked.

"Why'd you sell?"

"What's to keep you from selling them to Howie?" Warren Jenkins hollered.

"Quiet! Everyone. Just hear me out."

The room settled down.

Joel shook his head. "I'm not gonna sell Nathan and Patsy's mineral rights to anyone. I'm protecting them. Now, Nathan will buy Earl Appling's rights. Earl will buy Ellie's. In essence, Ellie is now protecting Nathan's rights by having sold to Earl. And so on until we've all bought each other's."

Pastor Seth stood. "I think I see how this works. We all will keep each other accountable, which is how life should be, given that we're neighbors."

"Yeah, I guess." Warren Jenkins's grudging acquiescence earned him a glare from Felix.

Joel made an *x* next to Earl Appling's name. "Nathan and I figured on a price of twenty-five thousand. It's reasonable. That money will basically pass from one owner to the next. He's buying the Applings' for the same amount. Ellie, we have you down to purchase Warren's rights, and so on." Joel laid the chalk down. "This morning, Felix asked the county clerk to bring everything we need to this meeting. She's here to begin the process. It's going to take a few days to work it all through, so y'all have to keep your lips zipped. But when we're done, nobody will own their mineral rights, yet all will be protected by their neighbor, and we'll have Howie Newlander and Xander Barlow hornswoggled."

"What about you, Joel?" Tom Fowler stood. "According to this plan, you're the only one who will be out of the money. Since Xander bought up Felix's and a couple of others' rights, there won't be anyone left to buy yours."

Joel exchanged a glance with Claire. "We talked it over." He took her hand. "We feel it's the best investment we could make. It's protection of our home and our way of life. And you know we'll never sell those rights, no matter what is offered."

Chapter 37

L acey took a deep breath. Dress rehearsal last night had been a disaster. Everything that could go wrong did. Actors forgot lines they'd known for weeks. The technical crew missed cues, and the new lighting system refused to work. If tradition held, it would be a wonderful opening night. A swarm of butterflies took flight in her stomach.

"Are you ready, sweet stuff?" Jake stood in the bedroom doorway, looking handsome in his tux. His eyes widened. "Wow! You look amazing."

She ran her hands down the midnight blue sequined gown. It followed every curve of her body, flaring at her knees. Chartreaux Katz designed and made it for her, a gift from Sunspots, and she'd fallen in love with it the moment she laid eyes it.

All of Chapel Springs was dressing up tonight. Of all their opening nights, this one was the highlight—the grand reopening of the Lola Mitchell Opera House. And her agent—oh, how she loved to say that, even if only to herself—had invited a Broadway producer. That sent the flock swarming again. Apparently, her agent also alerted the press.

"Thank you, but I'm so nervous my knees are shaking and"—she held out her hands—"so are my hands. I'm a mess."

Jake's expression and his dipping brows telegraphed his concern.

"But a happy mess. Come on. Let's go." She grabbed his hand and headed for the back door.

Jake stopped her. "We're not walking tonight." He bowed. "M'lady, your chariot awaits." He held out his hand for her to precede him.

What in the world? When he opened the door for her, a limousine waited at the curb with a uniformed driver beside it.

She snapped her head around to Jake. "Did you do this?"

"I admit I did not. Blythe did."

"Really? Why?" Lacey had been floored when the agent signed her. She was Carin's agent, and Lacey thought someone else in the agency handled playwrights. But Blythe said the other agent would guide her. She called Lacey a brilliant playwright and said she wanted to represent her.

"She believes in you, babe. As much as I do."

Nobody believed in her as much as Jake. "Crazy, but it sure is fun."

She thanked the driver, whose name was Ben, and climbed in the back seat for the five-minute drive to the theater. The hardest part of the ride was keeping her giggles silent. If Jake said one word to her—

"I'd offer you a drink but we're there."

Lacey clapped her hand over her mouth as her laughter erupted.

"You'll have to excuse my wife. She's enjoying herself entirely too much."

Ben smiled and held his hand out to help Lacey out. "It's been a pleasure, ma'am. Enjoy your evening. I'll be waiting to take you to the restaurant when you come out."

The moment her foot touched the sidewalk, it was like a scene from a movie about the Oscars. A camera flashed, and Jacquelyn Ford from WPV-TV held a microphone. Jake squeezed her hand and stood close to protect her.

"Ms. Dawson, congratulations. I've seen some of your plays and they're delightful. Rumor has it there will be a Broadway producer here tonight. Can you comment on that?"

Not a word about the accident. Peace fell on her. God knew what she needed before she even asked. She sent a quick thank-you heavenward, then answered Jacquelyn.

"Thank you for your kind words. My agent invited the producer. It's my hope he likes what he sees."

The reporter nodded. "I've no doubt he will. Thank you." She signaled the cameraman to turn off the camera. She lowered the mic to her side. "Lacey, you've been through a tremendous ordeal with your accident, not to mention a complete change in the way you look. When you're ready, would you share your story with others? I know several women who have experienced life-changing, tragic events and now suffer from the contrast between their former image and reality. You seem to be at peace with yourself. I'd love to know more about that."

She couldn't help the smile that stretched her lips. "Call me next week. I'd love to share that with you." She squeezed Jake's hand. Only he and a few close friends knew how much God had changed her. She still disliked being the center of attention, but if she could help another woman find the peace she had, it was worth the discomfort.

Jake escorted Lacey into the lobby, where an invitation-only party was taking place for the grand opening. Kelly Appling was gorgeous in a cream-colored gown, its soft material falling from an empire waist accented with a wide swath of rhinestones.

She waved when she spotted Lacey and clapped her hands to gain attention. "Here's our playwright."

It's a good thing Jake was behind her to support her or she'd have fallen through the floor, or would have if she could. Everyone cheered, and heat warmed her cheeks, but the well wishes of her friends took any fears away. She laughed at herself for being silly.

She and Jake made the rounds of all the theater patrons and the family members of the cast. Claire stood talking to Mel and her new boyfriend. Lacey smiled. In that sports coat and tie, he definitely didn't look like the stalker they'd thought he was. Poor Claire chewed a thumbnail and looked as nervous as Lacey had felt earlier. She wandered over to them.

"Relax, my friend." Lacey gave her a one-armed hug. "Joel does a fantastic job in his role."

"Oh, I know. But I'm so afraid he'll forget his lines. And I don't know why I should. He only has two and says them in his sleep."

The mayor crossed the room and offered his congratulations.

"Thank you, but I don't know why y'all are congratulating me. It's the actors and Kelly who truly deserve it." Writing the script was the easy part. "This cast is amazing, Mayor. Why, Eileen is perfect in her part. Wait till you see the chemistry she and Ellie project when they're onstage together."

The mayor stared at her like the doctor had attached antennae to her head. "Well, I haven't seen … uh … I'm looking … I've never heard you say so much at one time." The mayor clapped his hand over his mouth. His eyebrows dipped to his nose. "Good gravy, I'm channeling Claire Bennett. Forgive me for blurting that out." He scurried away, his face as red as a tomato.

Jake cracked up and Lacey couldn't help but laugh. The best part was that she was okay with it—another blessing from God. She loved the new "her." Not the face, but her inner self. That's what was new. The face was okay. Not *who* she was but simply part of the house. Jake understood that. So did her close friends.

Patsy put it so beautifully when she said, "It's as if God turned you inside out. Now everyone can see the beautiful inner you on your face."

Lacey only hoped the plain part became beautiful inside. For a while, she had worried about that. Her thoughts had been pretty ugly.

"God washed them all clean, sweet stuff." Jake kissed her cheek. He always knew her thoughts.

"He did what I couldn't do."

"Lacey!" Carin waved and came toward her with two people following her. The tall, slender woman exuded elegance. The silver-haired man's carriage—if not his silk, custom-made suit—spoke power and money. Lacey's heartbeat kicked up. It had to be Blythe, whom she hadn't met in person yet, and the producer.

"Sugar,"—Carin gestured to the woman at her side—"this is Blythe, our agent."

Blythe stepped forward and hugged Lacey. "I'm so tickled to finally meet you in person." She linked arms with her. "Let me introduce you to Preston Carmichael. He's read your script and—"

Mr. Carmichael thrust his hand forward. "I love it. I want it. If what I see tonight is even half as good as the written script, Blythe and I will negotiate the contract." He patted his breast pocket. "It's right here."

Lacey turned to Blythe. She opened her mouth but nothing came out.

Her agent laughed. "Get used to it, darlin'. This is going to happen to you a lot." She raised her champagne glass in a toast.

The lights blinked, signaling the play was about to start. The four of them, along with the cast's family members, were escorted to the front row. Wonderfully creepy music played in the background as the audience settled.

Then the lights went out and the curtain went up. And Lacey held her breath.

Claire couldn't have drawn a breath if her life depended on it. Joel was about to come onstage. She gripped the arms of her seat. When he appeared, her mouth dropped. He wasn't Joel. He was the fisherman who found the body. He even had a Northern accent. How did he do that? She glanced over her shoulder at her family, who filled the second row. They all wore the same expression—dumbfounded. Joel was good. Amazing even. Her heart did a little dance.

She leaned forward a bit and glanced to her left. In the center of the row, Lacey sat with Jake and two people Claire didn't recognize. The expression on Lacey's face warmed Claire's soul. Their playwright was delighted with what she witnessed. What must it be like to create people on the page and then see actors make them come to life? Was it similar to what she felt when someone fell in love with one of her creations? What Lacey did seemed so much more important.

Claire turned her attention back to the play. Beyond good, it was funny and yet intense. Though she tried hard, she could *not* figure out who the murderer was. And Ellie. Oh my. She was so good as the lead character. They seemed to have so much fun. Maybe next time …

The curtain closed to thunderous applause, and the lights came up for intermission. Everyone in the theater started talking at once. Several congratulated her on Joel's part. As if she had anything to do with that.

She patted several shoulders and said, "I'll pass your kind words on to Joel."

In the lobby, she and Patsy stood in line to get a Coke. Nathan wandered off to talk with Tom Fowler. Vince waved and joined them.

Claire looked around. "Where is Haleigh?"

He indicated the front of the lobby with a tilt of his head. "Waiting over by the door."

Claire found her and waved. "You know we approve, don't you?" Patsy's foot connected with Claire's ankle. "Oh, stop. It's my duty to help him." She turned back to Vince, who wore a cheeky smirk. Two could play this game. "You'd be a perfect daddy for that little girl of hers." She hated to tease him. No, she loved to tease him and he needed a push. She timed it perfectly because Haleigh was about to join them.

Claire grinned. "Why, Vince, sugar, I haven't seen you blush like that since you lost your swim trunks in the lake back in high school." She plucked the Coke from his hand and left him standing there. Haleigh's giggles and his loud laughter followed her as the lights dimmed, calling the end to intermission.

The second act accelerated as the clues mounted and accusations flew. Lacey's heart was in her throat, her hopes and dreams pinned on the producer liking it. The audience gasped when the murderer was revealed.

Jake squeezed her hand, and leaning close, he kissed her cheek. "I'm so proud of you, sweet stuff. It's a hit."

She shushed him. "It isn't until the reviews are in." Then the last line was delivered. The lights went out, and there was a moment of silence before applause broke out and "bravos" resounded from every part of the theater.

A man with a head full of thick black hair appeared at her side. He thrust out his hand. "Your agent didn't know I was coming tonight, Ms. Dawson. I'm Eldridge Smith. I want to produce your play. You're a fresh new voice in theater, and I plan to be the one to expose Broadway to you."

Two producers? Lacey didn't know what to say. She cast her eyes down the row for Blythe. There she was, standing beside Mr. Carmichael. She signaled for her to come handle this. Jake shook the man's hand and directed him toward her agent.

"What's Carmichael doing here? Is he trying to steal your script?"

Oh dear. She glanced helplessly at Jake.

Her hero took over. "Mr. Smith, why don't you talk to Lacey's agent?"

Smith nodded and hurried over to Blythe. Lacey tried to hear, but the actors called for her, and the audience took up the chant.

Jake escorted her to the stage where she received a bouquet of roses from the cast, took a quick bow, and just as quickly disappeared behind the curtains, trembling. She had hoped people would love her play, but like every writer alive, she still held some insecurity. *Thank You, God.*

Backstage, she and Jake were swallowed in a crush of actors and their families. Mr. Carmichael, who insisted on them calling him Roland, and Blythe found her a few minutes later, followed closely by Mr. Smith. How was Blythe going to handle that?

Eldridge Smith stepped forward. "Roland and I are going to find a quiet corner in which to make this a joint effort. We've co-produced before. Then we'll present a contract to your agent, Lacey. We'll see you at the party. Blythe?"

Her agent paused before joining the men. "It turns out they're friends. This should be fun." She winked at Lacey and disappeared into the sea of well-wishers and bouquets. Backstage was noisy and crazy. Lacey loved it. Jacquelyn Ford from WPV-TV congratulated her and said to watch the news tonight.

Jake put his arm around Lacey. "We'll have the TV on at the restaurant." When the reporter left, he kissed her cheek. "Are you ready to escape?"

She laid her hand on his arm. "Not yet. I need to speak with Ellie. Wait for me?"

"Go ahead. I'll be here." He leaned against the stage manager's podium.

Lacey found Ellie in her dressing room. "Hey. I wanted to thank you for making Alexa come alive for me."

The librarian wiped the cold cream off her face. "I loved every minute of it. There is a lot of Alexa inside me."

Lacey sat on the couch while Ellie finished removing her stage makeup. "I have to tell you, at the audition, I wasn't sure." Lacey locked her gaze on Ellie through the mirror. "You didn't fit my mental image of Alexa … until you said that first line. It absolutely shocked me." Lacey laughed, remembering the moment.

They shared their favorite lines, and then Lacey rose. "I'll let you change. We'll see you at the restaurant, right?"

"I wouldn't miss it. And Lacey,"—Ellie reached over the back of the chair and caught her hand—"we're all so proud of you."

Lacey closed the dressing room door. At the end of the hallway, her husband waited, love radiating from his eyes. The way it always had. No matter how she looked. No matter what she did. He loved her.

Chapter 38

Claire and Joel walked into Doc's office bright and early. Though his nurse had sounded cheerful when she'd set the appointment yesterday, Claire hadn't slept a wink and neither had Joel. They gave up and got up around five. Before the sun. They'd sat together on the back porch, drinking coffee and praying. Now, she reached for his hand as the nurse escorted them to Doc's office.

He was waiting for them with a smile that made Claire's knees wobble.

He came right to the point. "Good news. Your tests all came back negative. Not a sign of any cancer. You've started menopause, my girl."

Relief drenched her in a cold sweat. Great. And next, she could expect hot flashes? "So, am I going to grow a mustache?"

"Maybe." Doc winked at Joel. "And maybe not. Every woman experiences different degrees of some, all, or none of the symptoms."

"Oh, joy. So it's a crap shoot?" How was she supposed to prepare?

Doc's grin turned cheeky. "Pretty much."

"Let me understand this." Joel crossed his legs, an ankle resting on his knee. "I might need to wear waders to bed in case of hot flashes."

"As a precaution, yes." Doc folded his hands on top of her chart, nodding. "Some women can drench the bed."

Waders? Claire narrowed her eyes. Was he trying to be funny?

Joel ticked off symptoms on his fingers. "And her own razor for the mustache?"

"Good idea. Avoids dulling yours." Doc's eyes twinkled.

"Doc, what about mood swings? I've heard those can be wicked."

"Women can burst into tears at a moment's notice. I wouldn't worry too much about Claire coming after you with an ax, though. She's not violent by nature."

Men. "Are you two comedians finished?"

Joel reached for her hand, chuckling. "I'm nearly giddy with relief, babe. I'm sorry."

"We both are, Clairey-girl. You're like another daughter. I've been hovering over the phone, waiting for these reports." Doc stood, clearing his throat. "Now, I've got patients with real problems. You two scoot. And Joel, keep a stock of chocolate in the house."

When the door closed, he pulled her up and into his arms and held her tight for the longest time. Her safe place. *Thank You, Lord, for Joel.*

See? Perfect for you.

She snickered.

Joel leaned back and planted a soft kiss on her lips. "What's made you so happy?"

"How perfect you are for me. Come on. Let's go have breakfast at Dee's. Celebrate how you have to put up with me for another twenty-five or thirty years."

He crooked his elbow and she slipped her hand through. "Great idea. Then how about we go fishing?"

"What could we catch at this hour?"

"Nothing. That's the idea. Just us in a boat, drifting on the lake. Time to dream and make out. Find a secluded spot on the other side of Henderson Island." He waggled his eyebrows.

Joel didn't let go of her hand all the way to the bakery. When they opened the door, the bells jingled their familiar hello, but the noise level inside was crazy.

"What's going on?" Claire searched for Patsy. A hand rose above the crowd and motioned to her. "Patsy's over there. Hey, what's Nathan doing here?"

Joel shrugged. "Don't know. Is there a holiday we forgot? Tell you what, you go sit down with them, and I'll bring us coffee and something to eat."

Patsy lifted her purse from the seat next to her. "We've been waiting for you. Dad called me with the good news." She leaned over and hugged Claire. "I don't know what I would have done if it had been cancer." Her eyes shone with moisture.

Claire squeezed her hand. "Well, it isn't. So now you have to put up with mood swings and hot flashes, I guess. You should have heard your dad and Joel. A couple of real jesters."

Her hubby arrived with coffee and two of Dee's signature gooey cinnamon buns. Yum. She was hungry. Her appetite last night had been nil. Now she wanted to eat hers and his.

"What's going on?" he asked.

Nathan scooted his chair closer to Patsy as Joel sat down. "Everyone is reporting in. All the mineral rights have been purchased, recorded, and we're done. Turns out Newlander only got to three people. Felix was here a while ago and has called a council meeting for tonight."

Tonight? And he didn't tell her. "What for?" Claire had never seen Nathan so giddy over anything. He normally guarded his emotions, never putting them on display.

"He invited Newlander and Barlow. He let Howie think the town was capitulating."

Why—? She glanced at Joel, who gaped at his buddy. "Why would he do that?"

"He's hoping the shock will put an end to Howie's schemes once and for all."

Claire let her gaze travel around the room. Near the door, two rather sleazy men she'd never seen before leaned against the wall. Odd behavior for someone inside Dee's 'n' Doughs.

She leaned into the table. "Did you see those men by the front when we came in? Don't look at them."

"Claire, how can I see who you mean if I don't look?"

"Well, don't be obvious about it."

Both Joel and Nathan readjusted their chairs at the same time and looked. They turned around quickly when the strangers stared back at them.

"Van Gogh's ear. Some detectives you two would make."

Patsy frowned. "What about them, Claire?"

"They aren't tourists. I think they're part of Xander's group. They look like what I'd expect someone connected to that man to look like."

Joel cocked his head and snorted. "They could easily be reporters from a big paper like the *AJC*."

Patsy snapped her gaze to them and back again. "Why would the *AJC* be interested in Chapel Springs?"

Nathan stared at his wife like she'd lost her last marble. "Gold, remember?"

"Oh, yeah. I forgot."

Could they be reporters? Claire squirmed, looking for telltale credentials. Her cell phone vibrated in her pocket. Felix. A text he'd sent out early this morning. That was why she missed it. She'd turned her phone to silent when they went into Doc's office. She read it.

"Special council meeting 7 pm sharp. Xander & Howie invited. We'll show them. Spread the word."

She replied that she'd see him there. Then she sent him another message, asking when he sent the invitation to Xander.

"This morning. Why?"

That wouldn't have been enough time for anyone to get here unless they were in Pineridge.

"I guess they aren't part of Xander's group. Felix didn't invite him until this morning." While she was in Doc's office, receiving her wonderful news. The only other great news she wanted to hear was that the twins found a caterer. Hey, what about— "Did anyone see if Jake happens to be here?"

Patsy shook her head. "I didn't see him."

Claire leaned into Joel. "Would you mind terribly if we put the fishing off until later? It hit me that we still don't have the caterer. And don't start. I know you'd rather hang out in the kitchen, but you have other duties that day." She kissed his cheek. "I'm going to see if Jake and Dee will collaborate and do it."

Joel gave her his snarky grin. "Naw, I don't mind. I'll take Nathan. Just not to Henderson's Island."

So much for romance. But she had to figure out this problem. Pots o' paint. Her life circled from disaster to catastrophe and back again.

"Come on, Patsy. Help me talk Dee into doing the reception with Jake."

Claire sat at her desk with her list and calendar in front of her. Patsy's paintbrush swooshed across a new canvas, the last of her tour paintings. Claire loved the music of creating art. The whoosh of Patsy's brushes, the hum of her pottery wheel.

Right now, it was her brain that needed to hum on her list. Under the heading "wedding," she checked off caterer. Jake and Dee had agreed to cater the reception and were already working on the menu. Thank heaven for that. Her tour inventory was complete. The only thing left on her list of concerns was Howie, and he would be confronted tonight.

"Claire?" Nicole stood in the doorway.

"Hmm?" Oops, she still had one more piece to paint for the tour.

"Mr. Barlow is here asking to see you."

"Xander Barlow? Did he say why?"

"Yes. He's buying a house and wants some artwork for it."

Really? Why didn't she believe that?

"Tell him I'll be right there."

"Okay, then I'm going to pick up lunch."

"That's fine."

Patsy had peeked from behind her easel. "I'll come too. I don't trust him."

Claire hadn't fallen on either side of that fence yet. Something about Xander piqued her curiosity. The rest, she distrusted.

He stood looking at her display of whimsy vases and turned as she approached. "These are truly wonderful. Being in town for a while, I've seen the comical originals."

These were her origin— Oh. He meant the real animals. "You can't be here long without seeing them."

"Ms. Bennett, I've bought the Newlander house and want to change the décor. I'd like to get a few art pieces. Would you and Ms. Kowalski help me choose?"

He'd tried to charm his way into their confidence before. She wasn't buying it but she'd take his money. "We'd be glad to."

He selected three of Patsy's paintings, two vases, a large urn, and a platter. Claire carried each piece of pottery to the back. "I'll go wrap these. We'll deliver the paintings and the urn to the house."

Patsy followed her to the workroom. "I don't like leaving him out there alone. I'll keep an eye on him from the doorway."

"I doubt he'd steal anything, but still, it's a good idea." Claire was glad they had moved that cabinet away from the door. The space it left free was perfect for this kind of observation, but she never thought they'd use it to spy on customers. Actually, she wasn't sure what she thought they'd use it for or why they moved it, for that matter.

The door chime buzzed.

"Wha—" Patsy's finger flew to her mouth, and her whisper was tinged with panic. "We're being robbed. A man's out there with a gun!"

Claire gasped and almost dropped the platter. She tiptoed to where she could see into the gallery. But the man holding the gun wasn't picking up anything. His back was to them, and Xander had his hands in the air. Who was he? Wait. She glanced at Patsy and mouthed, "It's the sleazy-looking guy from the bakery."

She'd been right. He was part of Xander's group. And it looked like they specialized in funny money—drug or laundered.

Patsy clutched her arm, then pulled out her cell phone, fumbling it. Claire caught it, punched in 911, and gave it back to Patsy, who whispered into the phone. Then she clicked off. That may have been a mistake.

"Now what?" Patsy whispered.

Claire held her hand up as a signal to wait. She held her breath and listened.

"You thought you'd pull this over on us, Barlow?"

"I don't know what you're talking about. Pull what over?"

"The rights have been sold, but not to Newlander or you."

"What are you talking about?" Barlow's voice caught.

"The hillbillies bought each others'. Now move."

Hillbillies? *Hillbillies!* Humph. She'd show him hillbillies.

Mr. Sleazy jabbed the gun in Xander's neck. "We're going for a little walk."

Uh-oh. Was he was going to shoot Xander? With her heart pounding in her throat, Claire motioned for Patsy to follow her. She wasn't going to let this yahoo murder anyone in her town. She grabbed Patsy's hand and pulled her around to the back hallway entrance to the gallery. She only used that way to carry her heaviest pots to the display shelves.

Hidden by her pottery, they watched as the sleaze pushed Xander from the back corner of the gallery toward the door. In a moment, they would be in front of this display shelf.

Claire looked up. She nudged Patsy, and with an upward tip of her chin, indicated the top shelf where another turkey resided beside a large rooster.

Patsy's eyes widened and she grinned. They crossed their index and middle fingers, then locked pinky fingers for luck. They moved into place. Mr. Sleazy stepped in front of the display.

Now!

With all her strength, Claire pushed against the shelves. *Help us, Lord!* If this didn't work, they'd all be going for a walk.

At the same time, Patsy reached out and grabbed Xander's arm from the side, pulling him out of the way. The whole display tipped and rumbled. The turkey and the rooster leaped off the top shelf. The rooster hit the bull's-eye right on Mr. Sleazy's head. The turkey smashed against his shoulder, and the gun skittered across the room. As he crumpled to the floor, the rest of the display shelves landed on him, successfully pinning him.

Mr. Sleazy lay beneath the mess, out cold.

Xander stood over him, shaking. After a moment, he raised his eyes and sought Claire's. "Why? Why did you help me? I came here to set up a mine that would, in essence, ruin your town. He was your way out."

She snorted. "We aren't about to let anyone commit murder in our town. No matter who or why." She shrugged. "Besides, we already have you and Howie skunked. Your pal was right. We've bought each others' rights."

Xander stared at her for a long moment. What was going on inside his head? Then, a slow smile stretched his lips.

"I sure had all of you pegged wrong." He handed her his credit card. "You can return the card when you deliver the artwork. And I'll see you at the meeting tonight." He winked and disappeared out the door.

"I'll call Jim Bob." Claire pulled out her phone.

Xander's head popped through the door again. "Tell the sheriff he can call me. I'm in the raccoon cottage until Friday." He laid his business card on the counter and disappeared again.

Claire stared at Patsy. "What do you suppose he meant about tonight? I know he was invited, but he insinuated something. What could it be?"

"I have no idea."

Patsy called Dr. Vince while Claire explained to Jim Bob what happened. "Yeah, it did feel a little like déjà vu. But this time, you're not hauling me to jail."

Next, she called Felix and told him the news about the gunman and the change in Xander.

"Do you think it's for real?"

"Felix, if someone saved your life at the risk of theirs, wouldn't you be changed?"

"I wonder what that will mean for Newlander."

"He said he'd see us tonight. What that means for Howie, I'm not sure. But I wouldn't miss it for the world."

Chapter 39

When she walked into the bank's community room, Claire stopped. The place was jam-packed. Every year-round and summer resident was present. She raised an eyebrow at Joel. "Looks like Faye set her phone tree moving."

"I'm sure. After Jim Bob arrested your Mr. Sleazy, she and Felix spread the word. They even called me." He went to find a seat, and Claire headed to the council table.

She made her way through the crowd. Leaning against the back wall, Howie and Xander took it all in. Howie wore a smug, self-satisfied grin.

Just you wait, Henry Higgins. Just you wait. The tune played on in her head, and it took a concerted effort not to giggle.

Xander made eye contact with her, but his expression didn't alter. Had he changed his mind about them? It didn't matter if he did—although judging by Howie's demeanor, Xander hadn't clued him in. Interesting. This should be a fun night.

She found her name placard and, after speaking with Ellie, sat next to Doc. From the second row, Patsy, flanked by Nathan and Dane, waved. On the other side of Dane sat Megan, 'Lissa, and Sean. Behind them were the rest of Claire and Joel's brood and their spouses. *Thank You, Lord, for the blessing of my sweet family.*

Felix lumbered up to the dais, turned his back on the audience, and shot Claire a huge grin that was totally un-Felix-like. She bit her lips to keep from chuckling. He was almost swaggering because he was about to snooker Howie. Finally, the rest of the council joined her and Ellie at the table. Felix took a seat at the end near Boone. Claire searched the room for Warren, the only one missing. A moment later, he ran through the doorway.

Boone banged his gavel until all the murmuring stopped. After Pastor Seth gave the invocation, Felix rose and walked to the center of the platform. His gaze swept the entire audience. Then he raised the microphone.

"I called this meeting to address this business of mining. Newlander, come up here, please."

Howie swaggered through the audience toward the front of the room like he was about to receive the keys to the city. He didn't notice Xander hadn't followed him. Apparently, he didn't notice the rogue snicker from Joel either. She frowned at him, and he ducked his head, grinning. She understood. They all were deliriously happy to have hoodwinked Howie. He deserved the comeuppance he was about to get. She was glad Granny Newlander had passed on and never had to see her grandson's greed.

Howie advanced. She edged forward in her seat. When he reached the front, his lips stretched into a cheesy grin, and he held out his hand to Felix.

The mayor stared at it but didn't shake his hand.

Here it comes. Get him, Felix.

"Newlander, you've tried to scam this town several times." Felix held up his palm. "No, don't open your mouth. Just listen. We've got you this time." A snort escaped Felix's mouth.

Howie looked around, maybe for Xander, but he was all alone. He frowned at Felix.

"All the mineral rights have been bought up. By us."

Howie frowned and pulled his ear, probably not believing what he heard.

"Chapel Springs is ready to see the back of you."

"How did—what—" Howie sputtered. "You can't—"

Xander stood in the back of the room. "Newlander, accept it. They did. When you first contacted our group, we thought you knew what you were doing." He took a step toward the aisle. "You led us to believe the town was nearly abandoned. Your strange dislike of Chapel Springs has blinded you to common sense." He was halfway up the aisle now. "Frankly, I don't care if you found the Hope diamond in the woods. I don't want anything to do with you or your schemes." Xander stood nose-to-nose with Howie. "At this point, I highly suggest you make yourself scarce around here and don't come back."

Claire hadn't known what to expect when Xander stepped forward, but it sure wasn't that. Howie's jaw went slack and his face turned beet red. Balling his fists, he opened his mouth.

Felix held up his hand. "Not a word, Newlander." He pointed to the door. "The sheriff is waiting to escort you out of here. If you don't go peacefully, we'll make a new ordinance that will keep you in jail for a couple of years. Now git."

Not a sound was heard until the door closed with a bang. Then cheers erupted. Boone didn't even try to call them to order. He packed away his gavel and joined the rest.

Where was Xander? Claire wanted to talk with him. Ah, there he was, shaking hands with Felix. She approached them. "Xander, what are you going to do now?"

"Why, I'm going to get my things moved into my new house."

He was staying here? "But what about that man?"

He laughed. "With you and Miss Patsy here, I don't have any worries." He turned to Felix. "You should have seen them, Mayor. They were magnificent."

Felix smacked his ball cap against his thigh. "I've seen 'em in action before. But she has a point. Are there any more men upset with you?"

"No. Smith wasn't part of the regular investment group. He was someone Newlander brought in. I should have squashed it, but I learned about it after the fact. Still, I'm glad it happened. It opened my eyes."

"What did you see, Barlow?" Joel asked, stepping up beside Claire. He put his arm around her shoulders.

"That the people in this town have found the answer to what so many of us seek. Contentment. I watched you pull together, helping one another save Chapel Springs. You turned down a lot of money to keep what you have." He fixed his gaze on Claire. "But when you and Miss Patsy risked your own lives to save mine, I couldn't understand why. But I decided I had to stay to learn all I can from you folks."

"Well, I can te—" Claire clamped her mouth shut. She didn't need to tell him anything. The town and God could show him what he needed better than she could. Van Gogh's ear. Patsy would be shocked at what just happened. Looked like Joel was, too. "Close your mouth, dear."

Joel shook his head. "I never know what to expect with you, babe."

He shook Xander's hand. "How about going fishing with me and a couple of the guys Saturday morning?"

The gazebo never looked more festive. Claire pulled her hankie out and dabbed her eyes. She and Joel married here. Charlie and Sandi were married here, and now the twins. Three out of five kids wasn't a bad score. Adrianna would break the tradition by getting married in Nashville. And Wes and Costy broke it too, but that didn't matter. Not really. She loved Costy too much to allow it to.

The music started. Was she ready for this? Wes offered her his arm, and they started down the aisle to seat her. The twins, the last of her babies, were getting married. *Thank You, Lord. They've all made good life partners. You've blessed me—us—beyond measure.* Megan chose Dane and bound Claire and Patsy's families together forever. Charlie had already escorted her BFF to her seat across the aisle.

Wes patted her hand and leaned close. "At least this time, you didn't take a detour to talk with Great-aunt Lola first. Your dress remains clean, m'lady."

"Cheeky boy." No, not a boy any longer. Her youngest—her last-born—had grown into a fine young man. A good husband, and he'd make a wonderful daddy one day. She slid into the pew and wiggled her fingers at Patsy across the aisle.

The music changed. Claire's vision blurred. Joel escorted both girls, one on each arm, toward their grooms. Oh, the girls looked so beautiful. Their dresses were very similar, with slight differences. Just like the twins. Her little girls.

Joel kept swallowing, a sure sign he was emotional. When they reached the front, he stopped and lifted each girl's veil. He kissed their cheeks and stood next to their pew.

Claire's hankie was already wet. Then Seth stepped forward.

"Who gives these women to be married to these men?" Seth grinned. "Now that sounds strange. Let me rephrase that. Who gives Megan and Melissa to be … no, that won't work either. I know we rehearsed this. Well, y'all know what I mean. Who gives them to be married?"

Thank the Lord for Seth's levity. Her poor Joel would be mortified if he lost it and cried.

He cleared his throat. "Their mother and I do."

When Sean and Dane stepped forward to claim their brides, Joel reached for her hand and whispered, "It seems like yesterday that we were getting married. Where did the years go, babe?"

Claire shook her head, not trusting herself to speak. Her heart was so full. God had granted her desires. Her husband now shared her faith, her children all made happy marriages, and Chapel Springs was safe. She sent up her thanks in a silent prayer as Joel squeezed her hand.

Vows were repeated, unity candle lit, and everyone cheered as Sean and Dane kissed their brides. Somehow in her heart, Claire could see their lives play out as hers and Patsy's had with faith, family, and friends, surrounded by laughter. Life couldn't get any better than that.

Wes stood at the end of the pew, waiting to escort her back up—or was it down?—the aisle. In the foyer, the twins hugged her. She still didn't trust herself to speak without bawling. Oh, flubber.

"I'm so proud of you both. You look radiant and beautiful." She stopped and mopped her eyes.

Megan laughed. "And it's a good thing we did your makeup, Momma. It's waterproof. Now come on. It's time to party!"

The twins and their husbands led the parade toward Sandy Shores Drive, where so many had spent their time and love preparing it for the reception. The Drive had been cordoned off from the boat launch to the Chapel Lake Inn. Tents and long tables stretched down the center of the street, where Jake and Dee had prepared a feast. In the center of the table stood the most beautiful wedding cake Claire had ever seen.

After everyone had been seated, Joel stood and gave a beautiful toast, blessing the couples. Nathan added his remarks while she and Patsy mopped their eyes again. And laughed. But Dane and Sean stole the day when they presented the girls with their wedding presents to them. Sean gave Melissa the deed to the house he had bought. She squealed and threw her arms around his neck.

Dane had kept his present a big secret. Now he nodded to Felix, who turned and waved to Bud Pugh. Bud raised the guard gate, and down the street rolled one of those tiny houses on wheels. Megan didn't seem surprised, though. Claire glanced at her daughter, then Dane. What was going on? Dane took the microphone.

"Megan and I decided we wanted to go tiny and do some traveling before we start a family. But there's one thing we couldn't go tiny on." He turned to Megan. "Meg, I know the one thing you really were having trouble leaving. And so my present to you is …" Dane set down the microphone and walked over to the tiny house, opened the door, and out bounded a mastiff puppy.

Megan screeched and ran. She lifted the brindled bundle of wiggles into her arms. Claire's eyes filled for the umpteenth time. Dane knew her daughter so well. His wife now. He knew how much she loved Shiloh. Claire glanced around. Speaking of Shiloh, where was he? She turned to Joel.

"He's in the tiny house. He was babysitting Beauregard."

"Beauregard?"

"That's what Megan just called him."

What would Chapel Springs do with three English mastiffs in town? Carin and JJ had gone over to meet Beauregard. Megan let Shiloh out of the little house, and he and the puppy romped around everyone's feet.

Claire grabbed Joel's hand. "Come on. I want to see inside that teeny house."

"Tiny. It's a tiny house."

"It sure is."

As the afternoon wore into evening, twinkling fairy lights came on, and music filled the air. Joel moved to the floor to dance with his daughters. Dane took Patsy into his arms and danced with her, while Sean spun his mama around the street.

Soon though, Joel claimed Claire and they danced beneath the stars. What was it she'd thought earlier? Oh yeah. Faith, family, and friends— surrounded by laughter. Life didn't get any better.

Chapter 40

Claire turned in a circle, searching the corners of their room for anything she'd missed. Thanks to Joel, everything was stowed in the tour bus Avery had rented for them. He was already in New York, taking care of the last-minute details. Was she ready for this? Being a big fish in little Chapel Springs was one thing. But an art tour in famous galleries in big cities? She eyed the closet. Could she hide until the bus left?

"Ma? You coming?" Wes's voice carried up the stairs.

Not blooming likely. Her son, Patsy, or Joel would haul her fanny out quicker than a wink. Wes and Costy would stay at the house while they were gone. Shiloh would be in good hands.

Claire snatched up her turkey tote. One of Dee's cinnamon buns was calling her name before they left. Downstairs, she found Costy with Shiloh in the foyer.

She wrapped her arms around Claire. "I will miss you, Ma."

Her daughter-in-law blurred before her. She'd adopted Wes's way of calling her "Ma." Claire squeezed her. "I'll miss you too. But I'd better go before I decide I can't stand to be away."

Joel and Nathan were inside the bus, playing with the electronics. She stepped aboard.

"I'm heading over to Dee's 'n' Doughs for coffee. Do y'all want anything?"

"We'll be coming over shortly." Her hubby pulled his head out from beneath the dashboard. "Have you met our driver?"

"Not yet."

A man was still on his knees with his head where Joel's had been. He scooted back and stood.

Claire's jaw dropped before she could stop it. "Bud? Bud Pugh? *You're* our driver?"

"Not really, but my grandson, Jason, is."

Claire hadn't seen the other set of legs under the dash. What had they been doing under there? "Is everything all right with the bus?"

Jason scrambled to his feet. "Yes, ma'am. It's all good as grits. I was showing Pop and your husband how a few of the new electronics work. And where they're housed."

Boring. "Oh. Well, Bud, I'll see you when we get back." Which won't be soon enough.

The old man put his arm around her shoulder. "Take time to enjoy it, Claire. You worked long and hard to get here. The good Lord is showering you with blessings. Receive them, gal."

His eyes were lost in a sea of wrinkles, but his wisdom shone in each one. She leaned close and kissed his weathered cheek. "You're right and I will. Be good while I'm gone."

Joel pulled his head out of a cupboard. "We'll come pick you and Patsy up in a bit." He disappeared again. He and Nathan would have a ball on this thing. She slung her tote over her shoulder and set off for the bakery.

As she stepped onto the boardwalk, she could almost hear the wedding music float over Sandy Shores Drive. The night had been magical and perfect for her twins. Oh, how she loved this lake. Living in Chapel Springs was like a permanent vacation. Here, life slowed to a manageable pace.

Beauty surrounded her. Chapel Lake sparkled like diamonds in the morning's sunlight. The only thing missing was the cry of the loons, but they'd be back in the fall. Like she would. She swallowed the lump that lodged in her throat. Six weeks was a long time to miss life in Chapel Springs.

The bells on the bakery door jingled a merry welcome. Maybe if she installed one of those on the bus door, she'd feel at home when it opened. All her friends waved from their favorite table in the window. She waved, draped her tote over a chair back, and went to quiet that loud cinnamon bun. And get a pot of Dee's high-test coffee. She'd missed it when her stomach thought she was pregnant.

Lydia scooted her chair over to give her a little more room. "Are you excited? I know I would be. Lacey said you're going to catch her opening night."

Claire took a fortifying sip of coffee before she answered. "I'm looking forward to the opening. The tour part … I'm not so sure." She glanced at Patsy. "I think we're both a bit nervous and insecure."

Ellie stared at her like she'd suddenly grown another head. "Whatever for?"

"I know what she means," Carin said. "I experience that every time I finish a book. I wonder if I have another one in me."

"You're kidding, right?" JoAnn asked.

Nancy Vaughn shook her head. "I've seen it in Chartreaux. As a clothing designer, she's a creative person. All y'all are an insecure lot." She snorted a laugh.

"We are, I'm afraid." Patsy shrugged one shoulder as she lifted her coffee cup. "I guess it goes with being an artist, right, Claire?"

"Mrfaiph—" Claire held up her hand and finished chewing the mouthful of cinnamon bun. She swallowed and wiped the excess frosting from her lips. "I'm afraid you're right. Every artist I know, whether painter, sculptor, potter, or word artist, is the same way."

"Even Mama quivers in fear of not finding her muse." Patsy snitched a pinch of Claire's pastry and popped it in her mouth, her eyes twinkling.

Claire leaned toward her BFF. "Better on your hips than mine. Which reminds me, Dee, I want a thermos box of coffee to take with us and some pastries for the boys."

Dee left to get her order. While the ladies chatted about everyone and everything going on in Chapel Springs, Claire and Patsy shared a glance. They'd miss this.

Patsy leaned close. "You'd think we were headed to a prison sentence instead of a multi-city tour."

"That's the truth." Claire didn't know how to say it. If she were honest with herself, she'd admit she hated to not be in the middle of things. *Time to grow up, Grandma*. She squared her shoulders. "Look, the boys are here. Come on, girlfriend. We're going on a road trip." She grabbed Patsy's hand.

Dee followed them out, carrying an insulated, cardboard box of coffee and a bag of assorted pastries. The rest of her friends traipsed behind them.

Ellie had one foot poised on the bottom step. "Will you show us this thing, Claire?"

"Sure, come on up. It's really more a motorhome than bus. It even has two master bedrooms and crew quarters." Crew was a laugh, but Jason needed a place to sleep too.

Her friends inspected the entire bus, then she and Patsy went back out to say good-bye. JoAnn hugged her and whispered a prayer for safety and a good time. Over her shoulder, Felix rounded the corner, his face redder than a tomato.

"Gotta run," she whispered to JoAnn.

Grabbing Patsy's hand, they dove into the bus. "Quick! Close the door and get this thing moving. Felix is on the warpath."

Jason put the bus in gear, and they drove away, leaving the mayor behind. He threw his ball cap on the ground and stomped on it. Claire fell onto a couch next to Joel, giggling.

Mayor Felix Riley would catch up with her when they returned, but that was okay. It was all part of life in Chapel Springs.

Other books by Ane Mulligan

Chapel Springs Revival
Chapel Springs Survival
Home to Chapel Springs
The Chapel Springs Cookbook

Coming Home ~ a Tiny House Collection
When the Bough Breaks
Way Down upon a Suwanee Murder

While a large, floppy straw hat is her favorite, award-winning, best-selling author Ane Mulligan has worn many: hairdresser, legislative affairs director (that's a fancy name for a lobbyist), business manager, and drama director. Her lifetime experience provides a plethora of fodder for her Southern-fried fiction (try saying that three times fast). She's a novelist, a playwright, and managing director for a community theater group in her hometown. She still finds time to speak to book clubs and women's groups and to teach at writer conferences like ACFW, BRMCWC, and ACWC. She resides in Sugar Hill, Georgia, with her artist husband. You can find Ane on her website, anemulligan.com, her Amazon Author Page, or the theater website, pgatsh.com. If you enjoyed this book, please consider writing a review on Amazon.

CPSIA information can be obtained
at www.ICGtesting.com
Printed in the USA
BVHW032053260820
587411BV00001B/137